Byron guided Lin into his bedroom

He pointed at the bear.

For a moment, she just stared. Someone had attacked the stuffed bear? This was more than a little sick. But the bear had not been mutilated. Its furry limbs were neatly arranged on the covers. The dagger wound was precisely centered. The very neatness of the act scared her.

"They're coming after my children," Byron said.

"Don't panic. Did you find the room like this? Both windows open?"

"Yes."

She approached the bed. The silver dagger speared a sheet of lined yellow paper from a legal pad to the bear's fuzzy chest. Words clipped from magazines were glued to the paper. Not only an ugly warning, Lindsey thought, but a specific one. She read aloud: "I will kill you real slow. You will die by inches. You are not safe."

ABOUT THE AUTHOR

Though Cassie Miles lives in landlocked
Denver, Colorado, with her two daughters,
she had always been fascinated with the
ocean, especially with the mystique of living
on an island. However, her only extended
stay on Santa Catalina Island was definitely
not romantic: for two summers, many years
ago, she was a counselor at a Girl Scout
camp there.

Handle with Care

Cassie Miles

Harlequin Books

TORONTO • NEW YORK • LONDON
AMSTERDAM • PARIS • SYDNEY • HAMBURG
STOCKHOLM • ATHENS • TOKYO • MILAN

Harlequin Intrigue edition published November 1990

ISBN 0-373-22150-9

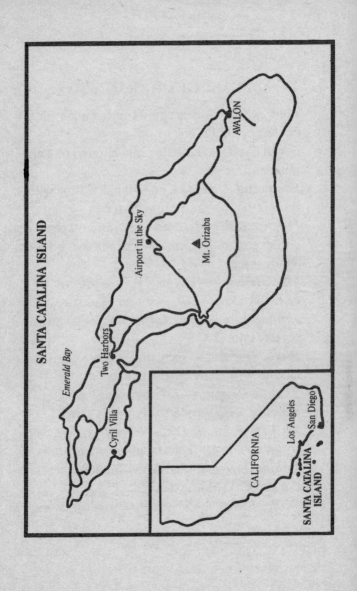

SANTA CATALINA ISLAND

Emerald Bay
Cyril Villa
Two Harbors
Airport in the Sky
Mt. Orizaba
AVALON

CALIFORNIA
Los Angeles
San Diego
SANTA CATALINA ISLAND

CAST OF CHARACTERS

Lindsey Olson—She could run from her past, but she couldn't hide.

Byron Cyril—Who hated him enough to want him dead?

Sonny and Amanda Cyril—Quality time with their father became a time of terror.

Helen and Reg McHenry—The housekeeper and gardener handled domestic affairs in a house of death.

Martin Rankin—Revenge for his brother's death would be slow, sweet and sadistic.

Jerrod Blake—An inventor. Had he created the perfect crime?

Estelle Dumont—A shirttail relative whose clothes were designer made.

Thomas Peterson—An ex-husband whose jealousy was exceeded only by his greed.

Dr. Bart and Julia Dixon—They would never forgive or forget their daughter's death.

Colonel Wright—U.S. Army Intelligence wanted the NORAD plans returned.

Walter Kirsch—A private investigator or a spy?

Prologue

The stripped-down pink Jeep from Minnie's Taxi had no doors, no roof except a giddy fringed awning and definitely no shock absorbers. But Lindsey Olson wasn't bothered by the bumpy ride along dirt roads to the far side of Santa Catalina Island.

She liked this secluded place, only twenty-two miles off the coast of southern California. Catalina reminded her of an unspoiled Mediterranean island with steep rocky cliffs and canyons, wrapped around by an emerald sea.

The taxi rattled past a small herd of goats, and she laughed at the antics of kids springing over scrub and cactus. Along the road from the tiny Airport in the Sky, they had seen few cars, a couple of hikers and a string of horseback riders. Lovely. She didn't mind the ride at all. What she minded was being late for her appointment. An hour late.

The taxi rattled down a gorge, rounded a curve and halted. "We're here," the driver announced. "The famous Cyril Villa."

At the speaker box outside the wrought-iron gate, Lindsey jabbed the white Ring button. Afternoon sunlight against the tall fence pickets cast prison-bar shadows across the road.

"Turn *zz* toward *zzzz*," said an electronically garbled voice from the box.

Lindsey jumped. "What?"

"*Zzz* camera. Turn toward *zzzzz* camera."

Smoothing her shoulder-length blond hair, Lindsey bent down to the one-eyed level of the lens and smiled.

"Wow," said the box clearly. "I'll *zzz* right out."

Lindsey straightened her long legs and hiked back to the taxi. The driver had hauled her four suitcases from the rear and set them on the asphalt. He stuck out his palm. "That'll be twenty-six dollars and thirty cents."

"Not until you deliver me to the doorstep, it won't be."

He tossed her a condescending gaze. "This is the famous Cyril Villa, you know? Nobody gets in here."

"Why not?"

"Dunno. Maybe they like their famous privacy."

Lindsey stared past the gates and the manicured grounds with displays of geraniums and roses to the sprawling, three-story stucco villa. There were wide terraces below and an oddly gabled, red-tile roof above. Rather fanciful architecture, she thought, like a dollop of vanilla ice cream topped with strawberries. It wasn't the most elaborate home she'd ever seen. In fact, she herself had lived in far more palatial surroundings.

A golf cart putt-putting down the long, curving driveway toward the gate convinced Lindsey that there would be adequate conveyance for her luggage. She paid the driver. "May I have a receipt, please?"

When the gates electronically wheezed open, she had her receipt and Minnie's taxi had disappeared in a cloud of dust and carbon monoxide.

The man from the golf cart sauntered toward her. He was large, blond and aggressively tan. The bulge of a shoulder holster ruined the line of his white jacket, but his ivory keyboard grin appeared friendly. He wasn't too bad-looking, she thought, if you happened to like the aging beach-boy type.

"Okay, babe," he said, shifting a toothpick clenched between his numerous teeth. "State your business."

"I'm expected. My name is Lindsey Olson. Not babe."

"That so? Well, Lindsey, babe, before you get inside, I gotta check your luggage."

His bleached blond charm was fading fast. "Who are you?"

"Daniel Danton, sometimes known as Dan-dan."

Better than dum-dum.

Though she wouldn't have thought it possible, he showed even more teeth. "And I'd better frisk you, too."

Lindsey rolled her ice-blue eyes and held her arms wide. She wore a sleeveless peach blouse and a full muslin skirt. "As you can see, I am unarmed. Frisking is unnecessary."

"It's my job. I'm in charge of security. Gotta do it."

"No, Dan-dan, I don't think so." She set down her shoulder bag and took a firm but easy stance. Her weight centered on the balls of her feet. Her knees were slightly bent, and her arms hung loosely at her sides.

He grabbed her suitcase. "Not to worry, babe, I won't tell what color panties you wear."

"Put it down. I don't want you touching my things."

He dropped the luggage with an inconsiderate clunk and peeled off his sunglasses for a close study of her. "Then you must be wanting me to frisk you first."

"In your dreams." And in her nightmares. What a jerk!

"I'll do it real slow." He cracked his knuckles and spread his palms wide, preparing for a thorough search of her breasts. "I mean, who can tell what you got hidden under that shirt."

"I'm warning you. Don't do this."

He gave a smug chuckle. "And how do you plan to stop me?"

She whirled and kicked. Her sandal made solid contact with his chest and he toppled with a heavy thud. Before he could react, she'd drawn the .231 Detective Special from her shoulder bag. The barrel of the gun aimed directly at his crotch.

"Hey, lady!" he gasped. "Who the hell are you, anyway?"

She tossed her head. Her straight blond hair fell neatly into place. "I'm the new nanny."

Chapter One

In an upstairs bedroom of the Cyril Villa, Estelle Dumont applied her cinnamon lipstick and smiled at her reflection. *Mirror, mirror on the wall, who's the fairest of them all?*

"I am." She turned her head from side to side, critically studying her jawline. Being the fairest was a great deal of work, especially when one had been thirty-nine years old for the past twelve years. Estelle would be needing another face-lift soon. So costly, but so necessary to appear at one's best.

She tucked a wing of shining black hair behind her ear, picked up the telephone and punched out a long-distance number. "Hello, darling. I'll be there rather late tonight, so don't bother to wait up for me."

After detailing her arrival arrangements for her trip to Cape Cod, Estelle drawled, "You simply won't guess who I've hired to watch my little nephew and niece while I'm away. Lindsey Olson, that's who."

Appreciative oohs and ahs hummed through the long-distance line, and Estelle congratulated herself. It really was clever of her to engage this nanny, who was also a body-guard. With the renowned Miss Olson on the job, *nobody* could accuse Estelle of leaving the homestead unprotected.

"So dreadful to need guarding," she said with a happily martyred sigh. "But the Cyril family must be so careful about kidnappings. And since I am bringing Dan-dan, my personal security man, with me..."

A glance through the window showed her that the golf cart had arrived at the doorstep. Estelle bid her friend farewell and draped her slender body on the chaise longue. Like Cleopatra, she awaited Dan-dan's report.

He tapped on the door to her boudoir.

"Enter." She patted the mauve velvet of the chaise. "Sit right here and tell me abut Miss Olson."

Dan-dan sat. "She's a cream puff."

"That's not her reputation. According to that old sow, Gracie Vanderhoff, Miss Olson single-handedly disarmed and captured three kidnappers."

"Big deal!" He flashed his wide smile. "No female is ever going to be as tough as a guy. Never."

"Is she...attractive?"

"A cheap blond." He glided his hand up Estelle's smooth thigh. "No real man wants a chick with muscles."

Though his opinion was blatantly chauvinistic, Estelle agreed. A woman's place was on a pedestal. There would always be things that men did better, and bodyguarding happened to be one of them. Of course, the rest of the world didn't think so, and that was why Estelle had hired the acclaimed Miss Olson.

Dan-dan's hand had reached her waist. His glittering teeth were inches away from her mouth.

"Mustn't kiss me, Dan-dan. I've just put on my lipstick." She uncoiled her slim legs. "Be a dear and load my cases while I deal with the nanny."

Estelle swept from the bedroom and descended the marble staircase. Her eyes narrowed when she spied the tall, healthy-looking blonde who stood in the foyer, sniffing the fresh-cut roses in a black-laquered vase. *Who is the fairest of them all?* "Lindsey Olson," Estelle said coldly. "I am Mrs. Dumont."

Lindsey gave Estelle's dainty hand a firm shake. "Sorry I'm late. I hope I haven't inconvenienced you."

"You have. I must depart immediately."

She preceded Lindsey into a front sitting room that was crowded with priceless antiques. Estelle went to the Chippendale desk and picked up a four-page document. "Your contract."

A cashier's check was paper-clipped to the upper right corner. Due to the impermanence of the assignment, Lindsey had requested double wages. And, amazingly, Mrs. Dumont had agreed.

Lindsey glanced over the check and the papers, verifying the prediscussed arrangements. She was to stay at the Cyril Villa for one month, during which time she would be responsible for the care and feeding of Amanda and Byron. "Mrs. Dumont, you haven't filled in the ages of your niece and nephew."

"Oh, really! I don't have time for this. It's enough for you to know they aren't babes in diapers. Byron's almost grown, quite tall." She tilted back her head, unable to resist a dig. "I expect you can handle him. You are rather large, aren't you?"

"Five feet, eleven inches in my stocking feet."

Lindsey took a pen from her shoulder bag, signed the contract and presented Estelle Dumont with her copy. "Are there any special arrangements I should know about?"

"There's a married couple, the McHenrys, who live in a cottage on the grounds. Mr. McHenry is the gardener. His wife does cleaning and cooking. The pool man comes once a week and a girl from Avalon does windows. But, of course, Mrs. McHenry handles the domestic chores. Your sole responsibility is to keep the children amused."

"I wondered about the extensive security precautions," Lindsey said. "The high fence. The need for a full-time guard. Have there been problems?"

"Problems?"

Lindsey clarified, "Has someone threatened your family? Or your lovely home?"

"This is not *my* lovely home." Estelle didn't bother to disguise her bitterness. "Oh, I take care of the routine hirings and firings, but the home—and the fortune, I might add—belong to the reigning heir. I'm only a Cyril by marriage. Tragically widowed, you know. And my husband left me penniless."

Lindsey assessed the perfect coiffure, the designer clothing and the diamond tennis bracelet that encircled the petite wrist of Mrs. Dumont. Penniless? Must be the Gloria Vanderbilt version of poverty. "About the security," she persisted.

"That's your problem, isn't it? And I will be taking the gentleman who met you at the gate with me."

Good, Lindsey thought, great.

Dan-dan himself appeared in the front doorway and Estelle floated toward him. When Lindsey noticed the blatant exchange of leers between the two of them, she tried not to gag. So that was the reason for a full-time guard; Estelle was having an affair with the aging beachboy.

"I must run," Estelle said. "My itinerary is on the desk. I'm summering with friends on Cape Cod, so please remember the time difference before calling."

"You're not leaving right now, are you? I really need to find out a bit more about the children and I wanted to ask—"

"By the way—" Estelle sashayed back toward her "—did you really capture those kidnappers single-handedly?"

"Well, yes, but the incident with the Vanderhoff children has been blown out of proportion. I'm a nanny. My job is to nurture children. If there is a serious security risk, I advise you to hire a professional, full-time bodyguard."

"Oh, you'll do quite nicely," Estelle said. "Yes, indeed, I believe you're exactly what I had in mind."

"Thank you, but—"

Estelle pivoted on her stiletto heels and whisked through the door, clinging possessively to Dan-dan's arm.

Lindsey doggedly followed. She had dozens of questions. "Mrs. Dumont," she called. "When do Byron and Amanda arrive? It was tomorrow, wasn't it? Should I pick them up in Avalon?"

"Mrs. McHenry will handle the details." With that minimal reassurance, Estelle disappeared into the yacht-sized black Caddy parked at the foot of the front terrace.

It was Dan-dan who offered a farewell comment before he climbed into the driver's seat. "Hey, babe, cool down. This place is real relaxing." He laughed. "And you're welcome to every boring yucca."

The Caddy rolled majestically around the driveway. Though Lindsey would have preferred more details, she was not disappointed to see them go. Mrs. Dumont set her teeth on edge. And Dan-dan was a world-class creep.

Boring yuccas would be a welcome change from her usual hectic pace. A month on sunny Catalina with only two children to supervise sounded delicious, especially when sweetened with double wages.

She dragged her suitcases from the front terrace into the foyer. Her next long-term assignment was for a New York City divorcee with three boys, but Lindsey welcomed this stay on Catalina as a time to regroup. She stretched and looked around. Since the Cyril Villa was home for the next month, she might as well explore. Possibly, she would find the elusive McHenrys.

Toward the rear of the house was a large, open room with comfortable sofas instead of priceless antiques. Here, she suspected, was where the family did most of its living. There was a casual dining area, bordered by a breakfast counter and a large kitchen. Sunlight warmed the room through two walls of French doors. Charming, she thought, and pleasant.

Beyond the French doors, a wide flagstone terrace stretched all the way around the house. The landscaping was marvelous—tubs of azaleas, bird of paradise, flowering cactus, citrus trees and palms among the indigenous pines. Lovely. The gardener—Mr. McHenry—must be a green-thumbed genius.

On the rear terrace, a swimming pool shimmered in the late-afternoon sun, but Lindsey was drawn to an iron railing that separated the flagstones from a steep cliff. Far below her, the Pacific boiled against crags of mollusk-covered rocks. She heard movement behind her and spun around.

"Lindsey Olson?"

Startled, she stared for a moment. He was over six feet tall, she noted automatically. His hair was chestnut. He was well-tanned and wore only khaki shorts and sneakers. His sharp features and slight squint gave him a short-sighted bookish appearance. But the thick whorls of black hair on his chest were strictly masculine. Was this Mr. McHenry? If so, Lindsey envied the missus.

Finally, she found her voice. "I'm Lindsey," she confirmed.

"I'm Byron Cyril. It's a pleasure to meet you."

"Byron?" Had she been hired to be nanny for this Byron? Surely that was impossible. But Mrs. Dumont had been coy about his age; she'd said he was nearly full-grown. "You're Byron Cyril?"

"Yes, I am."

The man was in his midthirties, probably a few years older than Lindsey herself. "I don't get it."

"There's nothing to get. That was an introduction." He thrust a pair of child's binoculars into her hand. "I want you to turn slowly and scan that big, gray cliff to the north."

"But you look like you can take care of yourself."

"Well, yes. I can tie my shoelaces and cut my own meat."

Was he joking? Being sarcastic? She wasn't quite sure. It was entirely possible that Byron Cyril was some kind of weird recluse, someone who appeared normal but required watching. Lindsey cursed under her breath. No wonder Estelle Dumont had been vague. No wonder she'd agreed to pay double wages. And the heavy-duty security? Maybe it wasn't to keep the world out, but to keep Byron in.

"Lindsey," he said. "Please look at the cliff."

Her lips compressed to a scowl. After her years as a nanny, this absurd turn of events shouldn't surprise her. She'd watched children on three continents and had been involved with weirdness on a royal scale.

"The cliff," he prompted again. "All afternoon I've had the feeling that I was being watched. I kept seeing flashes of light from that direction. So I got the binoculars from the playroom. But I haven't been able to identify anything."

Though Lindsey wasn't a qualified psychologist, Byron sounded paranoid. "I really don't think—"

"Humor me. I understand that your skills include some security training."

"I'm a nanny," she said. A nanny for children. How was she going to get out of this one? "I didn't expect for you to be here. I thought you and your sister were arriving tomorrow."

"My sister? What are you babbling about?"

"Why don't we come over to the pool and sit down?" Lindsey trailed her voice to a soothing level. She could handle a child's tantrum. But an outbreak from this man? "You see, Byron, I'm a bit surprised at your age. And I'm wondering if I'm the best person to care for you."

"For me?"

"My contract says Byron and Amanda. And you are Byron."

His grin was as sudden and bright as sun through the clouds. "Has it occurred to you, Lindsey, that I'm a little old to need a babysitter?"

"Sometimes chronological age isn't—"

"Ah, yes, I see. You've deduced that I'm the family idiot. The Cyril lunatic who should be locked in the belfry after dark."

Exactly. "Let's try to find your sister, shall we?"

"Amanda is my daughter. My son is Byron, Junior."

Lindsey gulped. With thudding embarrassment, the pieces fell into place. "Oh."

"He's Byron IV, actually. Also known as Sonny."

She gritted her teeth. Oh, marvelous. Calling the boss an idiot was a great way to start out an assignment. "I'm sorry, Mr. Cyril. Mrs. Dumont was a bit unclear about the arrangements."

"Let's start over, shall we?" He extended his hand. "Hello, I'm Byron Cyril."

His was a firm, very normal handshake. Lindsey boldly met his gaze. She'd made a fool of herself. So what? She'd bluffed her way through worse situations than this. "And your children? Are they here?"

"Arriving tomorrow afternoon at five o'clock." His gaze focused on the cliff again. "Despite your first impression, I'm not generally given to paranoid delusions. I really think there's someone trying to spy on me."

"Why? I asked Mrs. Dumont if there had been threats, but she was vague. Is there some sort of danger?"

He spread his hands wide as if to show there was nothing up his sleeves. In fact, there were no sleeves. No shirt. She dragged her gaze away from his distractingly bared chest.

"Listen carefully, Lindsey. I am a very average person. Not an idiot. Nor a powerful magnate who is in constant peril from kidnappers."

"Then I'm confused," she said. "You're saying that someone is spying on you?"

"Correct."

"But it's not dangerous."

Byron nodded and sucked in his cheeks to keep from chuckling. Though he didn't have time for this frivolity,

Lindsey piqued a silliness in him. She seemed so stalwart with her square shoulders and her straightforward gaze, but those wide blue eyes held an irresistible trace of vulnerability. He wanted to tease her, to hear the sound of her laughter.

"I want some answers, Byron."

"If there is someone watching me, they were probably sent by Jerrod Blake. He's annoying, but not dangerous."

"Why not?"

"Jerrod is family, an uncle twice removed or something like that—Estelle could give you his lineage. And he's an inventor of some prominence. Perhaps you've heard of him?"

"I've been out of the States for eight years."

"Have you?"

Interesting, he thought. Why had she chosen the life of an expatriate? How had she become a nanny? She wasn't at all what he'd expected when Estelle informed him that she'd hired someone to help with the children. Byron remembered his own governesses as grandmotherly figures who came equipped with cookies and warm milk rather than high, firm breasts and long legs.

"Byron? You were telling me why your uncle isn't a threat."

"Oh yes. The reason he's spying is because he and I are working on a similar project—a solar-powered engine."

"Are you an inventor, too?"

"I'm an architect. The engine is a hobby." The mention of work caused him to frown. He really shouldn't be goofing off—no matter how charming she was. His project needed to be finished tonight. Very quickly, he finished his explanation. "Jerrod is worried that I'll complete my experiments before he does. And, as it happens, he's right. My solar engine prototype is functional as a helicopter."

She sighed. This was average? "A solar powered helicopter?"

"I'll show you."

Byron led the way around the pool to a patio shaded by fragrant orange trees. A portable computer with an extra-large screen took up most of the space on a table beneath a gold-and-white striped umbrella. "My office," he said.

A fat gray cat slinked from behind an azalea-filled tub and rubbed its thick body against Lindsey's leg. She scooped the beast into her arms. It seemed odd to have a cat on an island with water everywhere. "Love your secretary."

"That's Smokey. His two missions in life are to catch lizards and to clog my computer with his fur." Byron flipped through a carrying case of computer diskettes, selected one and inserted it into the computer. He pointed to the screen. "You see. Here's the initial blueprint for the engine."

Lindsey squinted at the graphic on the screen. "Looks like the motor for a lawn mower."

"You're right," he said with some surprise. "Are you familiar with mechanical physics?"

"A little." She knew how to hot-wire a car. And how to soup up an engine. That knowledge had been an intrinsic part of growing up in the poor part of Los Angeles. "But I'm more interested right now in hearing about your kids."

"Sonny is twelve, incredibly gangly and has the appetite of a great white shark. Amanda is nine, kind of a tomboy. She loves baseball. This month on the island is our family time. I'm rushing to finish up a last few projects, then I can devote all my time to the kids."

"And are you planning to stay at the villa all month?"

"I had intended to." He punched a computer key, erasing the graphic. "Is that all right with you?"

Again, Lindsey was embarrassed. Why was she asking the owner of the villa if he planned to live in his own home? This sort of ingenuousness was unforgiveable. Why was she being a ditz? Perhaps it was Byron, his odd combination of intellect and virility, that was throwing her off. "Maybe it would be better if I spoke with the children's mother."

"They have no mother. My wife died three years ago. Cancer."

"I'm sorry." Once again, she'd stuck her foot in her mouth, but this gaffe was surely the most insensitive.

"I'm sorry, too," he said simply.

With practiced will power, Byron blinked away the memories that threatened to engulf him whenever he thought about his late wife, Maureen. Determinedly, he forced his attention back to the nanny. She set down the cat and strolled toward the blue waters of the pool. Though her pace was casual, those long legs moved with smooth athletic grace. He liked her straight posture, her wide strides and slim ankles. "Do you work out, Lindsey?"

"Not regularly. Do you?"

"When I'm here, I swim fifty laps in the morning and at night. Otherwise, I work out in a gym."

"Do you enjoy it?"

"Let me put it this way. I often work on the computer for twelve hours at a stretch, and I've found that an athletic regimen keeps my mind alert."

"A hundred laps a day is a rather strenuous schedule."

"I like to be tired when I go to bed."

Exhaustion helped him forget. He winced inside. During the first year after Maureen's death, he'd thought about her every night. Sleep only came when he was physically wiped out. Now he remembered less frequently. And that was frightening, too. As if he were truly losing her, saying a final goodbye.

His thoughts were interrupted by a flash of light from the cliff. "They're back. Dammit, Lindsey, someone or something is up on that hill."

"And they aren't dangerous?"

"Not at all. I'd just like to confront this rather obvious spy. To send him back to Jerrod with a message."

"You stay here," she said. "I'll go inside. I have high-powered binoculars in my luggage."

Without another word, she hurried into the house. Through the family room with the French windows, she went to the foyer, found her binoculars and ran up the marble staircase.

After establishing her bearings in the wide hallways on the second floor, Lindsey located a bedroom that had a perfect view of the hillside to the right—to the north—of the rear terrace. Jagged rock formations descended to the water. The upper edge sprouted with scrubby trees and shrubs.

From what Lindsey could tell about the topography of this coastline, there were three projecting fingers. The northern cliff where Byron had been seeing things was the highest, then came the more cultivated ground where the villa was located. To the south was another rocky projection that was even lower.

Scanning without the binoculars, she saw a flash. Byron had not been imagining it. She adjusted the focus and zoomed in on a man dressed in a dark shirt to fade into the shadows of the rocks. He, too, had binoculars. The flashing must have been sunlight against his lens.

She carefully searched his area, trying to find his route to the perch where he hid, barely visible behind an outcropping. Then she froze. Byron's harmless spy had a gun.

Chapter Two

Lindsey lowered her binoculars. She had seen a rifle. The spy wasn't aiming it, but he was a threat. A real threat.

She had to bring Byron inside as quickly as possible. But she didn't want to alert the potential sniper. Striving for a controlled tone of voice, Lindsey leaned out the window and shouted, "Byron, could you come in here. Please."

"Just a moment." He tapped at the keys of his computer.

"Now, Byron. I need you. Hurry."

With obvious reluctance, he rose to his feet, yawned, slipped into a short-sleeved shirt that had been draped over the back of his chair and sauntered toward the house.

Lindsey trained her binoculars on the cliff. The man was staring back at her. As she watched, he reached for his rifle.

She yelled out the window. "Run, Byron. He's got a gun."

"What?"

Lindsey dug into her shoulder bag. Her handgun was for close protection, inaccurate at long range. But if she fired, the sniper might think she was armed with a rifle.

A glance at the pool showed her that Byron was standing, hands on hips, staring up at her window. "What is it, Lindsey?"

"Run!" she yelled. Lindsey aimed skyward and fired two warning shots.

Finally, Byron responded, diving through the French windows into the house.

He was safe. Her binoculars focused on the jagged cliff, and she easily spotted the watcher's perch. But he was gone. Rapidly, she scanned. The man was nowhere to be seen.

Byron charged into the bedroom. "What the hell is going on?"

"You were right about being watched," she said. "But you were wrong about there being no danger. That guy had a gun."

"And so do you," he said quietly.

"Very observant." She wasn't about to apologize, especially since her gun might be the reason he was still standing here, staring disapprovingly.

"How'd you get past customs?"

The first thing she'd done upon landing in Los Angeles was to purchase a new .231 Detective Special. "It's not important. You're not in danger from me."

"That depends upon your definition. I don't like to have guns around my kids."

"I don't like it, either. But you and your kids need protection. You're wealthy. People want what you have. It's a fact of life."

"Whose life? Not mine."

"That man who was spying on you had a rifle." She spoke slowly, as if addressing a child. "I didn't recognize the make, but it had a long barrel."

"Is that all?" He shrugged.

"Pardon me, Byron, but a sniper on the hill doesn't exactly set my mind at ease."

Again, she searched the cliffside with her binoculars, but found no trace of the watcher. Had he hidden or run away? Was he, at this very moment, making his way toward the house? His disappearance worried her almost as much as his presence. "How long would it take for him to get from that cliff to the house?"

"A good fifteen minutes. He'd have to climb to the bluff and circle around. Or descend to the cove. There's a little beach down there and a path leading up to the house."

"I'll check it out."

"You're overreacting." He casually buttoned his white shirt. "Let's be logical. Number one, if he intended to shoot me, there's been ample opportunity. Number two, Jerrod has invented an air rifle. It makes a loud pop and is effective in stunning a small bird or a lizard. Your 'sniper' probably brought the gun to protect himself against creepy crawlies. Number three, It's virtually impossible to spot someone coming from that direction, especially in the dusk."

"If he's out there, I'll find him."

"If you insist. But I'm coming with you."

"Absolutely not," she said firmly. "It's not safe for you."

"These are my grounds and my cliff. If you want to get technical, it's my sniper. I'll come with you to search."

She wanted to sock him in the belly, to shake some common sense into his supposedly logical head. "Don't you get it? This guy was coming after you with a gun. Maybe he's been watching the house, waiting for your security guard to leave."

Byron chuckled. "Dan-dan? Oh, yes, he'd be a real deterrent to snipers. He could blind them with the glare off his teeth."

Why wasn't he taking her seriously? "If you want to ignore danger to yourself, that's fine. But I advise you to consider carefully before bringing your children into a potentially frightening situation."

Every trace of humor fled from his expression. "I would never do anything that would endanger Amanda and Sonny. There's not a problem, and I won't allow my time with them to be interrupted by this idiotic inconvenience."

"Inconvenience?" She gaped. "Running out of mayonnaise is inconvenient. A spy with a gun is dangerous."

"Not necessarily."

She waited for him to explain, but he did not speak. Lindsey went to the telephone on the bedside table. "I'm going to report this incident to the police."

"And what would that accomplish?" He stepped up beside her and clicked down the receiver button. "There's nothing the sheriff can do, except for embarrassing Jerrod and me."

"Take your hand off the phone, Byron."

As she glared up at him, she saw dark anger in his eyes. Tension shimmered between them like a heat wave on a desert highway. Then, with quick decision, he removed his hand from the telephone. "At least, let me explain."

Though their eye contact was broken, her apprehension remained, causing a heightened awareness of the slick plastic telephone, the fading light of sunset, the cries of terns and pounding surf. Yet she placed the telephone receiver back on the hook. She would not defer to his anger, but he deserved the chance to make sense of his behavior. "I'm listening."

He turned away from her, took two long-legged strides. Beneath the thin fabric of his white shirt, she watched his shoulder muscles relaxing. When he faced her, he wore a mask of calm geniality. "You might have noticed that I have a temper. And that I am dedicated to my work. My late wife's parents—Dr. and Mrs. Dixon—say that I am obsessed with work, that I am too stubborn and that I am not a good father. The possibility of a kidnapping threat would given them the ammunition they need to seek custody of the children."

"I see." Lindsey sat on the edge of the bed. Her gaze drifted to the telephone, then back to him. "But I can't ignore this, Byron. If there's any possibility of danger..."

"There is none. Just give me five minutes to explain about my family. I suppose Estelle told you nothing."

"That is correct."

He cocked an eyebrow. "And are you accustomed to moving into strange houses with no idea of what you will find?"

"Is this a strange house?"

"The proportions are a bit bizarre. My grandfather built this place. Years ago when Wrigley owned Catalina."

"What's the point, Byron?"

"My family, including Jerrod Blake, has a tradition of eccentricity. Grandfather is a good example. He founded the Continental Auto factory in 1924, using an engine he invented. Though his car designs were fairly standard, his eccentricities are obvious in this house—the jigsaw gables, three backup electrical generators and a workroom that makes Fort Knox look unguarded. My father was an excellent manager who increased our fortunes when other American car manufacturers were losing money. However, most of his decisions were made upon the advice of a psychic and an astrologer named Xeno."

"And this inventor uncle of yours? Jerrod?"

"Many of his inventions are for the military, and Jerrod is fond of spy novels and espionage. He planned all the surprise parties for the family."

She was beginning to understand, especially when she considered the obvious weirdness of Estelle Dumont. Family eccentricity? Perhaps Byron was right. On the other hand . . . "How do you fit this family profile?"

"I'm a bit of a black sheep—the wayward heir who chose to be an architect rather than pursue the family business. Despite this lack of qualifications, I inherited the chairmanship of Continental Auto when my father passed away six months ago. Plus a fairly extensive estate."

"I see."

His glance was sharp, almost challenging. "And you're not impressed."

"When you've lived in a castle on the Rhine, an oddly proportioned villa on Catalina Island isn't all that impressive."

Byron liked her response. Ever since his wife died, he'd been plagued by willing brides, women who were attracted to his money. Lindsey wasn't one of them. Or was she? He didn't think her lack of acquisitiveness was an act, but still he tested. "What if I told you that my inheritance puts me in the top twenty-five of the *Fortune* Five Hundred?"

Her only reply was a shrug. Though she sensed a hidden meaning in his statements, she was unsure of their purpose.

"I have a yacht," he said. "A private jet. A house in Detroit, condos in L.A. and New York. Two helicopters."

His listing of possessions was vaguely annoying. Somehow, Lindsey expected something different from Byron. She rose from the bed and returned to the window. After scanning the cliff and finding nothing, she gazed toward the horizon. The setting sun touched the glass surface of the sea. "Listen, Byron, I really don't care whether you're Daddy Warbucks or a clerk. My only concern is for the children."

"Mine, too." He sounded relieved. "All I want, Lindsey, is for the kids to have a good month here. This is our home, a place we can be together without interruptions. I don't want to be run off by some crazy scheme of Jerrod's."

When she looked at him, his eyes were warm as melting chocolate. She was convinced that his love for his children and his need to be with them was genuine. Keeping that in mind, it was inconceivable that he would ignore a real threat.

"Please, Lindsey." His voice was gentle as a caress. "Trust me on this one."

With her amplified senses, she perceived his sincerity, his strength. Worse, she felt herself responding to him on a level that was totally unacceptable. "I won't call the police."

"Then it's settled. May I show you to your room?"

He crooked his elbow and she had no choice but to slip her arm through his. Actually, she did have a choice. She could have ignored the tanned, well-muscled arm thrust toward her, but didn't want to back down.

His arm accidentally brushed the curve of her breast. She stiffened and relaxed. She could handle it. She could ignore these ridiculous butterflies that had started to flutter in her stomach. Lindsey was an independent, tough, untouchable woman—completely capable of maintaining professional distance.

Her bedroom was an airy corner room. There was a small balcony on one wall and a dormer window on the other. The double bed had a brass headboard.

"The closet is over there." He pointed, then crossed the Oriental carpet to a louvered door. "Here's the bathroom."

The bedroom was adequate, but the bathroom was incredible. White tiled walls and gold fixtures gleamed beneath a huge overhead skylight. There was a shower, double sink, mirrors and toilet. On a carpeted platform in the center of the room stood a huge oval bathtub.

"Hope you don't mind sharing the bathroom with me," he said, pushing open another louvered door on the opposite side of the room. "This is my bedroom over here."

"Do the doors lock?"

"Yes."

"No problem in sharing."

"Good." He stood close to her. "I like you, Lindsey. I think we'll have a good month together."

He was near enough that his natural warmth radiated toward her. She caught a whiff of his clean male scent. Earlier, the Cyril Villa had seemed too protected. Now she wished for absolute invulnerability. "If there's really no danger, Byron, why do you have such extensive security?"

"What security?"

"The high fence," she said, "the squawk box to monitor callers. The driver who brought me here said that nobody gets into the Cyril place. And Dan-dan wanted to frisk me. Why all the precautions?"

"The only threats are in Estelle's mind. Some of her friends have had kidnapping attempts, and she thinks we should keep up with the Hearsts."

"Family eccentricity? Again?"

"Getting to be a theme, isn't it?" He grinned. "Dan-dan frisked you?"

"He tried." Lindsey spun on her heel, not wishing to discuss Dan-dan's crude approach. "I'll get my things."

After they brought her suitcases to her bedroom, she searched through her smallest bag. Distance, she thought. She needed distance from him, needed to remind herself that he was the employer and she was the nanny. She found an electronic device that was the size of a cigarette pack. "Just in case," she said. "I'll sweep the room."

"Well, aren't you the little James Bond." He folded his arms across his chest. "What kind of governess are you, anyway?"

"My first nanny job was for an American family living in the Middle East." She moved around her bedroom, checking likely areas where bugging devices might be hidden. "They hired me because I have a brown belt in karate and—without bragging—I'm accurate with close-range firearms. Since then, I've taken courses in escape driving."

She took the bug sweeper into the bathroom. "I haven't had to use my skills often, but there have been occasions when they've come in handy. Kidnap attempts, mostly."

Byron trailed her into the bathroom. Though he could see that Lindsey was in outstanding physical condition, it was difficult to picture this graceful woman in hand-to-hand combat with a kidnapper. He watched her diligently inspect beneath the sink. "You're wasting your time, Lindsey."

The sweeper emitted a high whining noise. Behind the bathroom mirror, Lindsey discovered a small, round, silver object—an electronic bug.

Silently, she went through her bedroom and opened the door to the balcony, which overlooked the swimming pool. She flung the bug as far as she could over the railing to the rocks far below. "Yes, Byron? You were saying?"

"Maybe that was left over from when my father was living here. He was an international figure."

"And you've inherited his mantle," she pointed out. "Mrs. Dumont might have a valid reason for worry."

Before she could theorize further, Byron bolted toward the door. "I'll leave you to freshen up. Dinner will be in an hour. The McHenrys have the night off, so I was planning to throw together a couple of sandwiches and fruit."

"Don't bother on my account. I can raid the refrigerator by myself."

"It's no bother, and I'd welcome some adult conversation."

"But Estelle—"

He silenced her with a look. "*Adult* conversation."

"What about the work you were rushing to complete?"

"I'll make it a late night." His eyebrow raised. "Is there some reason you'd rather not share dinner with me?"

Maybe. Maybe she didn't quite trust herself to be alone with him. "I'm tired."

That was a good excuse. Lindsey had been traveling for nearly two days and flown halfway around the globe. Not to mention the twelve miles of bad road in a bouncy pink taxi. "I'm really tired."

"Yes, of course. Sorry. It was inconsiderate of me not to notice. I'll bring you a tray."

"That's not necessary."

But he was gone. When she heard him stride down the hall to the staircase, she made a quick sweep of his bedroom and found another bug in the telephone mouthpiece. Before destroying it, she studied this one carefully, noting that the technology was nowhere near state-of-the-art. Perhaps Byron was correct and these devices were left over from an earlier time. But just in case, she intended to stay alert.

She turned on the overhead light in her bedroom and expertly unpacked her suitcases, shaking the wrinkles from a jersey sundress. It was mint green and she knew it flattered her figure. Would Byron like it? Did she care if he did?

Her brain emitted a high whining warning. Byron's sexy presence might be more threatening than a couple of bugs in the bedroom and a sniper with an air gun.

Still holding the soft dress, she went out on her balcony. The evening dusk had rolled in from the sea creating a landscape of lush, enticing shadows. Below her, the swimming pool was lit and she watched Byron churning through the clear water. One hundred laps a day. He exercised at a driven pace. His late wife's parents were probably right, she thought. He probably was a workaholic—a hard worker with a taut, tanned body and well-developed thighs.

Which were none of her business. She stalked back into the bedroom, threw the mint-green dress onto a hanger and racked it in the closet. If only she didn't have such rotten taste in men. The fact that she found Byron the least bit attractive should be sufficient cause to sprint in the opposite direction. She'd run away twice before. From two disastrous relationships.

With fierce energy, she unpacked. Twenty minutes later, all four suitcases were empty.

"Lindsey?" Byron tapped on the locked door to her bedroom.

"Yes?" She stiffened. "What is it?"

"Are you ready for dinner?"

"No, thanks. I'm taking a bath, then going to bed."

In the hallway, Byron leaned against her bedroom door. To bed? Before he could stop himself, his imagination conjured a picture of Lindsey in bed—naked, of course—with her long legs stretched out seductively.

No way, he told himself as he erased the charming picture. Not appropriate. It would be too confusing for his children if he ravished their nanny. However, his imagination teased, the children wouldn't arrive until tomorrow. Tonight was his. And Lindsey's. Even the McHenrys had the night off and couldn't disturb them.

It wouldn't work. He shouldn't even think about it. She'd probably shoot him if he made overtures.

Byron hurried downstairs. Despite her protests to the contrary, he knew she was hungry. Should he ply her with champagne. Caviar? No, he decided, not prissy little canapés for Lindsey. She was a healthy woman who needed substantial food. Roast beef. Leg of lamb. By the time he reached the kitchen, he was humming.

Upstairs, Lindsey filled the marble bathtub and reviewed her professional standards. Even on Santa Catalina, no woman was an island. However, nothing good could come from a quickie affair with an eccentric millionaire. And that was that.

While the tub filled with bubbles, she fetched her robe, tucked her gun into her shoulder bag and brought the bag into the bathroom. Tonight she would fulfill her need for romance by wishing on the moon. With the bathroom lights off, she could watch the gathering stars through the skylight overhead.

Steam and bubbles caressed her as she eased into the hot water, eventually lying back and gazing up at the night skies. Beautiful. Beautiful and lonely in a bathtub designed for two.

A sharp click pierced her relaxation and she focused on the door from Byron's room. Pale starlight shone against the brass knob and she saw it turning. She'd locked that door; she was certain that she'd locked both bathroom doors and the hall door to her bedroom.

The knob turned. Very slowly. There was another click and the movement stopped.

Lindsey reached into her shoulder bag and drew her pistol. Overreacting? Perhaps. But better to be safe than sorry. Behind the mountain of bubbles, she concealed her weapon.

The door opened. A shadowy figure fumbled for the switch. When the overhead light went on, she blinked.

It was Byron. He balanced a silver ice bucket in one hand. In the other, he held a tray with sandwiches and a key.

"That door was locked," she said.

He turned with a start. "It was dark. I didn't think you were in here."

"I turned off the lights so I could see the stars." She indicated the skylight. "Do you have a key for that door?"

"Yes, but it didn't work very well." He sheepishly grinned. "I thought I'd surprise you with dinner."

And what else? "Didn't I say I wasn't hungry?"

"Yes."

Her eyes feasted on the heavily laden tray. "I lied. Thank you, Byron. This is very thoughtful."

He placed the ice bucket on the white tile floor beside the tub and displayed two bottles of sparkling water. "I hope water is all right." Slyly he added, "Or would you prefer James Bond's drink? A martini? Shaken, not stirred."

"I'm not really into espionage." Oh, sure. Right! And how was she going to dispose of her gun without looking silly?

He uncapped the bottles. "I'd like to propose a toast."

The half-opened door behind him flew open and crashed against the wall. There was a man wearing a red ski mask. His gun raised and aimed at Byron.

"No!" Lindsey's arm lifted from the bubble bath and she fired. The man stumbled. Yet his aim held true.

She fired again.

He screamed, but his gunhand did not waver.

Lindsey rose from her bath, braced her pistol in both hands and fired twice more.

The man staggered back against the white tile wall. The gun fell from his hand. He left a wide smear of blood as he slowly sank to the floor. He was still. Dead still.

Chapter Three

Would there be another? An accomplice? Kidnappers seldom worked alone.

Lindsey knew she should prepare for a second assault. She'd used most of her ammunition. She needed to reload. Yet, how could she think? How could she plan when the blood of another human being, the lifeblood she had spilled, marked the white tile wall and floor before her?

Act now, think later. Tomorrow, she would grieve.

Nimbly she leaped from the marble tub, grabbed a towel to cover her nakedness and raced into her bedroom. Her bullets were stored on a top closet shelf, away from the reach of curious children. She stretched on tip-toe and grabbed the box.

"Byron," she barked. "I need to reload."

He locked the door behind her. "I'll do it."

Thank God, he wasn't arguing with her. There wasn't time for discussion. She handed over the gun and ammunition, turned off the overhead light and warned, "Don't go near the windows."

"You think there's more than one?"

"I'm sure of it." In the moonlight, she pulled on a pair of shorts, a T-shirt and sneakers. "A kidnapping operation usually requires more than one person."

"Kidnapping?"

"An abduction? Holding you for ransom? It's usually a gang project, especially when the victim is an adult."

"Victim?"

"You, Byron. He was after you."

"I don't know. He didn't look like he was planning to take me alive."

"Chances for survival in an abduction are not terrific. Even when the ransom is paid."

She moved toward him, carefully stepping around the cedar chest at the end of the bed. When she touched his arm, he placed the gun in her hand. Flipping open the chamber, she checked her pistol. "Nice job, Byron. Not many people can reload an unfamiliar weapon in the dark."

"Thanks. What do we do now?"

"Call the police." She was surprised at the controlled tone of her voice. The ease and logic with which she responded. "Then we must leave this room. If there's an accomplice, he knows we're in here."

Byron crept to the telephone on the nightstand, punched out 911 and squatted on the floor. His hair shone black in the moonlight. His hand, gripping the telephone receiver, showed a sharp delineation of tendons and muscle.

"Damn," he muttered.

"Don't tell me. The phone's dead."

"No, but it's rung eight times. Not a real efficient way to handle emergencies." He spoke into the receiver. "Hello? This is Byron Cyril . . ."

The telephone wires weren't cut? Lindsey frowned. This had to be the most poorly planned abduction attempt in history. Or else there was another motive. She listened while Byron gave information and the address to the local sheriff's department.

He hung up the phone and hastened to her side. "Now what?"

A horrible thought occurred to her. What if this had been a bizarre family joke? Something Jerrod cooked up for laughs. "Byron, you didn't know that man, did you?"

"Let me search my memory. Red ski mask? Gun pointed at my face? Doesn't seem familiar."

"I'm not kidding."

"I can't be positive, Lindsey."

"He never actually fired a shot. This couldn't be a game, could it? Like the air rifle for shooting lizards."

"This seems too ugly and unplanned, even for one of Jerrod's stunts."

"But it could be." What if she'd killed an innocent man? That thought frightened her more than an impending attack by a hundred terrorists. "Maybe we should go back into the bathroom. Maybe he's not dead."

"He's dead. There's nothing we can do. In any case, we need to move, to assume he wasn't working alone."

Byron was right. If she'd made a ghastly mistake, they'd find out when the authorities arrived. In the meantime, she would treat the incident like an abduction attempt in progress. "Are there any other exits to this room?"

He took her hand. Staying low, he pulled her toward the balcony. "We can swing over the edge of the balcony. Hang by your arms and it's a short drop."

"How short?"

"Four feet. Five at the most."

"Onto a hard flagstone terrace?"

"Got any better plan?"

"I was kind of hoping for a convenient crawl space. Or an attic. Or a secret panel."

"Only a balcony."

Through the French windows on the balcony, she studied the terrace at the rear of the house. The surface of the unlit pool reflected darkly, but nothing else moved except the wind, tickling the shiny leaves of orange trees and rustling through palm fronds. "Don't you have lights back there?"

"Sure. Floodlights. But I don't use them unless there's a party. They attract bugs."

"Great." Now if only she could turn off the moon. "We're better off in here, Byron. The night is too bright. We'd be easy targets for anybody who might be hiding in the trees."

"What's our alternative?"

"Wait here. We can hold off an attack. There are only two doors into this room."

"And one gun," he said quietly.

"But the police will be here, soon."

"Twenty minutes," Byron informed her. "Even then, they're going to have to fight with the electronic gates."

Lindsey weighed the possibilities. If other attackers burst into her bedroom, there would be a gun battle at close quarters. She was an ace shot, but it was certain that someone would be hurt. And that someone might be Byron or herself.

"Okay," she decided. "Out the window."

"I'll go first. Then I can catch you."

Before she could object, Byron stepped onto the ornate wrought-iron balcony and climbed over the upper rail. He crouched on the opposite side and lowered himself quickly, holding on to the curlicue wrought-iron spokes. Then he dropped. She heard a thud, then saw him step out from under the balcony and wave to her.

Lindsey tucked her gun into the waistband of her shorts and swung her leg over the railing. In the glow of a waxing moon, she was visible and vulnerable. Her back prickled with apprehension as she copied Byron's move and dangled from the wrought-iron bars.

Her legs kicked in midair. How far down? She tried to remember the architecture of the house, to gauge the distance from the balcony ledge to the terrace. Was it only four feet? Or eight? She had to trust Byron, take a leap of faith.

What if she broke her leg on the terrace stones? Sprained an ankle? It might be safer to climb back into the room and face the gunmen. Though she ordered her fingers to loose their grip, her hands would not obey.

Byron whispered, "Don't kick."

She couldn't do it, couldn't drop without knowing what was beneath her. Then his hands touched her calves, anchoring her.

She let go.

Her body slithered gently into his embrace and he held her, protected her. For half a second, she felt utterly safe. Until she remembered that they were fleeing. "Byron, let's go."

They ran across the flagstones toward the small grove of orange trees where Byron's computer had been. Over another railing, and they were in the trees. When they ducked down, the handle of the gun bit into Lindsey's midriff and she stifled a cry.

With her pistol drawn, they waited. It was perfectly still. Apparently, their escape had attracted no attention.

Lindsey peered toward the house, almost hoping to see an intruder—a verification that she hadn't killed a harmless man. From the upstairs, lights shone from the bathroom and Byron's bedroom. On the lower level, lamps were lit in the large room with the French windows. Nothing moved. There was no sound but the constant echo of the surf against the rocky palisade.

In less perilous circumstances, she would have enjoyed the sultry night and welcomed the taste of salty sea breezes. But now, her mouth ached with metallic tension. Her palms were slippery with sweat and she wiped them on the tail of her T-shirt. She whispered, "Twenty minutes before the police arrive?"

"It takes at least that long to get here from Avalon," he said. "But they might be quicker. I've never reported an emergency before."

"A homicide," she dully corrected.

When his arm went around her shoulder, Lindsey did not object. She needed companionship, comfort against the turmoil she felt in her gut. Had the intruder been a prankster? Did she accidentally murder an innocent man?

"Lindsey." His low voice tickled her ear. "I want to compliment you on your quick thinking. You saved my life."

"And my own."

"I won't doubt you again," he promised. "When you tell me there's danger, I'll believe you. Your instincts were correct."

"But not altogether logical." She'd been alerted by the sniper on the hill, but there wasn't necessarily a connection between that danger and the masked intruder in the bathroom. Unless they were the same man. Unless Jerrod sent both of them.

She started to speak, then sensed movement behind them. A stealthy rustling in the hedges. Not the wind. No, this sound was different—more measured.

A glance at Byron told her that he'd heard it, too. He gave an almost imperceptible nod and took his arm from her shoulder. She whirled, her gun braced at arm's length, and came face-to-whiskers with Smokey, the fat, gray cat.

With typical feline disdain, Smokey glanced at the gun in her hand, stuck his nose in the air and stalked away.

Lindsey exhaled, then sank down beside Byron. Waiting for the police, they huddled together, surrounded by the fragrance of orange trees and azaleas.

The police? She stifled a shudder of dread. Though she hadn't broken any laws, old memories die hard. When she was a kid, growing up in the poor part of Los Angeles, the arrival of the police meant something bad had happened. Someone—maybe a friend—was going to be arrested. Someone had been hurt. Maybe someone was dead.

As a child, she'd thought the arrests and the selection of victims was arbitrary as a lightening bolt striking one tree in the forest while leaving the others unscathed. And she'd always feared that her time was due, that the cops would discover a secret sin. Someday they would be coming for her.

Almost to herself, she murmured, "I don't want to talk to the police." In the dim moonlight, her eyes sought his. "Worse than police, there'll be reporters."

"Not necessarily." But he sounded doubtful. "After we file the necessary police paperwork, it'll be done."

"But this is news. Even on Santa Catalina, reporters listen to police radios, and the attempted kidnapping of the Cyril heir makes for a good headline."

"I still don't think that guy was a kidnapper. There was no finesse, no skill, no apparent plan." He paused. "Lindsey, there's something else I need to tell you about. I don't think it's related, but—"

She raised her finger to her lips. "Not now. In case there is someone else, we'd better be quiet."

Byron nodded.

While Lindsey kept her senses alert and her eyes trained on the blank stucco walls of the villa, her mind journeyed backward through time. She remembered a day when she was sixteen and the police had come to the one-bedroom apartment she shared with her mother. It had been afternoon on a hot summer day. Lindsey was coming home from her job at a drugstore, trying not to sweat so she wouldn't have to wash out her pink waitress uniform. She'd seen the black-and-white cars, heard the sirens. A neighbor told her the police had come to her home, and she wished them away with all her heart. She'd prayed the neighbor was wrong, prayed for a miracle. But there wasn't much magic in the slums.

Her mother had been injured. Two cracked ribs and a shiner. Lindsey knew her mother had been beaten by her boyfriend, Deke, and they must have had a big, loud fight because somebody else called the cops. The officers had come to take Deke away. But her mother stopped them. In a moan, she claimed to have fallen down the stairs, refused to press charges.

Lindsey stood in the doorway and silently watched, knowing her mother's denial was street smart. Even if Deke were locked up for one night or two or three, he'd be back. And he'd be angry. He'd hurt her mother worse.

That was the moment, at age sixteen, when Lindsey decided to leave home for good. Unfortunately, she figured marriage would be a good escape.

Crouched in the shrubs beside the terrace of a vanilla villa, she recalled her adolescent foolishness. She'd thought marriage meant security, a white picket fence, a loving husband and a perky bride who wore an apron and baked bread. Though she'd never actually met this perfect couple, she'd allowed herself to dream that marriage would be like that—a glossy photograph in a women's magazine.

The groom she found couldn't have been further from her vision. But he did have ideals.

Chas Grakow was his name. He was tall with a scruffy beard and a scrawny body. His skin was pale as a vampire's. Chas wasn't much to look at, but his deep, resonant voice enchanted her. When he spoke of love, she almost believed her fantasies. On a more realistic note, Lindsey had figured that his parents were wealthy because Chas referred to them as capitalistic pigs. She'd married him and blindly accepted his counter-culture schemes.

They lived with a small band of similar-thinking radicals in a three bedroom bungalow. It was there that Lindsey learned the basics of karate and handling guns. Not that she ever expected to use those skills. Chas said that she only needed to know for self-protection. However, in less than a year, she discovered that while she was baking bread, the gang had perpetrated forays against the "establishment" that were nothing more than a series of armed robberies.

With a small hoard of cash and false identification that said she was twenty-one, Lindsey fled.

By the time she was really twenty-one, she'd gotten her own apartment, obtained her high school equivalency diploma and found a decent job for an insurance company. Every month, she sent money to her mother, a practice she'd continued until last year when her mother passed away.

She'd learned one valuable lesson from Chas Grakow—to be unprotected was to be dead. When it came to street smarts, Lindsey was a genius.

If only she'd run her personal life so cleverly, she wouldn't have married again after she started college courses at night school.

Her reverie vanished when she heard police sirens approaching Cyril Villa. If there was anyone hiding in the house, they would have to make their escape now. Her fingers closed on the butt of her pistol. She tensed, readied herself for action. But no one appeared.

The sirens came nearer. Against the stucco shadows at the side of the house, she saw the reflected whirling lights from police vehicles and a reminiscent shudder went through her. From her subconscious, the corner of her mind that had been occupied with memories, Lindsey blurted, "I don't want him to find me."

"Who?"

"My second husband. We're divorced, but he's unbelievably jealous. I haven't seen him since I left the States eight years ago. If there are reporters..." She chewed her lower lip. "I should never have come back. Never."

The officer wearing the L.A. County sheriff's uniform of tan shirt and forest-green trousers rounded the corner of the house. His pistol was drawn and ready.

When Byron bounced to his feet, Lindsey forgot her own inner struggle and yanked him down. "Don't do that."

"Why? He's on our side."

"Never surprise a man carrying a gun. Not even a cop."

He nodded, then called out. "Hey, Jackson. It's me, Byron. I'm over here by the orange trees."

Officer Jackson, a physically fit young man who had played tennis with Byron, approached. "Yo, Byron. Are you okay?"

"Well, I'd feel a whole lot better if I could get out of the bushes."

"Fine with me." Jackson's voice was casual, but his gun was still drawn. "Are you alone?"

"I have a lady with me."

"That figures." He kept his gun at the ready. "Whenever you're ready, come on out."

When they came near enough to Jackson that Lindsey could hand over her pistol, he relaxed. "You're a pain in the rear, Byron. You interrupted my coffee break."

"Too bad," Byron good-naturedly rejoined. "Next time I have my life threatened, I'll try to make it more convenient."

When he introduced Lindsey, Byron noticed that she didn't take part in their teasing. Her expression was aloof and cool. Her hands were trembling. Would he ever understand her? Who was this woman who knew so much about abductions, who'd had a jealous husband. He was curious and confused. Despite recommendation letters stating her honesty and integrity, despite her obvious intelligence and strength, this nanny had admitted to murky secrets. Clearly, Lindsey Olson was a woman with a past.

As they strolled around the house to the front entrance, Jackson asked, "So? What happened here?"

"I killed a man," Lindsey replied.

Chapter Four

"Once again, Ms. Olson. Did you know the deceased?"

"No."

"Never saw him before?"

"Never."

"Have you committed murder before?"

"Do I need to have an attorney present?"

Detective Edward Murtaugh of the Los Angeles Police Homicide Division puffed nervously on a cigar that looked as big as a rolling pin in his small hand. Throughout the questioning, his partner had sat sleepily on the opposite end of the sofa. Murtaugh glanced at him, then back at Lindsey and Byron, who sat opposite. "We'd appreciate your cooperation, Ms. Olson. Have you ever killed a man before?"

"No."

"It's irrelevant," Byron said tersely. "I told you what happened here."

"Yes, you did. And we believe your story that the deceased was shot in self-defense. We also believe that when you looked the deceased full in the face, neither of you recognized him. But this is homicide. And we have to investigate. Ms. Olson understands, doesn't she?"

"Of course, she understands," Byron muttered.

His self-control was wearing thin. He was sick of Murtaugh's badgering. He was sick of all of them: the county sheriff's officials, the homicide detectives from L.A., paramedics and representative from the L.A. Medical Examiner's office who declared the intruder to be officially dead. For the past four hours, his secluded villa had been busier than a beehive.

"Ms. Olson and I gave our statements," Byron said. "And we've repeated the story at least five times. What are you trying to prove, Murtaugh?"

"We're just covering our backsides, Byron."

"Are we?" Murtaugh's use of the royal *we* was beginning to annoy him. *We* need to know. *We* are investigating. *Our* backsides.

Murtaugh exuded a wisp of blue cigar smoke. "When a wealthy and influential person, such as yourself, is involved in a homicide, we must be extra thorough. So no one can accuse us of being blinded by the aforementioned wealth and influence."

"Fine," Byron said. "Shall *we* get on with it?"

"According to your statements, you were both in the bathroom?"

Byron nodded. "Both bedrooms connect to the same bathroom. Ms. Olson was bathing, and I had brought her a dinner tray."

"To her bathroom?"

"That's right."

When Byron glanced at Lindsey, she did not return his gaze. Through this tedious questioning, her blue eyes shone hard as topaz. When Murtaugh suggested looking into her arrest record, she had coolly informed him that he might also wish to check with Interpol.

Her identification papers had been in order, including her International Driver's License, and Byron learned that she'd been born in Los Angeles, that she was thirty-two years old and had no living relatives.

Murtaugh reiterated their statements and said, "We have two more questions."

Byron gave a resigned shrug. Though it was too sultry on Catalina Island for Murtaugh to wear a rumpled trench coat à la Columbo, the detective was doing a fine impersonation of a sly detective trying to trip up the witnesses in a lie.

"As near as we can figure, the alleged assailant slipped into the house through the French windows in this very room. The *unlocked* French windows . . ."

Shame on me, Byron thought. "As I mentioned before, Mrs. McHenry generally locks up for the night. But she and her husband are off on a fishing trip and won't be back until tomorrow morning."

"And he came upstairs," Murtaugh continued. "He tried to gun you down in the bathroom. My first question is, why?"

"I don't know." In a monotone, Byron repeated the theories he'd offered before. "Maybe he was a psycho. Or on drugs. Or an armed robber."

"We doubt this was a random attack. He apparently came here in a motor boat, stolen from the pier in Avalon and parked in that little cove at the south end of your property."

"A robber then," Byron said. "Though I don't keep a lot of valuables here, I showed you the jewelry and cash in my wall safe. A thief could have strolled away with nearly ten thousand dollars."

"Or he could have been a hired gun," Murtaugh said. "Do you have any enemies? Business associates? Disgruntled employees?"

"I won't pretend that I'm the world's most popular guy, but—as far as I know—nobody wants to kill me."

"What about personal enemies? Any lady friends who might have angry husbands?"

At this point in his life, Byron had a dearth of ladies in his life—married or unmarried. "No."

"The motive doesn't have to be as strong as hate. People are known to kill for strange reasons. A snub. Jealousy. Could be as simple as a guy who thinks you're making a play for his wife."

Byron recalled Lindsey's comment about her jealous ex-husband. But that was absurd. Lindsey had only been back in the States for a day, and she surely hadn't contacted the man. Besides, there was no reason for jealousy. Byron's relationship with Lindsey was purely professional.

"Or maybe," Murtaugh offered, "there's a contract you landed that put another fella out of business."

There was a new contract he'd won in bidding. But no, the award for the contract had not been made public. No one knew.

"I'll think about it," Byron promised.

Murtaugh turned to Lindsey. "We're confused about you, Ms. Olson. Why, exactly, did you have your gun in the bathtub?"

"I thought I'd heard an intruder. But it was only Byron bringing my dinner."

"Might be that you're a little trigger-happy?"

She did not reply.

"Regarding the job requirements for a nanny. Do most of you ladies carry pistols?"

"My responsibility is to protect the children in my charge, and I have worked in international hot spots."

"But you're back in the U.S.A., now. On sunny Catalina, that gun might not be necessary."

Byron rolled his eyes and flopped back on the sofa. "Safe in the States. Right, Murtaugh? I'm damn glad she had a gun and that she used it. Or else you would have been zipping us into body bags instead of that masked thug."

"In any case, we'll need to confiscate the pistol for ballistics tests. Ms. Olson, I'd appreciate if you did not purchase another gun until I return this one."

She nodded, but Byron had an immediate objection. "What if this guy was part of a gang? I'd prefer that Ms. Olson be armed if somebody else comes after me."

"Is there some kind of conspiracy that you're aware of?"

"Of course not. I'm an architect, not an activist. But my kids are coming tomorrow. I don't want to take chances."

"With what?" Murtaugh frowned. "Are you sure that you've told us everything, Mr. Cyril?"

He frowned. Everything? No, he hadn't mentioned Lindsey's jealous ex-husband. Nor Jerrod Blake. Nor had he revealed all the projects he was currently working on. "I've told you everything that is pertinent."

"Then there's nothing to worry about. This guy was probably a robber, working alone. You shouldn't have any more trouble."

When Murtaugh rose to his feet and signaled to his partner, the other man lazily stretched and rose. "Sorry," he said with a half yawn. "Nice little island you got here."

"Thanks." Byron bounded upright, readily nudging the homicide detectives toward the door like a couple of obnoxious party guests who had overstayed their welcome.

On the front terrace, he stood beside Lindsey on the top step, watching as the two men climbed into one of the black-and-whites used by the local police. The car chugged around the driveway, heading toward the open front gates.

Finally. The police were gone. Byron looked over at Lindsey. The bright lights that ran along the terrace illuminated her face as she turned toward him. Standing side by side, he realized that she was almost his height, almost eye to eye with him, but still unreadable. More than ever, she was a mystery woman. Tentatively, he patted her shoulder. "You handled that well."

"Oh, sure." Her tone was self-mocking. "I don't, as a rule, perform well with authority figures."

"You were terrific. Cool, calm and collected."

"And about as helpful as a fence post."

There was a popping sound. A sudden bright flash in the night. A camera, Byron knew. Dammit. Another flash.

He squinted into the velvet dark. "Where did it come from?"

Lindsey pointed and he saw a shadow stumbling through the dark at the right side of the house. A photographer. A pushy, nosy photographer who caught them in a near embrace.

Byron leaped down the three wide terrace steps and dashed in the direction she'd indicated.

With far less determination, Lindsey joined in the chase. She'd known that publicity was inevitable. At the edge of the driveway, she dodged to avoid being mowed down by a man on a motorcycle.

He sped away and she stared helplessly at the red flash of his taillight.

"Hey," Byron shouted after him. "Hey, you! Wait!"

The motorcycle zoomed through the gates and was gone.

Byron kicked at the grass beneath his feet. "I'm sorry, Lindsey. I didn't see that guy, don't know where he came from."

"Get used to it," she warned. "After the incident with the Vanderhoffs, we had reporters calling night and day. And that was in Greece where the press is fairly repressed. Not here, in the sunny U.S.A., as Detective Murtaugh would say."

"Too bad you don't still have your gun."

"Trigger-happy little old me?" She shook her head. "It's better that I don't. If I gunned down a reporter, Murtaugh would have a real homicide to investigate."

She would just have to hope that the story didn't get much play. Or that her ex-husband, Thomas Peterson, did not notice it. Even if he did, she thought, what harm could he cause? She wasn't the same scared woman she'd been eight years ago. Thomas couldn't hurt her now.

After they reentered the house, Byron locked the front door behind them, thinking that Murtaugh would be pleased. "I need to telephone the publicity department for Continental Auto. They can handle the press statements and we won't be bothered by a constantly ringing phone."

"I'll leave you to it. What I need is a good night's sleep."

"Me, too." He checked his wristwatch. "But I have a project that's due tomorrow. May I see you to your bedroom?"

"I know the way."

Her voice was tense, he thought. Throughout this harsh night of guns and body bags and police photographers and insulting questions from Murtaugh, she maintained an aura of cool poise. Yet, in the garden, when he'd felt her body against his, she was soft and yielding. He wished he could erase the slate and start over with her. In two strides, he closed the space between them, took her by the shoulders and placed a light kiss on her forehead.

"It's okay," she said. "I'll survive."

"You deserve better than mere survival."

"Good night, Byron."

With a show of energy, she bounded up the stairs. Alone in her room, Lindsey collapsed across the bed. She'd held herself rigid through Murtaugh's unending questions, not caved in to the abiding fear that he would charge her with murder. She'd kept herself from sobbing when she saw the face of the man she'd murdered. A young man. Couldn't have been more than twenty-five. His nameless face was forever branded on her memory.

She roused herself. It would be slovenly to fall asleep in her clothes and she wanted very much to feel clean. Tossing her shorts and shirt into a closet hamper, she slipped into a modest cotton nightshirt.

Time to wash up. To splash water on her face, to brush her teeth. But that meant going into the bathroom. Lindsey stared at the louvered bathroom door. Obviously she couldn't avoid that room all month. Might as well get it over with, she told herself. It was only a bathroom with spigots and commode and tile. White tile.

Quickly, she crossed the bedroom, flung open the door and flicked on the overhead bathroom light. Heavy smears of dried sienna-colored blood marred the tile wall. On the matching white tiled floor there were dark pools.

The police hadn't drawn a chalk outline, she noted. But it wasn't necessary for Lindsey to have a reminder of the position of the body. She would never forget the splayed arms and legs of that lifeless form.

Though repulsed, she went toward the wall and ran her fingers across the cool tiles. A reddish-brown chip peeled away at her touch. Had she really killed another human being? Taken a life?

Her stomach wrenched into a tight hard knot. The idea that she'd murdered a man was horrible, but there was no way to change the facts. It was over. Unchangeable. And best thing was to clean up the bathroom and get on with her life. Clean up the mess.

In the cabinet under the double sink, Lindsey found cleanser and a sponge. She returned to the place where the dead man had been and set to work—wiping at the puddles, rinsing the sponge in the sink and swabbing again. When Lindsey was small, her mother had complained that she was such a messy child—sloppy and always underfoot. In the way. Would mother be proud of the way she cleaned up this mess?

Water from the sponge melted the dried blood and turned the white tile walls and floor into a smeared fingerpainting. With circular strokes, she scrubbed. Who would mourn this dead man? Did he have a mother? There had been no identification on the body. Had anyone loved him?

A reddish swirl disappeared down the drain as she squeezed the sponge in the sink. Even after it seemed she had rubbed the wall and the floor a hundred times, there were discolored stains on the caulk between the tiles.

"Lindsey? What are you doing?"

She made another journey to the sink to rinse the sponge. "I wanted to tidy up before I went to bed."

"You're tired and hungry," he said. "Let me help you."

"I'm almost finished." She knelt and scrubbed. "Leave me alone."

"Lindsey?"

Byron's tone was gentle and she steeled herself, not wanting to hear sympathy or, worse, pity. She had a job to do. As long as she kept herself busy, she'd be all right.

"Lindsey, it's clean enough."

"But there's still a spot right here." Couldn't he see the discoloring at the edge of the tiles? She wasn't hallucinating. Lindsey knew that she had herself under control. She pointed to a fleck of sienna red. "Here. You see it, don't you?"

"Yes, I see it."

"Good." She nodded. "Maybe I ought to use bleach."

He took the sponge from her hand and firmly grasped her upper arms, pulling her toward him. "The housekeeper will take care of it tomorrow. You need to eat something and get to bed."

She tensed. Of course, he was right. She needed to maintain her strength. And she wanted to rest, to pass some of this burden to someone else. But she felt messy, uncertain. She glanced at the wall. Was it clean enough to wipe away her guilt? No, murder wasn't that easy to forget. Her conscience would never be pure white again. In her mind, she would always be able to see the man she had killed. His red mask and black clothing. His wounds. His blood on the white tile wall.

She took a deep breath and exhaled slowly, trying to force herself to relax. "I'll be okay. And, Byron, I'm really sorry about all of this."

He pulled her against his chest and she wrapped her arms around him, grateful for his warm support. In his arms, her tension eased. Her heartbeat seemed more calm. She felt like she was breathing properly again.

"Don't be sorry, Lindsey. I'm the one who should apologize. You've been through hell tonight. I should have stopped Murtaugh's questions. Should have seen you to bed and tucked you under the covers."

"You've behaved properly," she asserted. "You're my employer, paying me double wages, and I don't require for you to be my nursemaid, as well. It's the opposite. I'm the nanny."

"You're also a human being. It's all right to be upset."

She glanced back at the white tiles. The wall was clean enough.

"Are you hungry?" he asked.

She gazed into his concerned brown eyes. "I could do with a cup of tea."

His embrace became a companionable hug. Holding her hand, he led her away from the white tile wall, through her bedroom and down the stairs.

In the kitchen, he sat her down at the counter. While the teapot came to a boil, Byron shoved a variety of foods in her direction. Fruit. Nuts. A thick slab of chocolate cake. But all Lindsey wanted was the tea. Her throat was too tight to accept food. When he slid the tea across the counter, she wrapped her fingers around the warm earthenware mug and inhaled the aroma of orange pekoe. The liquid slid down with a soothing warmth.

"Are you sure I can't get you something to eat?" Byron hovered anxiously. "A muffin with butter?"

"Not right now."

"Then I'll offer scintillating conversation." He paused, thought for a moment, then said, "Read any good books lately?"

"You don't have to entertain me."

"That's a relief. I'm not sure of the proper protocol following an armed attack."

She sipped at her tea. "Possibly, you might give me some answers."

He groaned. "After Murtaugh's interrogation, I feel like I've been questioned out."

"But you didn't tell him everything. For instance, you avoided any mention of dear eccentric Jerrod Blake."

"You're right. I didn't want to sic Murtaugh on Jerrod."

"There was something else. When Murtaugh was asking about wild-eyed husbands and business associates, there was something else you held back."

"And how did you deduce that? Psychic powers?"

"Not even close." She felt the stirring of a smile. Perhaps everything would be all right, after all. "I've been a nanny for eight years. Which means that I've learned to tell when little boys are lying."

"I didn't lie."

"But you didn't tell the whole truth, either."

Her attitude had become very proper, he thought, very much the nanny. Her posture, beneath the cotton nightshirt, was perfectly straight. Her direct clear-eyed gaze accused him of holding back, and he decided there wasn't much chance for eluding her question.

"There was something," he admitted. "But it seemed so fantastic that I didn't want to say anything."

"I'm listening."

"A few months ago, my architecture firm put in a bid on renovation designs for a NORAD installation in Colorado."

"NORAD?" She blinked. "When you called yourself an architect, I didn't think you meant missiles."

He waved his hand dismissively. "I didn't. This isn't a technical renovation, nothing to do with the military hardware of air-defense systems. Believe me, Lindsey, I wouldn't know a warhead from a showerhead."

"Then why are you, a civilian, involved?"

"These aren't classified blueprints, and my firm won the bid for the job. I've take personal responsibility for the renovation plans for the NORAD visitor's center. Plus adding a few bathrooms and reapportioning offices for more efficient use of the existing space."

"If the job is that simplistic, why didn't you mention it? And why are you telling me about it now?" She considered, glad to have something to think about. "Are you suggesting that one of your architectural competitors hired that man to kill you so they would get this contract?"

"It's not that lucrative. Though the possibility of future government work might make a plausible motive."

"Then what are your suspicions?"

"I'm not sure. But the guys from army intelligence insisted that only one architect be assigned to the renovation project and that the blueprints, which were on computer disk, be stored in a secure manner."

"You have blueprints for a NORAD installation here?"

He nodded. "I keep the disks stored in my wall safe. In fact, the NORAD job is what I've been rushing to complete. Army intelligence telephoned this morning to verify that they would send someone to pick it up."

"Which telephone did you use for that conversation?"

"The one in my bedroom."

"I found a listening device in the mouthpiece of that phone. Byron, I think you should call army intelligence immediately and tell them about the attack."

"Why?"

"This sounds unbelievably far-fetched, but maybe this was some kind of espionage. Maybe that guy was an enemy agent."

"He was incompetent," Byron protested.

"Not all spies are suave. And his attack was fairly clever. A bathroom is a likely place to find people unarmed."

He had to agree with her logic. It was a lucky fluke that Lindsey had hidden a pistol under the bubbles in her tub. But espionage? Why would an enemy agent go to such lengths to obtain plans for the NORAD offices and visitor center? The classified areas had been deleted from the disk that was given to Byron. "What I have looks like the blueprints for any office structure, except that it's underground."

"And it's NORAD," she reminded him. "Please call."

"But I haven't quite finished with my designs."

She finished her tea and set down the mug. "Number one, I don't have my gun anymore. Murtaugh confiscated it. So we don't have any protection if the KGB comes blasting in here."

"The KGB?" he yelped. "Lindsey, you're getting carried away. And haven't you heard of *glasnost*?"

"Number two," she said coyly. "You promised me when we were hiding in the garden that you would not argue with my instincts again."

Trust a woman to remember a promise given in the heat of the moment. He had to grin at this evidence of Lindsey's paradoxical nature. In one breath, she mentioned the KGB, in the next, she chastised him in a lovely feminine way. "I'll call."

Army intelligence was far more certain than Lindsey had been. The agent who spoke with Byron brusquely informed him that the unwarranted attack and the possession of NORAD blueprints should not be regarded as coincidence. As soon as Byron mentioned the listening device in the telephone, the agent snapped, "You spoke to us from an unsecured telephone?"

"You might say that."

Abruptly, the agent rang off with a terse warning, "We'll be there shortly. Be careful."

When Byron went to tell Lindsey that army intelligence was on its way, he found her sitting up but asleep on the sofa. Her bare legs, neatly crossed at the ankles, stretched across the cushions. Her hands sprawled artlessly in her lap. Propped against the sofa's wide arm, she didn't look comfortable, but he wouldn't take the chance of waking her by repositioning her.

Quietly, he turned off the lamps and sat in the wing chair opposite her. Using moonlight coming through the French windows, he studied her features: sharply defined jawline, high cheekbones, full lips. Her blond eyelashes made pale crescents opposite her finely-shaped eyebrows.

After half an hour's contemplation, he decided that Lindsey was not a classic beauty. Her nose was a bit long. That sharp jaw had a stubborn jut. Yet, when her lips parted slightly and she mumbled in her sleep, he thought she was the most appealing woman he'd ever known.

Her eyebrows pulled into a scowl, then relaxed. What were her dreams? Was it a nightmare? With all his heart, Byron wished that tonight had never happened. If only he could have met her in another way, another circumstance.

The doorbell sounded. There was a loud hammering at the door and Lindsey's eyelids flew open.

"Relax," Byron whispered. "It's only army intelligence."

Chapter Five

Bleary-eyed and wishing she'd changed from her night-shirt, Lindsey padded after Byron. She was barefoot, disheveled and ill-prepared to greet agents from U.S. Army Intelligence. Or anyone else for that matter.

In the foyer, Byron turned toward her and a strange thing happened. A soothing communication passed to her. *Everything will be all right.* She knew that everything would be all right.

Without a word, Lindsey reached a new level of understanding. Their gazes melded and she thought the pupils of his dark eyes seemed dilated. His smile seemed changed. Before now, his expression had always been teasing or tense. He was different, suddenly genuine, more approachable.

He cleared his throat. "I need some advice, Ms. Security Expert. How do I find out if these people are from army intelligence before letting them inside?"

"What?" She blinked.

"The people at the door," he repeated. "How do I know they're not reporters? Or another attacker?"

"Obviously, you look through..." Her voice trailed off. There was no window in the carved oak door. "I don't get it," she grumbled. "This villa has massive iron gates and a full-time bodyguard but lacks a simple peephole in the front door."

"You're not real cheerful when you first wake up, are you?"

"Open up," came a shout from outside. "What's going on in there?"

"Dumb question," she said. "If I were an enemy agent, I'd hardly announce it to them."

She was definitely *not* looking forward to another confrontation with authority figures. At least this time, she wasn't the prime suspect.

"Who are you?" Byron shouted at the door.

"Army intelligence. Colonel Appleton and Captain Lantz."

"How can I verify?"

They shouted back a telephone number.

Byron frowned and turned to Lindsey. "That's a different number than the one I have."

"The ways of the government are mysterious. There's probably a whole bureaucracy devoted to verifying IDs." She shrugged. "Give it a try."

When he went to the telephone, she yelled at the door. "We're checking."

"Are you Miss Olson?" This time the voice was female.

"Yes."

"Good work on the Vanderhoff kidnapping attempt. And tonight. Excellent work."

Oh, really? Murder was considered an excellent night's work? Lindsey wished she could be that sure, that the lines between good and evil were so clearly defined.

Byron returned. "They're okay."

He unlocked the door and admitted a pencil-thin man in a gray blazer and a woman in a neat pastel suit who smiled at Lindsey, then frowned disapprovingly at her nightshirt.

"The computer disks," said the man.

Lindsey had been pushed around enough for one night. "I'd like to see your identification, please."

Both produced ID wallets, and Lindsey took her time studying the photos and showing them to Byron. Though she wasn't sure what U.S. Army Intelligence identification looked like, their papers appeared official enough. Still, Lindsey sensed something odd about these two. A lack of military bearing, perhaps? She nodded at Ms. Captain Lantz. "Nice picture."

"Thanks," she said briskly. "Now, may we have the disks?"

"How did you know there would be more than one disk?"

"I assumed so. Surely, Mr. Cyril made copies."

"I did," Byron said. "I tend to be kind of fanatic about making copies."

Lindsey maintained her noncommittal attitude. "Are you a computer expert, Captain?"

"She is," Colonel Appleton answered. His voice was properly authoritative. "The Captain works in EMDI which is Encodement, Microchip and Decipherment Intelligence. And she is stationed right here on Catalina. I happened to be visiting her."

"Which explains how you got here so quickly," Byron said. "And why you have a car."

When Lindsey threw him a confused glance, he explained, "Only residents are authorized to own and operate cars on the island. Except for those funny little golf carts that can be rented in Avalon."

Byron's attitude was awfully trusting, Lindsey thought. Was he being too gullible? Or was she being overly suspicious? These two people could be enemy agents, counterintelligence, kidnappers, anything. And she was virtually helpless.

On the other hand, she reminded herself, these two people could be exactly who they said they were. All she could do was follow when Byron led them into his private study where the wall safe was hidden behind a hinged section of the bookcase.

He opened the combination lock and produced two computer disk cases, which he placed on the desk. "The black case contains two back-ups, including an original of the blueprints. In the red case is my working copy. They're labelled NORAD."

"May I use your computer to check these out?" asked Captain Lantz.

"Be my guest." He flicked on the power for a duplicate of the portable computer he'd used on the terrace.

While Captain Lantz seated herself before the computer screen, the colonel stalked across the room and parked his skinny backside on the arm of a wing chair—a move that Lindsey considered to be out of character. In her experience, military men were excessively polite, always asking permission to sit. Then, when seated, their posture was ramrod straight.

"Okay, you two," the Colonel asked. "Want to tell me what happened here?"

"Not particularly," Byron replied. "We've been over this information a million times with homicide detectives from L.A."

"Their names?"

"Edward Murtaugh was one. And there isn't any more to tell than what's on the police report," Byron said. "A guy in a red ski mask broke in. He had a heavy-duty handgun."

"A modified .45 Colt Cobra," Lindsey supplied.

"Lindsey shot him," Byron continued. "With her .231 Detective Special."

The Colonel looked at Lindsey with new respect. "And you were accurate with that small pistol? Are you a marksman?"

"A marks*woman*," she corrected. "I'm a good shot, but this time it wasn't necessary. He was only a few feet away from me."

Captain Lantz came around the desk. While she walked, she filed the NORAD disks in a plain manila envelope that she'd taken from her purse. *Her purse?* Lindsey wondered why this official EMDI person was not carrying an attaché case.

"Finished," Lantz announced.

After Lantz and the colonel performed crisp salutes, turned on their heels and marched down the hallway toward the front door, Lindsey whispered to Byron. "You're going to think I'm paranoid, but there's something weird about those two."

"Maybe."

"Maybe you shouldn't give them those disks."

"I didn't."

He sauntered down the hall toward the foyer and Lindsey padded behind him in her bare feet. He didn't give them the disks? What was going on here?

She managed not to betray her confusion while she shook hands with Lantz and Appleton, but the moment Byron closed the door behind them, she blurted, "Am I still asleep or something?"

He held a finger to his lips. "You must be exhausted. Let me get you some coffee."

"Don't patronize me, Byron."

But he was already walking away from her, heading toward the kitchen. Without speaking, he wrote on the shopping reminder list that was attached to the refrigerator. "Bugs."

Lindsey squinted at the note. Bugs. For some reason, Byron suspected that they were being overheard by a listening device. She looked up at him and nodded.

"I'll have that coffee," she said.

While he filled two mugs and offered cream and sugar, which she declined, Byron suggested, "Perhaps I should show you the garage. You need to be familiar with our cars. So you can drive the children into Avalon."

The idea that they were being overheard made her self-conscious. In an overly-loud voice, she replied, "Good idea, Byron. Why don't you show me right now."

Down a narrow corridor with a laundry room on one side and a small bathroom on the other was the entry to the garage—a stainless-steel door with a combination lock in the middle, similar to a walk-in vault.

Lindsey whistled. "You must have some real valuable cars."

"My grandfather installed this," Byron explained as he worked the combination. "Since he used the garage as a workshop to build prototypes for Continental Auto, he worried about his competitors stealing his designs before they got to the production line."

"Who were his competitors? The ninth tank brigade?"

"I agree that the precautions are excessive. Eccentric, even." He tossed her a silly grin. "When I was a kid, I told Grandpa that Superman could blast right in there. And he seriously considered installing a kryptonite shell."

"But this heavy-duty security is kind of futile now, isn't it? I assume that the combination is common knowledge for everyone in the house who drives. Like Dan-dan?"

"Nope. There's another garage attached to the house for our everyday vehicles. Plus, the combination on this lock can be easily changed from inside. I'm the only one who knows it." He pushed open the heavy door and reached inside to turn on a light. "After you, Lindsey."

The slight quirking of his lips gave her pause. Byron was up to something and she would have been far more comfortable if she'd known what it was. The more she learned about him, the more she realized that he was not immune to his family's renowned eccentricity.

Warily, she stepped through the steel doorway into a large, high-ceilinged, air-cooled garage. The only car was a beat-up Volkswagen. In the center of the room stood a small helicopter with odd-shaped, oversize blades and a tiny cockpit. The frame looked as if it had been constructed from Tinkertoys.

"*Solar One,*" Byron said, closing the door behind them. "Isn't she a beauty."

"This thing actually flies?"

"Absolutely. I need a regular gas engine for take-off, but when aloft, I have found it possible, even efficient, to switch to solar power."

Lindsey shuddered. She wasn't fond of heights. "Lovely. But I assume you brought me here—to this unbuggable vault—to explain why you didn't turn over the disks to Appleton and Lantz."

"It wasn't a difficult conclusion. While I've been dealing with these NORAD plans, I've met several agents, all of whom delighted in displaying their identification wallets. The colonel and captain had forged papers. Nicely forged, but not quite right. Also—as far as I know—there are no agents stationed on Catalina. Plus, Captain Lantz didn't notice anything odd about the disks."

"Very observant," she approved. "And what disks did you give her?"

"Modified plans for an office building my company designed." Byron strolled to *Solar One* and fondly stroked the blades. "I guess I'm afflicted with spy mania, too. When I first received the disk and the *real* intelligence agents made such a fuss about security, I made up dummies and clearly marked them NORAD. The real disks are labeled Ronda."

"A girlfriend?"

"No, an anagram for NORAD."

She laughed. "You should work for Encodement, Microchip and Decipherment Intelligence."

"EMDI? A bogus unit, I'm sure."

"Agreed."

"What should we do about the bugs? Call an exterminator?"

"I think you already have," she said. "When the real intelligence agents arrive, they will certainly be able to sweep the house. Their equipment is far more sophisticated than my little sweeper."

"And until then?"

She shrugged. "We'll be careful about what we're saying."

"But in here, we're safe. And there is something we need to discuss." He posed the problem. "Who are the phony agents and the dead man in the red ski mask working for? Who's behind this?"

"You don't think it could be Appleton or Lantz?"

Byron gave a disparaging snort. "Neither of them struck me as a mastermind."

Lindsey sank down on a work bench and took a sip from the coffee mug she was still carrying. The twists and turns of their situation were becoming excessively complicated. There were snipers on the cliffside, attackers in the bathroom, photographers in the bush and now a pair of fake agents.

Somehow this must be connected with an attempt to steal the NORAD disks. But how? And why? Certainly, NORAD would never allow a civilian to have access to anything resembling secret information. But why else would Appleton and Lantz have tried this ruse? "If the NORAD plans were what they were after, why didn't Lantz know the blueprints you gave her were fake?"

"How would she know?"

"She must've had some idea. Why else would she have reviewed the disks on the computer screen? Besides, Byron, when you set out to steal something, you've got to know what it is."

Her only solace was an increasing reliance in Byron's intelligence. Not only had he deduced that Appleton and Lantz were imposters, but he outsmarted them without a risky confrontation. "I wish I had my gun."

"Oh, yes, that's another reason I brought you here." He yanked open a wooden drawer at the far end of a huge workbench and pulled out a pistol. "Here you go. Unfortunately, it's loaded with blanks and I don't have live ammunition."

"Why not?" She watched him flip open the chamber and remembered how easily Byron had managed to load her handgun in the darkness of her bedroom. "Why no ammunition?"

"No particular reason."

"I don't believe that. You might be eccentric, Byron, but you're not stupid."

"Thanks so much."

A sharp chill in his voice reminded her that she was out of line, behaving in a too familiar manner. Whether or not they'd shared danger and deliverance, she was still the hired help. "Sorry. It's none of my business. You're my employer and you don't have to tell me anything."

"It's not that." He sat beside her on the workbench. His scrutiny was so intense that she could practically feel it. "I've never talked to anyone about this."

"Fine. Maybe it's best if we maintain a proper attitude." Distance, she reminded herself. "A professional distance."

A pensive silence settled between them. In her peripheral vision, she was aware that Byron no longer gazed at her profile.

"When I was growing up," he said, "we always had guns around the house. Here, and at the family home in Detroit. I suppose it was a wise precaution because both places are fairly secluded."

Restlessly, he stood, stretched and paced toward *Solar One*. "My father taught me about rifles and handguns. He took me out for target practice, instructed me in safety procedures. I knew that the guns were dangerous. The idea was engraved on my mind and I assumed that everyone else understood."

She watched as he stroked the frame of his strange helicopter. His gestures were abrupt. He avoided looking directly at her, and she sensed that he was struggling with a painful remembrance.

"After my wife had been diagnosed and knew she was dying, we came here with the children. She was still beautiful then. With glistening hair that caught fire in the sun. And a firm, handsome little body. But sometimes, in the middle of laughter, her face would contort with pain—an agony made more terrible because of the hopelessness.

"I tried to ignore her illness, encouraged the children to play with her. I was chatty, full of platitudes about how she'd be well again." Bitterness tinged his words. "I refused to accept the depth of her despair until I found her with one of my guns held to her head. The children were playing in the next room, and she held a pistol to her temple. She wanted to die, to end the suffering."

Lindsey's breath caught in her throat. A strong empathy rose up within her urging her toward him, compelling her to comfort him. She held tightly to the workbench seat, ordering herself not to rise.

"But that's not why I pitched the bullets." He stared directly into her eyes. "I did it for myself. When I saw her terror, I couldn't stand it, I couldn't stand to see her dying by inches. Couldn't accept my own damn helplessness. When I took the gun from her, I knew that I would not have the will power to refuse if she asked me to end her suffering. That's why I removed the temptation. For myself. To protect us from my weakness. That's why I threw away the live ammunition."

His stiff posture warned her against solace that might be construed as pity. Gulping back her own feelings, Lindsey held his gaze. And waited.

"I've never told this to anyone else." More calmly, he continued, "Perhaps I've used the famous Cyril eccentricity to behave like a recluse, shutting out everyone else and

operating strictly on my own. Not that my family minded.
I don't really believe they give a damn.''

''Surely that's not true.''

''Oh, they came to her funeral, and they made the right
noises. But the only time I've seen real emotion from my
extended family was their panic after my father's will was
read and they realized that I was in control of the fortune.''

If Estelle were any sort of representative of the family attitude, Lindsey suspected that Byron's judgment was correct.

He drained his coffee mug and rose to his feet. ''Now, I
guess we ought to go inside and wait for the real army intelligence agents to arrive.''

Before he reached the vaultlike door to his workshop,
Lindsey caught his arm. ''You weren't weak, Byron. I think
you're the bravest man I've ever known.''

''A coward's courage. There was nothing else to do.''

''But you didn't run away.''

''I had no choice.''

There were always choices. Lindsey knew from her own
experience that there were always choices. She followed him
out of the workshop and through the house. In the kitchen,
he went to the refrigerator and pointed to his previous
note—Bugs.

Lindsey nodded. Their conversation must be censored
while they were in the house. Loudly, he said, ''Thank you
for the tour, Byron. But now I'm awfully tired.''

On a scrap of paper she wrote, ''I want to change
clothes.'' Aloud, she expanded, ''I think I'll go upstairs
now.''

''If you can't sleep, come back down.''

They exchanged good-nights, and she went up the
sweeping staircase. Though she was dragging, her brief nap
and the cup of coffee had recharged her enough to stay
awake. Which was fortunate because, of course, the *real*

army intelligence agents would arrive soon. She changed into a comfortable skirt and blouse.

Choices. Alone in her bedroom, she reviewed the choices she'd made in her life. Running away? That seemed to be a dominant pattern. She'd eloped from her mother's home, then fled from her disastrous first marriage. Not very brave, she thought, especially when she added the fact that she'd also run away from her second husband.

A familiar ache, deep as the marrow of her bones, trembled through her. She should have been able to make that marriage work. Even though she'd been young and frightened and felt very much alone, there should have been something she could have done.

So desperately, she'd wanted a conventional marriage with children, a home, a garden, security and love.

Lindsey shook herself. So dismally, she had failed.

Would she make the same decisions today? Certainly she was older and wiser. But was she more courageous?

Thankfully, a loud whirring and glaring lights interrupted her depressing reverie. She peeked through her bedroom window toward the front of the house. This time, it seemed, army intelligence agents would arrive in a helicopter.

When she joined Byron on the front lawn, Lindsey perceived a vast change in the climate of their situation—an absence of confusion. The gray-haired gentleman who disembarked from the helicopter wasted no time in taking charge.

He introduced himself as Colonel Wright, and Lindsey grinned. Wright? Wright makes might. The strong Wright arm of the law. The Wright way. The Wright stuff.

He escorted Byron and Lindsey away from the roar of the helicopter's rotor. "I've been in touch with L.A. homicide. The individual who attacked you has been identified. He's a petty thug by the name of Michael 'Mikey' Rankin, arrested twice for armed robbery. In my opinion, he's in no way connected with an attempted theft of the NORAD blueprints.''

''I'm not so sure,'' Byron said.

Wright gave complete attention to Byron's story about the fake agents. When Byron spoke of possible listening devices in the house, Wright nodded. ''Very probable.''

''So, is there a connection with the guy who attacked us?''

''Must be. It's too damn coincidental for you to be visited by both in the same night.''

''Unless . . .'' Lindsey put in, '' . . . unless the fake agents merely took advantage of an attempted robbery to make their appearance.''

Wright patted her on the back. ''Good thinking, young lady. And I will make more extensive inquiries into the past affiliations of the deceased.''

''Do you believe we'll be safe now?'' Byron asked. ''I had intended to have my children come here tomorrow. After you've taken the NORAD disks, is there any risk?''

''I don't believe so. Whoever is after the blueprints should leave you in peace once the disks are gone.''

''Then my children will not be in danger.''

''Not in my opinion. Of course, the impersonation is a serious business, but I cannot understand why someone would want those computer disks. They sure as hell—excuse me, ma'am—are not top secret. Why steal them?''

Why, indeed? Lindsey couldn't think of another explanation. It wasn't until Byron took the disk cases from his safe and handed over the NORAD disks to Colonel Wright that she made a connection with something he'd said earlier.

While Wright's men swept the house for bugs and located several, Lindsey turned the thought in her mind, examined it from several angles. But she waited until after the colonel and his helicopter departed to drag Byron into his newly debugged study. ''Open the safe.''

"Can this wait until morning? I think we've got everything under control. Let's leave it to Wright and Murtaugh, okay?"

"Please, Byron."

"I know, I know. I promised to trust you." He twirled the combination lock and pulled the door to the safe open.

"Take out the boxes," she instructed. "Is this where you keep all your disks?"

"Everything that's current."

"Then, I think I know who sent the fake agents. Remember how Captain Lantz looked at the disks while the alleged Colonel Appleton distracted us." She perched on the arm of the chair, mimicking Appleton's nonmilitary posture. "While we were occupied with Appleton, Lantz had ample opportunity to remove other disks from those boxes."

"So what? I don't have anything top secret."

"Solar One," she said.

Byron flipped through the disks. "It's gone. Both the original and the copy."

"And we can guess who took it."

"Jerrod Blake." Byron's expression was halfway between rage and laughter. "That old son-of-a-gun. The bugs must've been his. When he knew about the intruder—Mikey Rankin—and listened in to my call to the NORAD people, he took the opportunity to sneak his people in here and steal my research for *Solar One.*"

"Eccentric?"

"Obnoxious," Byron said. "Tomorrow morning, very early, we're going to pay my dear uncle Jerrod a call."

Chapter Six

In first light of dawn, Lindsey stood on the rear terrace, sipping from a fresh mug of coffee and watching the rise and fall of the shimmering Pacific tides. Soaring white gulls swept across the pale blue skies and Smokey the gray cat sprawled beside her, watching the birds while he sunned his round belly.

Behind her, from the swimming pool, Byron surfaced and said, "We should fly to San Diego in *Solar One*. It's quicker than anything else."

"And how safe is this experimental helicopter?"

"Well, it hasn't been approved by the FAA."

"Not very safe, then," she said as he splashed away for another lap in the pool.

Not safe. In the tranquil morning, it was difficult to believe the events of last night had taken place. And yet, when she observed the interplay of muscles in Byron's well-tanned shoulders as he churned the pool waters into a froth, she was reminded of another danger. Her desire to touch those shoulders, to feel their supple strength beneath her fingers. Not a very safe idea at all.

He surfaced again, rested his forearms on the edge of the pool and peered up at her. Droplets of water clung to his eyelashes. His wet hair shone like the healthy coat of a harbor seal. "Taking *Solar One* would save an incredible amount of time."

"Much as I'd love to risk life and limb, I've got to refuse. We're in enough trouble, Byron. We don't need citations from the FAA, do we?"

A sound from the house caused her to turn suddenly, spewing her coffee in a wide arc across the terrace stones. Even without her pistol, Lindsey was instantly prepared to battle whatever bad guys were lurking.

"Relax," Byron said, climbing from the pool. "It's seventhirty, which means that the person in the kitchen is probably Helen McHenry."

"The housekeeper." Lindsey recalled her conversation with Estelle Dumont. Was it only yesterday?

"Let me introduce you and tell Helen that she needn't bother with breakfast."

He towelled himself dry and flashed a grin that was cool as the azure sea on a summery morn. His attitude, Lindsey thought, was rather annoying. How could he behave as if yesterday was just another day in an island paradise? How could he rise from his bed and nonchalantly follow his morning regimen of exercise? Though she'd managed to catch a few winks last night, her sleep hadn't been restful.

She followed him into the kitchen where a comfortablelooking woman with wispy brown-streaked-with-gray hair frowned at the shopping reminder attached to the refrigerator. "Does this say bugs? I should shop for bugs?" She glanced in horror at the gleaming kitchen floor. "Or does this mean we have bugs?"

"Actually, I meant to write bags," Byron said smoothly. "Helen, I'd like you to meet the new nanny, Lindsey Olson."

Helen's handshake was firm and strong. She was nicely plump, as befitted a good cook.

"Pleased to meet you," Lindsey said.

"Same here." Helen refilled Lindsey's coffee mug. "Sit, Lindsey. You can tell me what happened here last night."

"Not now," Byron said. "I'm going into San Diego and Lindsey is coming with me."

"The children arrive at five o'clock this afternoon," Helen reminded. "Should I pick them up?"

"I'll take care of it."

Lindsey had been employed in enough households to realize that Helen McHenry would take a proprietary interest in the events of the previous evening. She also knew that the best way to ensure a good stay in Catalina was to be friends with the housekeeper. She nodded to Byron. "Would you mind if I got acquainted with Helen while you get dressed?"

"No problem." He consulted his waterproof watch. "I'll be ready to leave in fifteen minutes."

The moment he left the room, Helen turned to Lindsey. "Talk fast, young lady. You have some explaining to do."

"The police haven't questioned you, yet?"

"Lordy, no! My hubby and I were off fishing yesterday and we spent the night on the boat. The minute we got home this morning, a reporter fellow popped out of the hibiscus hedge. Like toast from a toaster, he was. And full of questions. What happened?"

"Last night there was an intruder. A man in a red ski mask broke in and threatened us with a gun." Lindsey swallowed hard. "I shot and killed him."

"Yes, yes. I know that part. But were you naked?"

"As a matter of fact, I was in the bathtub."

Helen gaped. "With Byron?"

"He was in the bathroom, but not in my tub. You see, he'd brought me a dinner tray, but the door to my bedroom was locked so he came in through the bathroom." Lindsey sighed. "I know this sounds awful, Mrs. McHenry."

"Sound perfectly natural to me. You're both young and healthy. It's high time for Byron to take an interest in something other than his work and his children."

"I'm not an interest," Lindsey said.

"Don't tell me, tell them." Helen placed the morning edition of the *Daily Herald*, a Los Angeles tabloid, on the counter. On page four was the photo of Lindsey and Byron on the terrace, arm-in-arm. The headline read, Auto Heir Saved by Nanny. The brief accompanying article mentioned the elegant bathroom, the fatal wounds of the intruder and Byron's wealth. Lindsey groaned as she read the description of herself as a "statuesque blonde and an ace marksman."

"Byron needs a woman in his life," Helen said. "And his children need a mother."

"But, I'm not—"

"Probably not," Helen said gently. "But there's no harm in trying, Lindsey. He's a handsome catch."

"But I'm not fishing for a relationship."

Skeptically, Helen propped her fists on her sturdy hips and studied Lindsey. "Really?"

"I've been married before." Twice, she added to herself. "I'm not looking to try again."

Helen bobbed her head once. "But I was all set to lecture you about not falling for Byron and having your poor heart broken. Should I save my words for Byron himself? You won't hurt him, will you?"

"Of course not. In the first place, there's nothing between us. And I wouldn't want to hurt him. He seems to be a . . . good man."

Such an inadequate description, Lindsey thought. Byron was intelligent, witty, sensitive and virile. A very, very good man. And good men were hard to find.

Helen bustled in the kitchen, gliding a redolent pan of fresh muffins from the oven. "I'm sorry we weren't here last night, but my hubby had his heart set on an outing."

"It's best that you were gone. It was dangerous. That man came in with his gun drawn. I guess the police have decided that he was a robber."

"Probably on drugs," Helen said authoritatively.

"But why would a drug-crazed maniac come to Catalina? And why wear a ski mask?" Lindsey shook her head. "I'm afraid the attack is more personal. Do you know if Byron has any enemies?"

"Not really. Right before his wife's death, he had some terrible rows with her parents, the Dixons. But I wouldn't call them enemies. And there's always bickering among the family. About the inheritance, you know."

"What about Jerrod Blake?"

"Nasty man. But he does like my cooking." Helen's eyes widened. "You don't think Jerrod had anything to do with this?"

"No, not with the intruder."

Byron strode into the kitchen. "We have to leave right away, Lindsey." He turned to the housekeeper, who pitched him two blueberry muffins. "Thank you, Helen. By the way, you'll probably be talking with the police today—a Detective Murtaugh. Give him your full cooperation."

"I certainly will."

"However, if there are telephone calls or visits from reporters, say nothing."

He plucked the newspaper from the countertop, saw the photo, read the article and tore out the offending page. "Of all the dumb, idiotic—"

The telephone rang and Byron went to answer. "This is how I want you to handle phone calls, Helen."

He grabbed the receiver. "No comment."

"How dare you say that to me, Byron."

"Hi, Estelle." Byron crumpled the sheet of newsprint into a tight ball. "How's Cape Cod?"

"Dreadful. My eyes are baggy from not sleeping. And I had to threaten mayhem with your nasty publicity department at Continental Auto to allow this call to come through." Her tone was imperious. "How dare you ignore my messages!"

"There's nothing to worry about," Byron said. "Everything is under control."

"This isn't my fault, Byron. Even if I did take Dan-dan with me and leave you virtually unprotected. People aren't blaming me, are they?"

"Gee, Estelle, I don't know. There hasn't been time for a survey."

"Put Miss Olson on the phone."

Byron gazed at Lindsey and lied. "She's not awake yet."

"I must insist that you fetch her. Immediately. I wish to speak with that little slut."

"She saved my life," he said, coldly.

"Don't be an ass, Byron. Can't you see what she's after? I knew. I knew the moment I laid eyes on her. Oh, I should have known better than to hire a young single woman."

"Goodbye, Estelle."

Though his aunt stung the telephone wires with her loud protests, Byron hung up. He turned to Helen. "If Estelle calls again, you have my permission to disconnect the telephone."

"Yes sir." Helen beamed.

"We'll be back in time to pick up the kids." He gestured to the rear of the house. "Let's go, Lindsey."

He hurried across the terrace and opened a small gate that led to a hewn rock path. After a few wide stairs, the path wound narrowly down a steep cliff to a cove. An inverted canoe was beached on gray sands and a motor boat was moored at a short pontoon pier.

He helped Lindsey into the boat, fired up the motor and carefully maneuvered away from the cove. His yacht was moored at the marina in Avalon, but he'd already decided against taking it. The weather was clement enough that the motor boat would suffice for their crossing to the mainland. And Byron was too hurried to bother with the larger craft. He needed to settle this matter with Jerrod before Sonny and Amanda arrived.

They made good time across the open sea, and as the mountains of Catalina faded behind them, he relaxed. Lindsey appeared to be enjoying the ride. Her blond hair streamed behind her as she faced into the wind. The fabric of her lavender blouse molded against her breasts. When she turned toward him, an errant breeze caused her blouse to gape slightly, offering him an enticing view of delicate flesh.

Immediately, he lifted his gaze to her face. No point in putting her on guard again. But he couldn't help noticing her femininity. How could he be a man and think of anything else? Byron teased, "*Solar One* would have been faster."

"Not if we were stopped by the FAA," she retorted. "What did Estelle have to say?"

"Predictably, she was worried about gossip. Would people think the attack was her fault because she'd taken Dan-dan with her?"

"It's possible."

"More likely, he was a friend of Dan-dan's." Byron pointed at the waves to the south of their boat. "Flying fish."

Like silvery torpedos, the fish skimmed the tops of the waves. Lindsey watched delightedly, then gazed back at the two-thousand-foot peak of Catalina's Mount Orizaba. An enchanted island guarded by shimmering fish. Were the waters really clearer here? Were there really more birds?

She wished to ride on the glass-bottomed boats in Avalon, to swim in Emerald Bay, to explore the cliffs with Byron as her guide. A lovely fantasy, but not for today. Her attention turned forward. Though the Pacific was relatively smooth and the sun shone brilliantly, the California coast was not yet visible.

"Seriously, Byron, do you have any reason for thinking Dan-dan is involved?"

"The possibility of an inside job has occurred to me. Especially since Mikey Rankin came by boat. Not many people know about our little dock."

"Surely there are plenty of piers on Catalina."

"Not on the seaward side of the island. The current's too strong. During storms, we get high breakers against the cliffs. We're lucky to have that little cove."

"But anyone could have discovered the cove," she said. "Why else would you suspect this was an inside job?"

"Maybe I'm forcing logic into an irrational event, but there are indications. Mikey Rankin didn't waste time going through the house, searching for valuables. Suppose he knew from an inside informant—a former employee or an acquaintance or even some disgruntled second cousin—that I didn't leave cash and jewelry lying around. The only way I can be robbed is for someone to force me to open the safe."

"So Rankin intended to force you at gunpoint to unlock the safe." She completed his thought. "He could have robbed you, tied you up and escaped. With that mask, you couldn't identify him."

"Inside knowledge would also explain how he happened to pick a night when the McHenrys, Dan-dan and Estelle were gone. Even if he knew you were coming, he would expect for you to be exhausted and asleep after your long trip."

"There are a lot of missing pieces, Byron." Though she hated to mention a difficult topic again, she said, "Until we have answers, it might be best to take the kids somewhere else."

"No," he said. "I'm sure the danger is over. If this was an inside job that failed with fatal results for Rankin, another try seems unlikely. If the intruder was connected to the NORAD disks, there's no problem because the disks are gone."

Another possibility fluttered at the edge of his conscious. It wasn't logical or rational, but an intuitive sense.

"What else, Byron?"

"Would you please quit reading my mind."

"Tell me."

"Just an idea. You know how that old wives' tale—when death comes, your life passes before your eyes. That's how I felt last night. When that guy crashed into the bathroom, the seconds felt like hours. An infinity of slow-motion replay. I knew I was about to die." He'd seen his death in the eyes of the intruder. Mikey Rankin was the predator. Byron had been the prey. "That guy meant to kill me."

"But why? You don't even know him."

"You're right. It makes no sense." He pointed to the eastern horizon. "That's Newport Beach ahead of us."

"I don't like this, Byron. He might have been a professional hit man."

"And where does that leave us? I'm not familiar with criminal protocol, but it seems that if he was a hired gun, his contract failed. All bets are off. It's over."

"Maybe not. What if it's not over?"

The worried note in her voice sounded clearly above the motor's whine and the cries of seagulls. And Byron was touched. Though Lindsey barely knew him, she was honestly concerned for his safety. Or was it only a professional concern? He looked into her tense blue eyes. "I guess it wouldn't look good on your résumé to have your employer murdered in cold blood, huh?"

"This isn't a joke."

"I know."

When he grasped her hand and squeezed, he saw the muscles in her forearm tighten. What a lovely contradiction she was! Guarded, yet vulnerable. Last night, she'd killed a man. Today, she was magnificently female—caring and concerned and everything a woman should be.

Gently, he brushed the hair away from her face. His hand rested at her nape. His darkly tanned arm contrasted with the pale gold of her flesh. Strands of her blond hair twined around his fingers.

He leaned toward her. Aware that he was crossing a forbidden boundary between them, Byron moved slowly, allowing her the opportunity to refuse. But she did not object. Instead, he saw affirmation in her clear eyes. Her lips parted.

He slanted his mouth across hers, lightly savoring the damp delicate texture. He pulled away, stared into the faceted depths of her blue eyes, then his lips joined hers again, tasting more deeply of her special flavor mingled with salt spray.

When Lindsey kissed back, her mouth was hungry. She knew their intimacy was terribly unprofessional, but that knowledge vanished in the wake of sensation when her tongue readily engaged with his.

Her heart beat faster. Arousal surged through her body, wakening dormant needs that had been buried deep. Her arms coiled around him. Her breasts pressed against the flesh of his chest and tenderness overwhelmed her.

Wind from the sea whipped around them, cushioning their hot embrace with cool salt breeze.

And then their kiss ended. A mistake? Perhaps. But she wouldn't exchange that moment for anything. She trained her gaze on the approaching landscape.

At the San Diego pier, Byron placed a phone call to a local Continental Auto dealership. Moments later, a car was delivered to their phone booth. With great deference, the driver turned over the keys to a sporty little red sedan.

Most women would have been impressed, but not Lindsey. "A sports car," she complained. "Not exactly subtle, is it?"

"Am I missing something here?"

"What if we're being followed?"

"In this little baby, we can outrun them." Byron climbed behind the steering wheel, waved his thanks and headed toward the hills where Jerrod Blake's workshop was located.

Half an hour later, at the foot of a deserted hill, Byron parked. "There are two ways into the workshop." He indicated a steep, winding cedar staircase that disappeared into a grove of palm trees. "That twists upward for over seventy-eight steps."

"What's the other way?"

"I can circle around to the rear door. That means announcing our arrival at a gate, which is usually locked and guarded by three rather unfriendly great Danes."

"What is it with you Cyrils? Doesn't anyone in your family live on Main Street, U.S.A.?" Lindsey opened the passenger door. "I guess we should take the stairs."

"I was afraid you were going to say that." Byron exited the sports car and stretched his legs. "After you. And don't bother being stealthy. I'm sure he already knows we're here."

When Lindsey rounded the last switch in the staircase, she was face-to-face with a thin gentleman who had, last night, identified himself as Colonel Appleton. Today, he wore thick eyeglasses and a white lab jacket. In his hands, Appleton held a long, odd-shaped rifle.

"Out for a bit of exercise?" he asked.

Lindsey gauged the distance between herself and the barrel of the gun. "Where's your friend? Captain Lantz?"

"She's off with Jerrod."

Byron trudged up the last three stairs. "You mean Jerrod isn't here? I came all the way up for nothing?"

"Perhaps it will save you a phone call. Jerrod said to tell you that his solar engine is far superior to yours."

"You know what? I don't give a damn."

Byron didn't slow his momentum but stalked right up to Appleton and took the rifle from his hand.

Without protest, Appleton allowed himself to be disarmed. If anything, he seemed relieved as he stuffed his fists into the deep pockets of his lab jacket.

Byron glowered. "I won't put up with this anymore, Appleton. That is your name, isn't it?"

"Yes. And I must say that I agree. I'm tired of charades. I'm a scientist, not an actor. Nor a surveillance person."

"So you were the person who was watching from the cliff?"

He gave one brisk bob of his head. "Yes."

"Did you plant bugs in the house?" Lindsey questioned.

"I did. But I wasn't happy about doing it."

"No stomach for spying?" Byron guessed.

"Spying doesn't bother me, but poor technology does. The listening devices I used were inefficient and archaic." He pivoted and started toward the lab. "You might as well come inside."

They followed him toward an average-looking cedar house. Through the palm trees, Lindsey could see that this pleasant home butted up to a much larger structure, nearly barn- sized. A high chain-link fence topped with barbed wire surrounded the grounds behind the house.

Inside was a nondescript room, rather like a doctor's office. While Appleton served coffee in mugs, Lindsey marveled at this self-proclaimed "scientist's" transformation. Last night, when he had been portraying a colonel, Appleton was authoritative and aggressive. When he'd been the watcher on the hillside, she'd sensed danger from his blackclad appearance. Today, he was the very epitome of a nerd.

"We've reviewed the information on your computer disks," he informed Byron. "And Jerrod happens to be far ahead of you in the development of his solar-powered engine."

"This isn't a race," Byron asserted. "And, by the way, you people are in deep trouble with army intelligence. Those guys don't take kindly to being impersonated."

Appleton shrugged.

"If you return all the computer disks to me, including the faked NORAD disks," Byron offered, "I just might be able to convince the real intelligence agents that last night was only a prank."

"Jerrod has the disks." Appleton's grin was smug. "And he did leave a message for you."

He produced a tiny cassette recorder from the base of a lamp and punched the Play button. A cheery voice resounded.

"Welcome, Byron. Too bad I couldn't be home to welcome you, but I've always been one step ahead, haven't I? Your disks haven't showed me anything I didn't know, but I suppose you want the silly things back."

"That's right," Byron muttered.

"I will meet you exactly one half hour from the moment you leave the lab. At the Riverdale Airfield. In hangar number four."

He gave detailed directions to which Lindsey paid strict attention.

The voice on the tape concluded, "Right now, Byron, you're thinking that I am hiding in the lab behind the house. Rest assured that I am not and you are not permitted to enter my workshop. The locks are so programmed that my handprint is required to enter. See you soon, nephew."

Byron glared at Appleton who was obviously enjoying his employer's little joke. "Would Jerrod have given me this information on the telephone?"

"My instructions were not to answer the phone."

"I see. So, Jerrod wanted to make this visit as troublesome as possible." He rose to his feet and drained his coffee mug. "We're leaving now, Appleton. I suppose you have your instructions on how to start the countdown."

Descending the staircase wasn't quite as strenuous as the climb. At the car, Lindsey asked, "Shall I drive?"

He tossed her the keys and sank into the passenger seat. "I can't belive this. How does Jerrod think he can get away with fake intelligence agents? And robbery? And sending that idiot Appleton to spy on me?"

"Eccentricity?"

"There comes a point when it's no longer charming."

Lindsey flicked the key in the ignition. While Byron stewed, she negotiated the hairpin turns down the hill from Jerrod's lab, enjoying the quick response of the little red sports car.

At the first stoplight, she noticed a gray Chevy in the rearview mirror. There had also been a Chevy trailing them down the hill. Were they being followed?

Lindsey made a sharp right and circled back to the same stoplight.

"What are you doing?" Byron asked. "These weren't the directions."

She watched as the gray car appeared in the rearview mirror. It was three cars back and in the next lane over. There was no doubt in her mind. "Damn," she said. "We've picked up a tail."

Chapter Seven

Byron stared through the rear window. A tail? "That gray car with the frosted windows?"

She nodded.

"Great. What do we do now?"

Her eyes gleamed. Her lips curled in a grin. "Fasten your seat belt, Byron."

She punched the accelerator and swerved across three lanes of traffic. With a flick of her wrist, she changed lanes again and again. Her speed was far beyond any posted limit for in-town driving. The sporty red car darted and danced like a willing partner in a vehicular waltz. "I might be a little rusty," she said, "but I have taken instruction in escape driving."

Byron gripped the dashboard as she whipped an illegal U-turn. "Why don't I feel reassured?"

Their tail made a less graceful move to follow Lindsey. They were almost a block behind when she pulled into a nearly empty parking lot surrounding a shopping mall. "How's the suspension on this model of car?"

"I don't know. Why?"

"I thought we might try jumping something." She chuckled at his look of panic. "Just kidding."

Instead, she revved the engine and the car squealed through the lot. With a hard crank of the steering wheel, she spun in a one-hundred-eighty-degree turn and disappeared behind the rows of mall shops. After a quick backtracking through side streets, they returned to the route Jerrod had described.

She didn't slow down until the zippy red sports car came to a dust-swirling stop in front of a high chain-link fence. Lindsey read the rusted metal sign: Riverdale Airfield.

She squinted through the windshield. Not a thriving center of activity. In fact, there was no movement at all unless she counted the occasional tumbleweed. Dry, maize-colored weeds obscured the tarmac runways. Four hangars, badly in need of paint, hulked before them.

"Riverdale Airfield looks like it hasn't been used since the biplane era. Are you sure this is the right place?"

"I'm sure. It's typical of Jerrod to select an obscure, deserted rendezvous." He peeled his tense fingers off the armrest. "About your exhibition of escape driving—"

"I'm good, aren't I?"

"Just wait until I get you up in *Solar One*."

"I'll hold my breath. Speaking of alternate means of transportation, who do you think was following us?"

"I'd bet it was army intelligence," he said. "I expect that when Wright swept the villa for bugs last night, he planted a few of his own. He's probably following us, hoping we'll lead him to the fake agents."

"You don't think it was Uncle Jerrod? Wouldn't it be his style to set a tail on you?"

"But why? He's planning to meet us here." Byron checked his wristwatch. "In about two minutes. So, I'd better get the gate open and go to...which hangar?"

"Number four."

Byron went to the gates, untwined the chain that held them closed and pushed the gates wide so Lindsey could drive through. Before returning to the car, he replaced the chain.

The little car bumped across the rutted blacktop. The furthest building from the gate was marked with a black-painted four.

"This must be the place," she said. "Hard to believe that a nice civilized suburban development is less than a mile away."

"I wonder what Jerrod has hidden here."

"*Solar Two?*" she suggested.

"I doubt it. We're both working on solar-powered engines, but it's unlikely that we've both decided to test our concept on helicopters."

"Unlikely seems to be the rule," she muttered.

Like being followed. The chance to swing into action with her escape driving had been fun, but the idea of someone tailing them was not. She climbed out from behind the steering wheel and stared at the hangar, wishing that they'd taken a few extra moments to purchase ammunition for Byron's handgun.

There was something ominous about the dilapidated hangar and the desolated airfield. A premonition of danger slithered down her backbone. "Byron? Are you superstitious?"

"Not in the usual way. Black cats crossing my path don't frighten me, and I don't mind walking under ladders." He came around the car and stood beside her. "But there are some psychic phenomena that defy logical explanation."

"Such as?"

"Déjà vu—the idea that you've been in a place before. Or the sense of knowing someone who you've never met before. I feel that way about you."

She glanced up sharply, unable to decide whether he was teasing or not. "How so?"

"There's a connection between us. A destiny that's waiting to be fulfilled."

She hadn't been thinking of that sort of superstition. Rather, her focus had been on the unexplainable tension that warned her against entering the hangar. Yet, when he spoke, she was aware of how sensitized her emotions had become. And how confused she felt. "Let's get this meeting with your eccentric uncle over with."

They entered through the huge open center doors. Though overhead bulbs were lit and sunlight peeked through cracks in the corrugated tin roof, the air hung thick and gloomy over a few stacks of crates, a beat-up station wagon and a shiny little one-propellor plane.

"I'm here, Jerrod," Byron shouted.

"I can see that."

The tall, lean man who stepped out from behind the small airplane did not fulfill Lindsey's expectations of a mad inventor. Jerrod Blake wore a magnificently tailored sports jacket. He was tall, like Byron. His dark eyes were like Byron's. They might have been brothers, except for Jerrod's steel-gray hair. His movements were elegant as he took her hand and gave it a firm shake.

"Please accept my apologies," he said, "for any inconvenience I may have caused."

No matter how charming he was, she was not willing to forgive and forget so quickly. "Small annoyances, sir? Such as snipers, bugs and imposter intelligence agents."

"Snipers?"

"Appleton on the cliffside with the airgun," Byron explained. "Actually, we should thank you for that. Appleton's presence put Lindsey on the alert. So she was ready for the intruder in the red ski mask."

Jerrod gave a thin smile. "Shocking business, that gunman."

"You wouldn't happen to know anything about him, would you?" Lindsey asked. "Like who he was or why he came."

"Certainly not."

"And you didn't have us followed from the lab to here?"

"Why should I do that?" He nodded toward the small plane. "I flew."

Jerrod was smooth, she thought. Like Byron. But there was a difference. Jerrod's self-possessed air was lacking in vulnerability. She doubted that anyone or anything truly touched him. "I have one last question for you, Mr. Blake. Byron's children will arrive this afternoon. Is there any possibility of danger to them? Or to Byron?"

"None that I am aware of," he replied. "Of course, I'm not familiar with all of Byron's enemies."

"What enemies?" Byron practically shouted. "Who the hell are these invisible enemies that everyone assumes I have?"

"You're more offensive than you know." Jerrod's voice was deliberately cutting. "It goes without saying that you're often unreasonable."

"What do you mean?"

"Don't be obtuse, Byron." He paced away from them and slapped the hood of the old station wagon for emphasis. The metallic clang echoed in the hangar. "Surely you're aware of the antagonism caused by your refusal to distribute father's inheritance. Frankly I'm surprised that your intruder in the ski mask wasn't one of the distant Cyril cousins." To Lindsey, he added, "The family loves their little pranks."

Byron struggled for control. He knew the strategy that his uncle was using; Jerrod was deliberately trying to get under his skin. Byron forced a grin. "This isn't a case of whoopee cushions and sugar in the salt shaker. We're talking about attempted murder, Jerrod. I agree that I might have annoyed some of the family, but we're not the Borgias."

"Likewise, your absentee management of Continental Auto has caused great hostility. You might wish to investigate your executives in Detroit. Or, possibly, one of the architects you fired for incompetence."

"That's absurd."

"I can remember, even when you were a tot, that you had enemies. Your first girlfriend. The boys on your baseball team when you lost the play-off game with a wild pitch. Miss Olson will appreciate the fact that two of your nannies quit in a huff. I seem to recall that your late wife's family, the Dixons, didn't much care for you. Even your mama and father were frequently disgusted with you. Estelle despises you. So does her muscle-bound boyfriend." Jerrod frankly sneered. "You see, Byron, your assumption that you have no enemies is naive."

"Is it?" Though Byron had no wish to engage in mudslinging with his uncle, his pulse was hammering. He gulped back his anger. "Perhaps you could make a list for the police. And do be sure to include the members of my Little League team."

"For those fools who patrol Catalina? I'll make no list for them. They are unimaginative idiots."

Byron recalled the reason for Jerrod's hostility and explained to Lindsey. "About five years ago, the sheriff's department on Catalina gave Jerrod a hard time because of an explosion in the marina at Avalon."

"It was an experiment," Jerrod snapped. "No one was hurt, and I paid for the damages. And your military friends were quite impressed with my peanut-sized grenade."

"Speaking of the military, there's a Colonel Wright who was not amused by Appleton's impersonation last night."

"But that's really not a problem, is it? Since the supposed NORAD disks were fakes. I've broken no law. I have never actually been in unauthorized possession of military documents."

"How did you know the disks were phony?" Lindsey piped in.

"I didn't until I glanced at them last night. That was, of course, after I had reviewed your solar-engine disks, Byron. And I don't mind telling you that you're on the wrong track. An interesting track using the helicopter, but wrong, nonetheless." Jerrod went to a stack of crates and removed a large briefcase from behind them. He opened it, took out a manila envelope and handed it to Byron. "And now, I'm bored with these games. You may have your disks."

Byron checked the contents of the envelope and nodded. "Thank you."

"That concludes our business," Jerrod said dismissively.

Byron gazed pensively at the envelope. Was he really on the wrong track? It was impossible for him to tell if Jerrod was lying. He, too, was tired of playing games. Byron took a deep breath and laid his cards on the table. "Look, Jerrod, I'd like to forget our differences. The solar engine is an important project. I would very much like to work together on this."

"Not a chance. I won't have you taking credit for my work."

"I don't want credit," Byron said. "I want to share our discoveries and complete the task."

Jerrod was horrified. "Stop it, Byron."

"If you won't work with me, I'd like the opportunity to make the first offer on your solar engine when it is completed."

"Whatever for?"

"Think of the possibilities, Jerrod. If we could adapt a solar engine for cars and mass-produce the engine, we could greatly alleviate pollution. Think of the benefits—the global benefits."

"I'd rather think of the profits. Really, Byron, this display of idealism is tawdry and disgusting."

Byron stiffened. "May I bid on your invention?"

"Of course. I'll accept bids from everyone—even you. Now, goodbye, Byron." He bent slightly from the waist. "Goodbye, Miss Olson. It was pleasant to meet you."

When she and Byron turned toward the door of hanger number four, it swung open. Four men holding guns entered. They all wore ski masks.

"Nobody move," came the shout.

Lindsey dodged behind a crate. A glance over her shoulder showed that Byron had instinctively followed her. They looked back at Uncle Jerrod, standing like a statue.

"I can't leave him," Byron said.

Before Lindsey could stop him, Byron was in motion. He grabbed his uncle and dragged him behind the beat-up station wagon.

"Freeze, dammit." The guttural yell resounded through the high, empty hangar.

Peering around the edge of the crate, Lindsey saw three men running toward the car. The fourth man remained at the hangar door. Their only chance was for her to get past the sentry and go for help. Was there another way out?

Crouched down, she scurried toward the shadows by the wall and yanked at a board. It was firm. And she'd make too much noise trying to break through. What now? There wasn't much cover near her.

But her hand rested on a wooden ladder. She looked up. Shafts of sunlight pierced the corrugated sheets of tin that formed the roof of the hangar. If she could climb up, she might be able to squeeze through a crack onto the roof.

Climbing slowly to avoid attracting attention, Lindsey went up the ladder. She reached a small ledge in the eaves and flattened herself upon it. Her perch was hotter than a kiln from the sun beating directly on the tin roof. Gasping, she looked down. Two men circled around the station wagon where Byron and Jerrod hid. Byron seemed to be arguing with his uncle, who suddenly stood, straight and tall.

"I demand to know what's going on," Jerrod snapped.

One of the armed men darted around the car, his pistol trained on Jerrod. "Put your hands up, old man."

"I most certainly will not."

A third masked man appeared behind Jerrod. Without comment, he clubbed Jerrod on the back of his head. Jerrod Blake crumpled in a heap.

In a sudden burst, Byron shoved away from the car. He knocked one man off his feet and fled to the far end of the building. Like Lindsey, his first thought was to pry a board from the wall. He hurled himself against the wall. It seemed to crack. She watched as Byron worked furiously at one of the loosened boards.

"Don't move," shouted the man who had hit Jerrod. "Or the old man is a dead man."

She saw Byron freeze.

"Get over here."

Lindsey almost cried out. *Don't listen to him, Byron. They'll kill you anyway. And your uncle. Break through the damn wall. You're almost through.* She knew these were not honorable men.

Desperately, she inched along the eave, aiming toward a large crack in the roof. The corrugated tin burned against her back. Once on the roof, how would she get down? Jump? Though she'd surely break an arm or leg, Lindsey knew her chance of safety was better on the roof than facing those men in red ski masks.

She looked down. Byron was surrounded by the three men. His hands were laced on top of his head. The man he'd knocked down tucked his pistol in the waistband of his trousers. He cracked his knuckles, drew back and unloaded a rabbit punch into Byron's torso.

With a groan, Byron bent double.

"Get your hands back up." Another man stabbed Byron in the ribs with the barrel of his gun.

"Where's the girl?" shouted the man by the door.

Lindsey lay utterly still.

The man who had punched Byron stepped into the center of the hangar. "Hey, girl! What's your name? Lindsey.

That's it, right? Hey, Lindsey. If you don't show yourself, your boyfriend is going to be in a lot of pain.''

"Don't do it," Byron yelled.

"You, shuttup." The man drew his gun. "If you don't show yourself by the count of three, I'll shoot. But he's not going to die. One." He lowered the barrel of his gun, aiming toward Byron's knee. "Two."

"I'm here," she shouted.

"Where?"

The street-smart part of her mind cursed her weakness. Why had she said anything? She knew better than to trust anything these men said. But she hadn't been on the streets for a long time, and she couldn't stand by and watch them hurt Byron.

"Where are you, Lindsey?" There was a sly, cajoling note in the man's voice. "I'm counting again. One. Two."

Weakly, she waved. "Up here."

The man by the door moved into a position below her. His gun was braced in both hands. "Get down here, Lindsey."

She wriggled backward. By the time she'd descended the last rung of the ladder, two masked men with guns stood waiting. They spaced themselves carefully beyond her kicking range. Not that it made a difference. She couldn't fight four armed men.

"Move it," one of them ordered.

Reluctantly, she complied, walking with slow, measured strides to the center of the hangar where Byron stood with his hands on his head.

The man who'd threatened to shoot Byron came toward her. When he stood only five feet away from her, he slowly pulled the red ski mask off. She knew that face. Thick lips, low heavy eyebrows. It was the face of the man she'd murdered, and he grinned like death.

She squeezed her eyelids closed. It couldn't be him. Mikey Rankin was dead. She'd killed him.

When she looked again, the man had moved to within a few paces of her. His eyes were opaque. His hand reached toward her and she recoiled when he touched her cheek. She needed to strike back, but she was numb, senseless.

He slapped her face. "You killed my brother."

Stinging pain from his blow wakened her like a splash of cold water. "Mikey," she said.

"That's right. Mikey Rankin. My baby brother."

He swung again, but this time she was in control of her reflexes. Lindsey ducked, deflected his hand.

He prudently stepped back a few paces. "You're a pretty good driver, Lindsey. You lost the first car that was tailing you. But you didn't lose me."

"There were two tails?"

"Yeah. Like the old man said, Byron has got a lot of enemies." He nodded to the other men. "Go ahead and take off your masks."

His command shot dread into Lindsey's heart. If these men didn't care about being identified, it could only mean one thing. They did not intend to leave witnesses.

Unmasked, she saw four men in their late twenties, dressed in casual southern California style. They weren't frightening, not even Mikey's brother now that she knew he wasn't a reincarnation from the grave. Except for the pistols in their hands, they could have been a golf foursome.

Good businessmen, she thought. Adept at crime.

Carefully, she avoided looking at Byron. If she hoped to survive, Lindsey could not allow herself to think of the probable consequences. She needed to be tough, to meet these guys on their own terms.

Mikey's brother, who was apparently the leader, extended his hand to her. "Take my hand, Lindsey. And don't try anything cute or your boyfriend's dead."

Unflinching, she met his gaze. His eyes were the pale shade of blue that reflected an emptiness within. His full lips formed a straight line. Not tall but muscular, he was broad-shouldered beneath his blue knit shirt.

When she accepted his hand, he tightened his grip unmercifully. She gritted her teeth to keep from crying out.

"I'm Martin Rankin," he said. "And you're shaking hands with death, lady."

Lindsey did not question his statement.

"Last night, you killed my little brother." He threw down her hand and backed away from her. "Today, you're going to pay."

"Then let me pay," she said, matching his coolness. "You can release these other two."

"I don't care about the old man," Rankin said, "but Byron Cyril was my brother's contract, and I'm going to clean up this loose end for him. You're both going to die."

"I'll pay you," Byron said. "Let us go, and I'll pay triple what anyone else would pay."

"No deals." Rankin chopped the air. "I'm not doing this for the money."

"But you're a professional. Name your price." Byron raised his voice. "I'll make you rich. All of you."

One of the other men spoke up. "That sounds pretty good, you know. We can make some bucks here."

"We're not doing this strictly for the cash, buddy. Don't you get it? I loved Mikey."

"Come on, Rankin. I need a new car."

"Dumb." Rankin spat out the word. "You think he's not going to call the cops? You think you'll get a chance to spend that money?"

"I won't say a word," Byron said. "I swear I won't."

"Besides," Lindsey put in. "You haven't done anything yet. We won't press charges."

"Yeah? But if Byron here gives us money it's called extortion. Understand? You guys understand?"

Rankin was a dangerous combination of brawn and street-smart intellect. But he also had a temper. Lindsey didn't doubt for a moment that Rankin's desire for revenge was sincere; that same fanatic light had shone in her first husband's eyes. She'd have to use Rankin's temper to drive him into a dumb mistake.

"I was doing my job," she said. "Don't blame me if your brother blew the contract." She appealed to the others. "Am I right? Mikey Rankin messed up."

There were slight nods of assent. Lindsey took that small encouragement and expanded on it. "I was faster than your brother. A better shot."

Rankin's mouth curled in a snarl. "And who are you supposed to be? The nanny from hell?"

There were chuckles from the others. Good, Lindsey thought, excellent. They were relaxing, letting down their guard. "I'm a darn good shot."

"What about hand-to-hand combat?"

Quick as a striking rattlesnake, Rankin grabbed her wrist and twisted her arm.

Lindsey gasped. *Not yet. Don't fight back yet.* She fell to the ground, effectively breaking his hold without appearing to retaliate.

"Hey, Rankin," one of his men complained. "Let's just do them and get out."

"Okay, but we're going to do them good." He glanced around the warehouse. "Terry, see if the keys are in that airplane. If they are, start it."

With a shrug, Terry moved to the small single-engine plane.

Lindsey noted that Terry had slipped his gun into the waistband of his jeans. Now two of them—Terry and Rankin—were unable to fire an immediate shot. Still kneeling on the concrete floor of the hangar, she looked over at Byron.

His expression was tense but alert. She could feel how much he wanted to comfort her, to help her.

The propeller at the nose of the small plane whirred to life, stirring the dust in the hangar. Blocks at the wheels kept the aircraft from moving.

"Hey!" Terry shouted. "Look at me! I'm a pilot."

"Looks good on you," Rankin said. "We ought to buy you an airplane, kid. Now get out of there." He coughed heavily. "The dirt in here is disgusting. Terry, go open the doors."

The huge wooden door opened and a crack of light poured into the hangar. Lindsey saw her escape. Rankin yanked her to her feet. Stumbling forward, she remembered to appear helpless, to cry out. "What are you going to do to me?"

He gripped her forearm and thrust her hand above her head. "This hand killed my brother. Now, I'm going to chop it off."

He dragged her to the front of the airplane. The others, including Byron, followed.

When she stood only a few feet away from the silver blur of the airplane's propeller, Lindsey understood his intentions. He meant to stick her hand into the whirring blades. She whitened. Absolute horror seethed through her, but when she heard Rankin's chuckle, she thrust fear away. This would not happen to her. She would not allow it.

She needed a diversion. She needed for Byron to make some kind of move so that she could get the drop on Rankin.

Rankin stepped behind her, his body shoved her forward, closer to the blades. He forced her arm upward and forward. Toward the propeller. She screamed and struggled—purposely being ineffectual, holding back, not letting Rankin guess at her strength or expertise.

Then Byron did it. He dove forward, shoving a block out from beneath the small plane's wheel. The plane started to turn. Rankin's men dodged out of the way.

And Lindsey reacted. With all her strength, she drove her free elbow into Rankin's chest. There was a satisfying crunch. A broken rib, she hoped as she elbowed again. His grip on her arm loosened. She reversed their hands and expertly flipped him to the floor. He reached for his gun. In a whirling movement, she kicked his arm. The gun went flying.

"Lindsey!" Byron was in the cockpit of the plane. "Over here. Quick."

The other men had recovered. She heard the discharge of a gun as she raced to the plane and leaped into the cockpit beside Byron.

"Hold on," was all he said.

They moved forward, through the hangar doors. Into the sunlight.

Chapter Eight

The engine sputtered but the small plane kept rolling across the weed-covered tarmac.

Swivelling in her seat, Lindsey saw the four men come through the door of hangar number four. Though she was pleased that Rankin was walking doubled over, the ping of bullets on the rear of the plane reminded her that she and Byron were still not safe. "Take off, Byron. They're still coming."

"Take off? Take a look at the left wing. I hit one of the doors."

The wing drooped pathetically, shattered at the tip. Ducking down in her seat, Lindsey's nostrils twitched. "What's that smell?"

"Fuel. We've got to ditch this plane before one of those bullets sets off an explosion."

Rankin's men ran after them for only a moment, then they headed back toward their car.

"I'm taking the plane near the fence," Byron said. "We can jump out, hide and hope they follow the plane."

"Jump out of a moving airplane?"

He gaped at her, then burst into laughter. "This from a woman who just faced maiming and certain death?"

"Maybe I've used up my quota of luck."

"You've got to push it," he said. "We're not moving that fast. Open the door, climb out on the wing and jump."

Easier said than done, but she agreed, knowing that Rankin's car would easily overtake the little airplane. Lindsey crept onto the wing. The weedy blacktop zoomed beneath her. Logically, she knew it wasn't far to the ground, but the motion created a sense of vertigo. *Don't think about it, just do it.* She looked up, saw the fence, took a deep breath and jumped.

From her martial-arts training, she knew how to fall and roll. But she was unprepared for the dizzying sensation of tumbling in an uncontrolled flip-flop.

Lindsey ended in a wide-legged sprawl beside the chain-link fence. She shook her head to keep the world from spinning. Her eyes blinked wider than two fried eggs.

Byron crouched beside her. "Are you okay?"

"I'm going to throw up."

"Later."

He propelled her toward a fortress of high tumbleweeds and pulled her to the ground where they were hidden from view. Before he'd bailed out, Byron had managed to twist the steering wheel, and the plane wobbled away from them in a loopy circle.

In a slow-motion moment, he waited. A midsized white sedan with a lot of chrome roared from behind the hangar and squealed across the airfield toward the little plane. Which way would Rankin go? Would he follow the plane? Or would he guess they'd bailed out?

Byron held his breath. If he and Lindsey were spotted, there would be no escape. Rankin couldn't be cute this time. No oddball tortures. No games. This time, Byron knew he'd be shot through the head.

His heart wrenched beneath his ribcage and he held Lindsey closer to him. She'd been so brave, so clever. If there were justice in the universe, she would not be harmed.

Then, it happened. Rankin's men chose to follow the erratic course of the plane.

But there wasn't time for Byron and Lindsey to savor their good fortune. As Rankin's car sped away, Byron whispered, "Let's go. Come on, over the fence."

Though her knees trembled and her head was still dizzy, Lindsey tried to do as Byron said. He hoisted her halfway up the chain-link fence. Automatically, she hung on. There had been hundreds of fences like this when she was a girl, hundreds of times she'd run from bullies twice her size. They hadn't caught her then. They wouldn't catch her now.

She grappled with her fingers and toes until she was up and over, crouching on the ground opposite.

As Byron gripped the chain links, he heard a roar behind him. He looked over his shoulder and saw the plane, unmanned, careering straight for him, the silvery blades dicing the sunlight.

In a flash, Byron scaled the chain links and dropped on the other side. There wasn't time to plan or select the best route through the arid treeless landscape. He grabbed Lindsey's hand and gave a one-word direction. "Run."

Apparently, their supply of luck had been depleted. As the plane bashed up against the fence, Rankin's men spotted them. Byron heard their shouts. In a moment, they'd be lined up against the fence, firing their guns.

Byron raced through the high weeds, tugging Lindsey behind him. Toward the road. He saw a car. If they could make it to that car... if the car would stop...

A volley of gunfire echoed through the deserted hills. Byron ran. Not much farther. They had to make it. They couldn't have come this far only to be brought down by a bullet.

He hit the road running, waving to the car. It pulled up at the gate to Riverdale Airfield. Byron yelled, "Hey! Help!"

Two men in suits leapt from the rear of the car. They took a braced stance and aimed their guns. "Freeze," they shouted. "Army intelligence."

Freeze? Byron glanced over his shoulder. Rankin's men were at the fence. They were taking aim. Freeze? There was no way he could stand still. But these army guys looked like they meant business.

"Freeze," one of them barked again. "Now, buddy, and I mean it."

Byron dove to the hard-packed earth at the shoulder of the road, flattening himself and pulling Lindsey along with him. He watched as the intelligence agents became aware of the situation and understood that Rankin's men were firing in their direction.

A spray of dirt kicked up beside Byron's elbow and he pulled it in, trying to make himself as small a target as possible while shielding Lindsey's body with his own.

Army intelligence had begun to return the fire of Rankin's men. Byron heard a yip of pain from the fence behind him.

"Good," he whispered. "I hope it was Rankin."

"He scared me," Lindsey mumbled. "I thought he was..."

"Mikey?" He felt her trembling beneath him. "It's going to be all right? It's okay, babe, it's going to be okay."

"Byron?"

"Yeah, babe?"

"Don't ever call me babe."

The gunfire ceased and Byron raised his head to look around. Colonel Wright was striding through the weeds toward them. Behind him, Byron saw Rankin's men streaking across the airfield in their chrome-covered car.

Pointing back at Rankin's car, Byron bounded to his feet. "They're getting away."

"Not necessarily," Wright said. "My men are going after them."

As Lindsey staggered to her feet beside him, Byron saw that the army intelligence car had pulled through the gates into Riverdale Airfield. "We've got to go back in there," he said. "My uncle is in hangar four. He's unconscious."

"I will be delighted to pick up your uncle. Jerrod Blake?" Wright halted only a foot away from them. "Your uncle was responsible for the two persons who impersonated U.S. Army Intelligence officers last night, wasn't he?"

"Perhaps you should ask him."

"You should have told me, Byron. It's my job to deal with these things. Instead, I wasted half the morning following you through San Diego, losing you and doubling back to Blake's lab to find out where you went. What were you trying to prove with that wild driving?"

"Trying to lose a tail," Lindsey said. "And Byron wasn't driving. I was."

Wright peered at her with an eagle eye. "I should have known. Then, this was your idea. Is that correct, Ms. Olson? Or should I address you as Mrs. Peterson? Mrs. Grakow?"

"Call me anything you like."

"We've done some checking on you, Ms. Olson Grakow Peterson."

She kept her gaze steady and her chin firm. But Lindsey crumbled inside. Wright knew her secrets. He knew about her first husband and her second.

For years, she'd dreaded this moment—a person in authority confronting her with her past. What now? As far as Lindsey knew, she hadn't broken any laws. But her first husband had. And her second husband was fully capable of fabricating a charge.

"I wonder," Wright said coldly. "How much does Byron know about your background?"

"Everything I need to know," Byron said. He clasped Lindsey's hand in his. "She's saved my life. Twice."

"Your sense of loyalty is admirable, Byron, but—"

"Thanks for your concern, Colonel Wright," Byron interrupted. "But it's misplaced. While you were checking my nanny's qualifications, we were attacked by a sadistic professional killer."

Wright nodded toward the airfield. "Them?"

"Their leader's name is Martin Rankin. The intruder from last night was his brother. Another of his gang is named Terry. Those are the people you should apprehend and investigate."

"Possibly."

Byron felt his temper rising. What did it take to get some action? "For all I know, Rankin and his brother and his whole damn gang are enemy agents. At least check it out."

"Let me warn you, Byron, if your Rankin is—as you claim—a professional killer or hit man, he's not my problem."

"No? It was my impression that the military was dedicated to protecting and defending citizens."

"Not on a one-to-one basis."

"Wonderful!" Byron threw his hands in the air. "What do I have to do to get some action? Get hit by an MX missile?"

"Your hit man is a police matter. Not my jurisdiction."

"Then don't lecture me about what I should or should not tell you. And don't threaten Lindsey about how she should or shouldn't drive. I won't be treated like a criminal while the real crooks walk away."

"Listen, mister. Your attitude isn't helping anything."

"Nor are you."

Byron pivoted away from the colonel and spoke to Lindsey. "Let's go the car. There's a lot to do before the children arrive." When he looked into her face, his take-charge attitude melted. Her teeth were clenched. Small lines of tension pinched her eyes. Against pain? "Oh, my God, Lindsey, are you all right? Can you walk? Maybe you should wait here and I'll bring the car."

Though her hip ached and her knees felt weak, Lindsey stood straighter. She'd rather hobble on a broken leg than spend one more minute with Colonel Wright. "I'll come with you."

With slow but determined footsteps, Lindsey and Byron limped along the blacktop road that led inside Riverdale Airfield. He braced his arm around her waist, encouraging her to lean on him.

Wright shouted after them. "A word of advice, Byron. We can't protect you from a professional hit man. No one can. If I were you, I'd seriously consider leaving town."

Over his shoulder, Byron retorted, "You're not me."

Once they were beyond Wright's earshot, Byron asked, "Are you really okay, Lindsey? If you want, you could sit here and wait for me."

"I'll live. Apart from what I suspect is going to be a Technicolor bruise on my hip, I'm okay. And it's better for me to keep moving. If I sit down, I'll stiffen up."

"I'm so sorry," he said softly. "Maybe I should do as Wright says and get out of town."

"Run away?" She offered a weak grin. "I've tried that and it's not too bad. After a couple of years, I even stopped looking over my shoulder."

"If it meant danger only for me, I'd rather stand and fight. But there are the kids to worry about." He exhaled a sigh of pure frustration. "This month on Catalina is supposed to be special for them and for me. It's the one time during the year when we're together without interruptions. I don't want to lose this time with them, Lindsey. Dammit, I don't want to run away."

"It's your decision," she said. "But I doubt we'll get much protection from Wright. Or from Detective Murtaugh or the Catalina sheriff's department. And it would take a private army to defend your house."

Byron considered while they dragged wearily toward the hangar. Should they stand? Or run? Obviously, it would be stupid to simply return to the villa and wait for Rankin to come after them. But where could they run? And how? It purely went against his grain to run away. Then he recalled Lindsey's words and a slow smile touched his lips. A private army.

By the time they reached the sporty red car, Byron's spirits had lifted. Why not a private army? He could afford it. He glanced at his wristwatch. It was noon, five hours until the children would arrive. Quite a lot needed to be done before then.

He was glad to see Jerrod Blake coming from the hangar. Despite a blood-matted contusion on the back of his skull, Jerrod was as imposing and cantankerous as ever. The first words out of his mouth were, "Where's my plane, Byron?"

"It made an unscheduled flight. I'll replace it."

"Oh, good. I wanted a new one, anyway."

Colonel Wright and the other army intelligence agents pulled up at the hangar and disembarked from their car. Crisply, Wright confronted them and announced, "My men were unable to apprehend Rankin. His car broke through another gate and my men lost them on the street. Though we will attempt to trace their car license number, I suspect it will lead to a false end. I'm afraid, Byron, that your enemies are at large."

"Who are these people?" Jerrod snapped. "More of your friends, Byron?"

"Friends?" Byron's eyebrow raised. "No, I wouldn't say that Colonel Wright is my friend. In fact, I believe he has more to discuss with you than with me."

Byron performed the introduction and stood back, cheerfully awaiting the clash between these two formidable gentlemen.

As soon as Colonel Wright shook Jerrod's hand, he made the first assault. "Mr. Blake, I believe you are responsible for a scheme to impersonate military-intelligence officers."

"Indeed?"

"Indeed, yes."

"Last night, I performed an experiment. I'm an inventor, sir. Perhaps you're familiar with some of my patents."

Jerrod paused to list several of his devices that had been adopted by the military, ranging from a sophisticated fuel-injection system to a disposable can opener.

"It has long been my contention," Jerrod lectured, "that identification procedures for all branches of military and civil law enforcement are sadly ineffective. I have spoken to several of my close associates in the military about this."

Again, Jerrod whipped through a list that ended just short of the White House.

Though Wright was not intimidated, he dared not be too aggressive. "Perhaps, we could discuss this in further depth. Would you come with me, Mr. Blake?"

"I'd be delighted, Colonel."

As Jerrod and the colonel strode together toward the colonel's car, Byron had no doubt that Jerrod's infraction of the law would be easily dismissed.

"Your Uncle Jerrod's good," Lindsey said, watching the car pull away. "From that conversation, it doesn't seem that Jerrod is being taken into custody for questioning. It seems more as if Wright was offering him a ride. Humbly offering."

"It's amazing, isn't it?" Byron rested his hand on her shoulder. "Jerrod marches to a different drummer, but he can always make other people hear his beat."

Byron wished that he were so skilled. Instead, he had inadvertently offended some unknown person so deeply that he hired a professional killer. But who? Who wanted him dead?

Of course, that question required some serious consideration, but Byron despaired of discovering an easy answer. What was it that Murtaugh said? Motives for murder—in this case, hiring a murderer—did not always make sense.

Byron decided to leave that thinking for later. More important was dealing with the current problem: his life was in danger. And he did not want to run away.

When he needed to be, Byron was an excellent manager, capable of organizing and activating complex plans. He'd need that ability to fight Rankin.

Carefully, he helped Lindsey into the car, noticing that she sat awkwardly to avoid putting her weight on her hip. "Should you see a doctor?"

"For a bump on my butt? No, I don't think so."

Byron slid behind the wheel and aimed through the arid landscape toward the San Diego dealership from which he'd obtained the car. There, at the first available telephone, he would begin to put his thoughts into motion.

"Byron?" Lindsey said. "What are you thinking?"

"I have a couple of ideas."

"Tell me."

"I intend to enjoy my children's visit, to relax with them." His voice became wistful. "I should spend more time with my kids. It seems like every time I see Sonny, he's grown six inches. He's almost a man, Lindsey. Twelve years old. And Amanda is so beautiful, even if she won't wear dresses, hates bathing and . . ."

She listened as he spoke lovingly of his children and she wished that she could categorically reassure him that they would be fine, that nothing would happen to them. But Lindsey had to be realistic. The awful possibility was that Rankin might strike at Byron through his children. And somehow, that very obvious fact had escaped him.

Gently, she interrupted, "They sound like terrific kids. We'll have to be sure they're protected."

"Oh, of course. Absolutely."

"Where shall we take them? You have a yacht, don't you? We could load up the children and sail away to parts unknown."

"No. I want to stay at the villa, and that is exactly what we will do."

Surely he didn't mean that. Lindsey frowned. She'd been the one who had a bump on the head, but Byron was behaving in an irrational manner. "I don't quite understand."

"At five o'clock we'll pick up the kids, take them back to the villa and stay there for the month."

The determined tone in his voice made her nervous. Staying at the villa was suicide. If the decision had been hers alone to make, Lindsey would book immediate passage to another continent. After all, she'd fled from less dangerous men than Rankin.

But this time, she wasn't alone.

Byron was with her. And his children were joining them. They were united in danger, bound together by threads of terror. She studied his dark profile against the hazy skies. His brow was pinched. His jaw thrust forward stubbornly, daring her to challenge his stupid decision to stay at the villa.

Again, she tried the gentle voice of reason. "I know that Colonel Wright isn't your favorite person right now, but his advice was solid when he suggested getting out of town."

"I won't run. I hate the idea that scum like Rankin can disrupt my life."

"But it's true. He can disrupt your life." Her patience was almost gone. "Dammit, Byron. Rankin can end your life. And mine. And the lives of your children. It's smarter to run, Byron. Rankin is a killer and he's after blood."

"Try to be logical, Lindsey."

"Me?" she squeaked. "You think I'm being illogical?"

"I can't hide. Much as I'd like to be anonymous, I'm not. Even on vacation, I have businesses to operate, decisions to make, employees to direct. I can't vanish and be out of touch for a month."

"Even if it means putting your life in danger?"

"But I won't be in danger. I'll stay on Catalina as planned, have lots of time with the kids and maintain my necessary business contacts."

"And how do you intend to do that? Did someone turn you into Superman when I wasn't looking?"

"You gave me the idea," he said, "when you pointed out that it would take a private army to defend the villa."

"I was joking."

"But I'm not. I can afford a private army, Lindsey. And I intend to hire one."

She leaned back in her seat, inadvertently putting weight on her bruised hip. The pain startled her to a more erect posture, but she still stared disbelievingly at Byron. "A private army?"

"Why not? Now, let's concentrate on the truly complex issues at hand. Who hired Mikey Rankin? Why?"

"You're changing the subject."

"I'm elaborating," he said. "Here's a question—How did Rankin manage to track us down at Riverdale Airfield?"

"He tailed the car."

"But how did he know we were going to visit Jerrod? Colonel Wright swept all the bugs last night, so Rankin couldn't have overheard our plans. And we traveled by motorboat, so he couldn't have followed us from Catalina."

Despite her confusion, Lindsey's mind engaged. "We picked up the tail after we left your uncle's lab. Maybe Jerrod hired him."

"Doubtful. My uncle's style is oneupmanship, planting bugs and sending impersonators. He wouldn't hire an assassin. Besides, Rankin's men knocked Jerrod unconscious."

"Maybe to throw us off," she suggested.

He raised one eyebrow. "Maybe."

"Or maybe Jerrod wasn't involved with Rankin at all. What about Appleton? Even in a lab coat, he's a smarmy character."

Byron nodded. "Appleton contacted Rankin, then Rankin followed us."

"Right," she said.

"But Appleton was with us the entire time we were at the lab. He didn't use the phone."

"But he knew we were coming before we actually came face-to-face. All it would take is one phone call to Rankin."

"How about Lantz? We never saw Ms. Captain Lantz who supposedly runs a craft shop on Catalina. She could have contacted Rankin."

Byron pulled up at a stoplight. "But it doesn't make sense. I don't even know Appleton or Lantz. Why would either of them hire someone to kill me?"

"The standard motives—greed, revenge, lust."

"Lust?"

"You've never heard of crimes of passion?"

He drove into the Continental Auto dealership. "We will figure this out. In the meantime, however, I'm going to work on our safety."

"By reserving space on the next flight to Alaska?" she asked hopefully.

He turned off the purring engine and faced her. "Not a chance. I intend to mobilize."

It almost sounded like a threat.

Chapter Nine

Byron was nuts. Lindsey was absolutely sure of it. At fever pitch, he launched a high-level frenzy of phone calls, faxes and communiqués that made Donald Trump look like a slacker.

Watching him in action surprised Lindsey. She'd known him as a father who was desperately concerned about his children. As a swimmer and a fighter and a thinker. She'd seen him as a casual, bare-chested executive who plugged information into a computer while improving his tan. But now Byron Cyril, CEO of Continental Auto and owner of his own architectural firm, was behaving like a tycoon. Or a typhoon, she thought, because he blew over every obstacle and countered every objection.

Back at Catalina, she'd given up on trying to understand what he was doing and opted for a long soak in a hot bathtub. Her body ached from the battering she took leaping from the moving plane, and her face was swollen from Rankin's slap. But she didn't feel beaten. Not the way her mother had been.

When she'd changed into a jungle-patterned shirt and wide-legged beige shorts that were long enough to conceal the bruise that spread down her outer thigh like a map of the Florida peninsula, she returned to the lower level of the villa.

Byron waved to her from the table in the big open room with French windows. Every inch of tabletop was covered with documents. "Lindsey, meet Walter Kirsch."

She shook hands with the huge red-haired man who didn't bother to conceal his shoulder holster. A sprinkle of freckles across his cheeks seemed incongruous—as if Huckleberry Finn had grown up to be a soldier of fortune.

"Kirsch is a private detective," Byron said. "He was recommended by both Colonel Wright and Detective Murtaugh."

Lindsey gave a noncommittal nod. "Pleased to meet you."

Kirsch rumbled, "Same here."

"Sit down," Byron offered, pulling out a chair for her. "We're in the final process of selecting men."

"No thanks." The sprawl of paperwork, maps and weaponry catalogues held no appeal to her. She simply didn't feel up to plotting the first line of defense. Likewise, though she saw Helen McHenry fluttering busily, Lindsey didn't join in the kitchen activity. "I'd rather rest before the children arrive."

"Yes, of course." Byron smiled and went back to work.

Leaving them, Lindsey felt unoccupied, idle. But this was what she had wanted, wasn't it? Idyllic relaxation on an island paradise? Finally she had a chance to relax, and she felt dull and without purpose. Wandering into the library, she found a magazine, eased into a chair, taking care to protect her bruises, and listlessly flipped the slick pages.

Without thinking, her hand touched her sore cheekbone. Her jaw ached, too. When she frowned, the bruised area smarted sharply. How had her mother been able to stand being beaten? Lindsey closed her eyes.

Only yesterday, she'd visited her mother's grave. She hadn't planned to. The stated purpose of her stop in Los Angeles was to purchase a new handgun, and there hadn't really been time for anything else. In fact, it was the side trip to a humble cemetery that had caused Lindsey to be an hour late in arriving at Catalina.

Yet, she had gone for a last visit. Bitterness mingled with guilt when Lindsey found the small marker at her mother's grave. She wasn't exactly sure what to do. There were no more tears she could shed for her mother. Dead at age sixty-one of unknown causes. Another beating? Or had she finally been consumed by her own tragic hopelessness?

Should she say goodbye? Lindsey knelt and touched the cold marker. She hardly knew this woman. And had never understood her despair. Lindsey had tried to help. After she left home, she'd always sent money. Every month, no matter how tight her budget.

But the cash hadn't helped. Not really. Her mother was too determined to be one of life's victims.

It hadn't always been that way. Lindsey had soft, misty memories of childhood laughter and games. So many years ago. When her father was alive and her mother had been so pretty—more lovely than an angel. Was she in heaven now? With a harp and a flowing white robe. Ethereal and meek.

Lindsey smiled at her fantasy. Though she didn't believe in angels anymore, she was very sure that her mother had gone to a better place than earth.

With a sigh, Lindsey slept.

When she woke, it was after five o'clock—rush hour for most towns and cities. But not here. The island wasn't run by a timeclock. She wandered out to the terrace. Below her, the white-capped waters swelled and splashed against the cliffside, making a soothing liquid roar. The orange trees and palms ruffled softly in the breeze, catching the reflecting sunlight.

Amid all this natural beauty, the ugly violence of this day seemed inconceivable. Yet, the huge bruise on her hip throbbed a painful reminder of the horror at Riverdale Airfield, and she concentrated on remembering. Terror too easily forgotten could lead to carelessness.

The back of her neck prickled, and she pivoted to face Walter Kirsch, the man who had been recommended by both Colonel Wright and Detective Murtaugh.

"Excuse me," Kirsch said. "This terrace isn't the best place for you to be standing. There might be snipers."

Reflexively, she glanced up at the cliff. "There's someone up there."

"You bet there is. We've got two teams posted on that cliff."

"That's comforting," she wryly returned.

"There's another four guys in the little cove to the south. And those are our men on the fishing boat." He pointed out to sea. "This is a tough place to protect, and I'm going to need your cooperation, Lindsey. Especially after the kids return with their father."

"You're right," she said. "And I'm sorry if I sounded flippant. What can I do to help?"

"Well, Byron doesn't want his kids to think they're living in an armed fortress."

"Which is exactly what this is." She winced. "Sorry, again. I guess I'm not too thrilled with the idea of being constantly observed."

"If we can't see you, we can't protect you. Now, the way I figure, the front perimeter of the grounds and the seaside approach are covered."

"How many men?"

"By tonight, there will be thirty-six, including the crews on the fishing boats. Plus we're installing cameras to observe movements on the grounds and at sea. My problem is the possibility of an air attack."

"From Rankin? I doubt it. He didn't strike me as being that sophisticated."

"Can't second-guess a killer." Behind his dark glasses, Kirsch was watchful. "I know. I was a cop for twelve years. And this Rankin sounds like one slippery fish."

An involuntary shudder went through her. A slippery fish? Hah! Rankin was a shark. She'd heard the police report from Murtaugh: Martin Rankin, age thirty-five, had been tried and acquitted for fraud, extortion and laundering money. But not for murder. Not for assault. Rankin's crimes had been chillingly white collar. He left the dirty work to his associates. And to Mikey, his younger brother.

After reviewing the rap sheets, Murtaugh had suggested that Martin Rankin never actually intended to murder them, but had some extortion scheme in mind. Though Lindsey considered the possibility, her gut told her that Murtaugh was wrong. Rankin wanted her dead. She would never forget the excitement in his eyes when he held her hand to the whirling blades.

She turned back to Kirsch. "What can I do?"

"Arrange the kids' activities so they'll be close to the safety of the house. There's an alarm system on the roof, sounds like a foghorn. If you hear it, you take the kids into that vault Byron calls a workshop until the alarm sounds an all-clear."

"Fair enough."

"Same procedure. Day or night." He frowned. "It's too bad that the kids have bedrooms at the opposite ends of the upstairs floor. But Byron insisted that we not move Sonny's bedroom closer to yours."

"I know. Byron wants to believe that the children won't notice thirty-six armed security guards patrolling the grounds."

"Another problem," Kirsch said. "Byron has forbidden us to wear uniforms. The only way you can recognize my men is that we're wearing these laminated plastic badges with our photos."

Lindsey grinned, recalling Jerrod's story about creating unassailable identification for military and police. "Is there anything useful I could do right now?"

"You could go inside."

She nodded and obeyed, listlessly strolling through the lower floor of the house. Byron would soon return with Amanda and Sonny. And then what? Her ideas about professional distance had been mangled during the course of the afternoon. And her crisp, efficient nanny persona seemed ludicrous. As far as she knew, Mary Poppins had never been menaced by a thug like Rankin.

Nor had Ms. Poppins kissed her employer.

Of course, she couldn't greet Byron's children with a cheery wave and the confession that she was mightily attracted to their father. Her behavior would be a balancing act, and she feared there was no way to prepare for it. In the meantime, she wanted to keep busy.

Lindsey aimed for the kitchen area, where she could hear Helen McHenry slamming pots and pans. "Hi, Helen. Need another pair of hands?"

"Yes," Helen said emphatically. "Sit here and peel potatoes."

"Thanks, I'd rather stand." Lindsey touched the painful bruise on her hip.

Helen hefted a ten-pound bag onto the counter, then a peeler and a paper sack to hold the peelings. "All of a sudden, I'm a short-order cook for thirty men."

"Thirty-six," Lindsey said.

"I can't feed all those people," Helen wailed.

Her husband, Reg, stalked through the rear door and glowered. "They're ruining my garden, Helen. Some moron set up camp in my roses. And now they're bringing in dogs."

Lindsey held out her hand. "You must be Reginald McHenry. I'm Lindsey, the nanny."

His calloused hands felt hard in hers, but he looked very much the gentleman—small and tidy. His speech was flavored with a light British accent. "Can't say as I'm too pleased to make your acquaintance, Lindsey. You're to blame for this invasion, aren't you?"

"Now, Reg," his wife chided. "If Lindsey hadn't shot that man, Byron would be dead."

"But dogs?" He gave a disapproving snort. "Have you any idea what dogs will do to my bulbs?"

"Much of this is my fault," Lindsey admitted. She began scraping peels into the sack. "I'm supposed to be handling security for the villa. But, please believe me, I never would have ordered up this private army."

"Byron took over," Reg said wisely. "Just like his father, he is. I started as a valet for the late Mr. Cyril, you know, and he drove me wild with his outrageous clothing."

"It wasn't much better when you became gardener," his wife reminded.

"No, indeed. I'd say, 'What a pity that roses don't take to this climate.' Before I knew it, he ordered four dozen rose bushes to be planted." Reg snorted again. "Learned to zip my lip, I did."

"I'll keep that in mind," Lindsey said as she deposited a peeled potato in a huge stainless-steel pot. "But perhaps I could have a talk with Byron about the logistics of this army. Obviously it's impossible for Helen to cook for them."

"I won't have Byron hiring helpers for me," she said. "It's more work to instruct an ignorant staff than to do it myself." Her ample bosom heaved as she let out a heavy sigh. "What I really regret is that I won't have time to spend with the children. Our two are grown and gone, you know."

"Off to college," Reg said with a proud snort. "Succeeding very well at it, too. Those two will make more of themselves than their mum and dad."

The loud blast of a foghorn shook the house and Lindsey dropped the potato peeler. "That's the alarm."

Kirsch's instruction to run to the workshop was worthless; Lindsey didn't know the combination. But the alarm immediately went silent, and Kirsch popped in from the rear terrace. "Sorry, folks. Nothing to worry about. It's just Byron and the kids at the entry gate."

Lindsey and the McHenrys hurried to the front door, and Lindsey was not surprised to find herself subtly placed at the end of a row that went from Reg to Helen to her. They were the staff, Lindsey remembered. The gardener, the house-keeper and the nanny. Though she'd shared intense inti-macy with Byron, Lindsey stood straight in her position. To do otherwise would have created animosity in the Mc-Henrys.

When Byron stepped out of the big, black Cadillac with tinted windows, she had a crazy urge to run to him, to throw herself into his arms. He'd cleaned up for the arrival of Sonny and Amanda and he looked incredibly handsome. His dark tan contrasted handsomely with the white shirt he was wearing. In the presence of his children, his expression showed a fondness she had not seen before.

Or had she? Lindsey recalled the night before the fake intelligence officers arrived. She'd been sleeping. And when he wakened her, his eyes held a similar glow. But that wasn't possible, she told herself. She must have dreamed it.

Sonny emerged next from the back seat of the Caddy. The twelve-year-old boy was tall, probably over five feet, eight inches. Though he was beginning to develop a man's shoul-der breadth, Lindsey's first impression was one of gawki-ness. Sonny's long legs, clad in worn jeans, were stiltlike. His wrists seemed huge. His hair, which was black like his father's, was an unruly mop.

Nine-year-old Amanda followed her brother from the car. Though she'd jammed a baseball cap atop her thick brown curls and wore jeans and a faded T-shirt, this young lady simply could not disguise her innate femininity. She turned back to the Caddy and pulled out a giant teddy bear, ex-tremely beat-up, that was nearly as tall as she was.

Sonny bounded up the stairs and shook hands with Reg McHenry. He gave Helen a hug, and they exchanged whis-pers about chocolate pie. Then he came to Lindsey.

With a serious demeanor, he extended his hand. "Dad told us about some of the stuff you did. You don't look like a nanny."

"Appearance can be deceiving."

Lindsey shook his hand, not allowing him to have the firmer grip. While projecting an aura of confidence, Lindsey wondered exactly what Byron had told his children. Her curiosity increased when Amanda bounced up to join them. The girl's green eyes shone with unqualified approval. "Will you teach me karate?"

"Absolutely."

"Good, because then I can beat up Sonny."

"You wish," he said with a sneer.

Apparently that was the end of their introduction, because Sonny bolted through the front door. Lindsey could hear him thundering up the staircase. From prior experience with preteen males, she half expected Sonny to be difficult. He was at the age when nothing made sense to him, but he thought he knew all the answers.

Byron had reached the top step. He stared through the open door at the space his son had occupied only seconds before. Then he looked at Lindsey. Byron's gaping confusion was priceless—a parental combination of worry and outrage. "What do I do?"

"Some people count to ten," she said. "Others grin and bear it. In some wise primitive cultures, they drive the adolescents from the village with long, sharp sticks."

"There's definite merit to answer number three."

When his gaze met hers, she saw little trace of their former intimacy. He wasn't cold to her—not by a long shot. But his mind seemed occupied, as if too many other emotions vied for his attention. Could she help? Could she take some of the worry from him? Lindsey stood straight and tall, her erect posture showing nothing of her inner doubt. Or her fear. Her lips pressed together to keep from blurting an improper comment that she was afraid to speak.

"Don't worry," Helen McHenry advised them all. "Sonny will be downstairs for dinner. I made his favorite dessert."

"Not that chocolate pie," Byron said. "We all go into sugar shock after eating that pie."

Archly, Helen replied, "Sonny needs to gain weight."

The housekeeper swept toward the kitchen. Reg snorted and headed toward his probably vandalized rose garden.

The two security guards who had driven Byron to pick up the children had faded into invisibility, and Lindsey suspected that Byron's instructions had emphasized that they should be unobtrusive.

Byron grabbed Amanda's bear and one of her matched red suitcases. Lindsey took another, but when she reached for Sonny's brown leather luggage, Byron said, "Leave it. He's old enough to carry his own bags."

"Me, too," said Amanda as she lifted her carry-on satchel.

After they deposited the bags in Amanda's room, Byron excused himself and stalked down the hall to Sonny's lair.

"May I help you unpack?" Lindsey asked Amanda.

"Sure." The girl placed the life-size bear carefully on her bright yellow coverlet and spun around. "I really like it here. Dad says there's going to be lots of security guards, but that's okay. I bet we have enough for a baseball team."

"I bet you're right."

"Did you know that the Chicago Cubs used to have spring training here? On the island?"

"No, I didn't."

"Well, it's true. Mr. Wrigley owned the Cubs and owned Catalina, too."

Lindsey opened the largest suitcase and found a jumble of clothes, ranging from party dresses to bicycle shorts. She made no comment; Amanda was of an age when she should be choosing her own outfits.

"Did you ever play baseball?" Amanda asked.

"Sure." But Lindsey knew it wasn't the kind of baseball Amanda was accustomed to. Rich kids played baseball on manicured green fields. She'd played stick ball on the street or in weed-filled vacant lots. "When I was your age, I used to listen to the L.A. Dodger games on the radio. Vin Scully was the announcer. And Don Drysdale was on the mound."

"It's Orel Hershiser, now. He's great."

They discussed the starting lineup and the Dodgers' chances for the pennant, and soon the clothes were unpacked and put away. Lindsey found herself enjoying Amanda's company. The tomboy attitude might be a front for the real Amanda to hide behind. But it was harmless, even healthy.

When Helen called them for dinner, Lindsey realized that she hadn't made time to chat with Sonny. Perhaps she was avoiding it. Conversations with angry young men did not rank among her favorite pastimes. Or was it Byron she was avoiding?

She sent Amanda to wash up and went downstairs. In the dining room, she met Byron. The moment she saw him, an uncomfortable tension knotted her stomach. Her throat constricted, making it impossible to speak. Which was just as well because Lindsey didn't know what to say. She forced a tremulous smile.

"Good evening," he said.

She nodded.

"What do you think of Sonny and Amanda?"

She swallowed the lump in her throat and spoke. "Amanda is a terrific kid. I haven't had a chance to get to know your son."

He nodded. Was he feeling the same tension? In a few quick strides, he came toward her. Byron had never looked so strongly masculine. His hand lifted, as if to touch her, then his fist clenched, catching a pocket of air.

In a strained voice, she asked, "Would you rather have this dinner alone with the kids?"

"I'd prefer that you were here. Please sit at that end of the table. It's where my late wife always—"

"If you don't mind, I'd rather sit by Amanda." She definitely did not want the children to think she was trying to fill their mother's shoes.

"What do you think of my private army?"

"We're protected, all right." Lindsey remembered her conversation with the McHenrys. "But I would like to discuss logistics with you—such as feeding of this multitude and keeping the dogs out of the flowerbeds."

"Tonight," he promised. "After the children go to bed."

Before she could reply, Sonny stomped into the dining room, shot them a disgusted glare and took his place at the table. "Well, nanny," he said, "how many times did you shoot that guy?"

"I'd rather not discuss it."

"What kind of gun? Some kind of heavy-duty Magnum, huh?"

Lindsey riveted her attention on the gangly young man who sprawled in the chair opposite hers. Her voice was stern, no-nonsense. "Murder and guns are not appropriate dinner conversation."

"How come? Are you embarrassed?"

"I did what I had to do. But I won't discuss this with you, Sonny, because I refuse to glamourize or trivialize violence. A man died here. At my hand. And I'm not proud of that."

Before looking at him again, she sat, unfurled her napkin and placed it on her lap. "Do you like to swim?"

He shook his head.

The atmosphere lightened when Amanda burst into the room. "Have you seen the dogs outside?"

"Those are guard dogs," her father said, "not pets. And you're not to play with them."

The meal proceeded with hesitant conversation. Quarter-pound hamburgers and mountains of potato salad were devoured before Sonny spoke again, "Listen, Dad, I don't want to hurt your feelings, but I don't want to stay here for the whole month. Can I visit some friends back in Detroit?"

"This is our month together," Byron said.

"Yeah? But it's not exactly private."

"The security men won't interfere with us. They'll keep out of our way, and their presence is not going to be a problem."

"I wasn't talking about the security men." Sonny jabbed his fork at Lindsey, then laid it across his plate. "May I be excused?"

"Before the chocolate pie?"

"I'm not hungry anymore." His chair went back with a squeak and Sonny left the room.

"What a jerk!" Amanda said. "He just wants to lock himself in his room and play with his computer. That's all he ever does."

Lindsey tried to smile and managed to chat with Amanda, but her thoughts focused on Sonny. The young man was behaving badly. He was hurting his father and making an already difficult situation more intense. But when had a child ever timed his problems for a serene moment when the parent felt capable of dealing with them? She needed to talk strategy with Byron before confronting his son again.

Though it was dark after dinner, Byron went for his evening swim. And Amanda joined him, splashing and kicking and bobbing through the blue waters of the pool while her father swam laps.

While Lindsey stood watching them, Kirsch approached her. "I don't like this," he said. "The pool is lit. The hills are shadowy. It's a perfect setup for snipers, and my men can't be everywhere."

"Perhaps," she said. "Are your men equipped with night scopes?"

"Sure they are. But, listen, could you talk to Byron about doing his swimming earlier, in daylight?"

"Tell him yourself," she said irritably.

"But I thought you and Byron, were, you know, close."

"I'm the nanny. Byron and I have been in some tight situations, but I only came here yesterday."

"Yeah, I know. Right before all the problems started."

She looked up sharply. Did he think she was somehow connected with all this? Kirsch's expression was noncommittal, but his implication stood. Why? Then Lindsey remembered that Kirsch had been recommended by Murtaugh *and* Colonel Wright, and that Wright knew her background. It was altogether possible that Kirsch had been instructed to keep an eye on her.

"I'll try to set up a meeting with Byron tonight," she said. "After the children go to bed, you and the McHenrys and I and Byron can discuss our various complaints. All right?"

"Suits me."

Before he could return to the shadows, the foghorn alarm sounded. Kirsch leaped into action. He pulled Amanda from the pool and directed her and Byron toward the vault.

Lindsey bolted up the stairs to Sonny's room. The foghorn was still blasting. Not a false alarm, but real danger. She yanked at the doorknob. It was locked.

"Open up, Sonny. We've got to go downstairs."

"Leave me alone," he shouted back.

"This isn't a game. Open the damn door this minute."

"Make me."

All right, you obnoxious little adolescent. I will. Ignoring the ache from her hip, Lindsey aimed a full-force karate kick at the door near the lock. She heard the wood begin to splinter, but the door remained closed.

She kicked again and the door crashed open.

Sonny, with his eyes bulging, sat on the bed.

In two strides, she approached him and firmly grasped his arm. "Let's go. And I mean now, young man."

Sonny obeyed and they raced downstairs to the opened door of Byron's workshop, where Amanda and Byron stood waiting with the McHenrys. Even inside the heavily insulated vault, they could hear the echo of the foghorn's scream.

It was a full five minutes before it died. Kirsch spoke through the intercom. "Hello, in there. Byron, there was an intruder at the front gate. He was unarmed and my men have taken him into custody."

"Good," Byron replied. "Lindsey and I will be right out."

Side by side, they went down the corridor to the living room. Though still in his swim trunks, Byron was the unquestioned leader.

In the living room, two security men flanked a befuddled-looking blond man in an expensive business suit. Lindsey knew immediately that this intruder was not a harmless person.

He was Thomas Peterson, her second husband.

Chapter Ten

Thomas Peterson, the man Lindsey had run away from, looked pale and ineffectual between the two armed security guards. His hair had thinned. His long, sensitive fingers plucked nervously at his necktie. Thomas was extremely thin with hollows beneath his cheekbones and a narrow brow. At one time, she'd thought he was aristocratic-looking.

She'd been married to him. But had she ever loved that man? Had she ever really cared for him?

"There's been a misunderstanding," She said to Byron. "I know this man."

Kirsch reported, "He was peeping at the front gate but didn't ring the bell. My men thought he might be reconnoitering the place."

"I repeat," Lindsey said more loudly. "I know him. He's not part of Rankin's gang."

Byron drew her aside for a more private conference. His touch on her arm was warm, gentle. "Are you sure?"

"Why wouldn't I be sure?"

"You've been gone for eight years, Lindsey. The people you knew before might have changed."

"I should be so lucky. Byron, that man is my exhusband."

Byron opened his mouth and closed it again. He turned back toward Kirsch and steepled his fingertips, a peculiarly civilized gesture considering that he was only wearing a pair of Speedo swim trunks. "False alarm, Kirsch. This man is visiting Lindsey. You may release him. And tell the Mc-Henrys and the children that they may leave the workshop. Lindsey and I will be with this gentleman in the front sitting room."

Kirsch frowned disapprovingly but gestured to his men. In a moment, they had vacated the living room.

Lindsey cleared her throat. "Byron Cyril," she said, "this is Thomas Peterson."

When the two men shook hands, the contrast between radiantly healthy Byron and Lindsey's former husband was amazing.

"Pleased to meet you," Thomas said.

Byron nodded and led the way to the front sitting room. With all the antiques, it was easily the most impressive room in the house, and Lindsey was glad Byron had chosen it.

The opulent setting was not wasted on Thomas. As Byron closed the door, Thomas blinked like a cash register ringing up the final tab. "Well, well, I can see you're taking good care of my Lindsey."

"I am not *your* Lindsey. Not anymore."

"Perhaps not ever," he said, philosophically. "I saw your photograph in the newspaper. You're still quite lovely, my dear. However, if the accompanying article was correct, you've become a bit more violent during the years we've been apart."

He hadn't changed. His style was always to give a compliment followed by a criticism. He built her up, then knocked her down. It used to drive her crazy, but now she merely shrugged. "Why have you come here, Thomas?"

"I have a bit of business with you." He pointedly stared at Byron. "It's confidential."

With utter unconcern, Byron ignored the hint. He settled himself on a delicate damask sofa and stretched his long legs out in front of him.

"You may speak freely in front of Byron," Lindsey instructed, enjoying her ex-husband's discomfort. "Please, Thomas, tell me why you've come."

"For old times' sake. I wanted to see you, Lindsey. I wanted to see if it meant anything to you. The time we spent together."

His cultured voice cut through her, spilling unpleasant memories. Quickly, she replied, "That was a lifetime ago, Thomas. I'm different now."

"I'll say." He turned to Byron. "When we first met, she was an ignorant little nothing."

"I was in my senior year of college at night school," she corrected. "I had a full-time job in an office, my own apartment and a car."

"But I taught you how to behave, how to speak, how to dress. I told you what books to read. I was an English professor, an educated man. Surely, you can't deny my influence upon you. I formed you."

She had heard this lecture before. While they were married, Thomas had frequently repeated it. But the sting was gone.

"Admit it, Lindsey. You barely knew how to order in a restaurant. And look at you now. Confident, bright and strong. A fit companion for someone like Byron Cyril."

"Have you finished?"

"No."

"Well, I'm finished listening."

"Don't be rude," he chided. "It doesn't become you."

"Yes, Thomas. No, Thomas. Very well, Thomas." She whirled away from him. "I'll be the first to acknowledge that you did educate me. And I was such an apt pupil—the ghetto kid, striving to improve herself, to please her husband, to make something of herself. But not too much. Right, Thomas? I was supposed to sparkle, but only as an ornament."

"I haven't the vaguest idea what you're talking about."

"Memory is a funny thing," she said. "You probably recall the first time you took me shopping. You and the salesgirls had a good laugh about my tasteless choices. But I'll bet you've forgotten the day when you forbade me to take additional classes so I could qualify to be a teacher. Your exact words were, 'There are already too many incompetent educators in the world.'"

"Merely stating an opinion."

Lindsey held her breath for a second, then let it out slowly. It wasn't worth arguing, pointing out that he'd held the purse strings in an iron fist and wouldn't allow the extra money for her tuition. Or that all her time had been occupied with typing and retyping his definitive textbook.

At the beginning of their marriage, she'd blindly trusted him and turned over every penny of her savings and salary to him. She'd accepted the role of inferior and dedicated all her efforts to making him look good. Perhaps if she'd been willing to fight for what she wanted, Thomas would have learned to accept it.

But he'd been so erudite, so slick, that she felt utterly helpless. And she'd chosen to run away.

"I never forced anything upon her," he said, again addressing Byron. "Please attempt to be realistic, Lindsey. I never beat you or kept you chained to a wall, did I?"

"Not physically."

But emotionally, he'd been brutal. Lindsey paused. She had the momentary sensation of looking into a mental mirror and seeing her mother's face reflected there. Her mother's victimization. Perhaps they hadn't been so different, after all.

But Lindsey had chosen to end it. She'd made her peace with the mistakes of long ago. And, during the past eight years, she'd grown up. She wasn't a ghetto kid anymore. And not a victim. "What's done is done."

"I'm delighted that you are capable of understanding. Perhaps now we can deal more efficiently with this small loose end.'' He reached into his inner jacket pocket. ''You must sign this document. It pertains to a small investment I made in your name.''

Her brow wrinkled. ''I don't remember.''

''It was nothing, inconsequential. However, when I saw your photograph in the newspaper, I saw an opportunity to tidy up my portfolio. And it's a benefit to you, too. After you've signed, I'll return a portion of your initial investment to you. Shall we say half?''

''Shall we say . . . I'll study the document before signing?''

''Really, Lindsey. Let's take care of this immediately. You know how I despise unfinished business.''

That was true. Thomas was disgustingly fastidious. And, in light of that character trait, his request made sense. Yet, she sensed an anxiety in his manner. If only she could recall the investment he was talking about.

''Here, Lindsey.'' He placed the sheaf of papers in her hand. ''Place your signature on the lines I've indicated with an *X* and I'll be on my way.''

She picked up the papers and folded them. ''I'll read this in the morning,'' she said, ''and mail it back to you.''

''I'm afraid that won't do. I'm engaged to be married again, Lindsey, and my new wife certainly would not wish for us to begin a correspondence.''

Tilting her head, she studied him. There was definitely something weird going on here, something connected to those papers. ''Good night, Thomas.''

''I'm not leaving without your signature.'' There was a harshness in his educated intonation. ''Oh, hell, Lindsey. I should have known you'd be difficult. Please forget I came. Return those papers to me.''

''I don't think I will.''

''Dammit, Lindsey. I'm in no mood to play stupid games with you.''

When he made a move toward her, Byron stood. His glower convinced Lindsey that he would love to throw Thomas through the bay window. Though she didn't need protecting, the masculine ruffling of feathers pleased her.

Byron's voice was a growl. "The lady said good-night, Peterson."

"I'm not leaving. Not yet." Thomas jabbed a long finger at her. "After all I did for you. How can you treat me like a common intruder?"

"Oh, but I'm not," she said smoothly. "If you read the article in the newspaper, you must know that I generally shoot intruders."

"How dare you threaten me."

He turned away from Lindsey and spoke to Byron in an attitude of confidentiality. Man to man, Lindsey thought. Or, in the case of Thomas, worm to man.

"I appeal to you, Cyril," Thomas said. "I came here to transact a simple business procedure, and she's carrying on outrageously. Help me talk sense into this woman."

Curiously, she awaited Byron's response. Would he get physical? Actually throw Thomas out? That might be fun, she thought. Immature, but fun.

"Your dealings with Lindsey are your own affair," Byron said diplomatically. "However, I believe she wants you to leave. Is that right, Lindsey?"

She nodded.

"Frankly, Peterson, I also want you out of here. Now!"

"You're under her spell," Thomas sneered. "Mark my words, Cyril, she'll turn on you, take you for all you're worth."

"Just for the record," Lindsey put in. "I never asked for or received a dime in our divorce settlement."

"I tracked you all over the globe. You never answered my letters. You've been nothing but trouble." He drew his gaunt, well-tailored body erect. "Give me my papers, Lindsey, and you'll never see me again."

"They're mine now," she said.

When Thomas made a snatch for the sheaf of documents, Byron blocked his path. He easily caught Thomas's hand in midair and held it. "That's enough, Peterson."

With a fierce effort, Thomas swung at Byron. A telegraphed punch, Lindsey thought. It pleased her to see how easily Byron deflected the blow.

"You want to step outside, Peterson?"

"What are you suggesting?" he dithered.

"Well, we're a couple of gentlemen, aren't we? I suggest that we settle our differences in the time-honored fashion. A duel? A sparring match?"

Thomas held up his hands in a gesture of surrender. "I'm not a fighter."

Byron held the door for him and called out for one of the security guards. "I'd appreciate it, Kirsch, if you'd escort this gentleman to the gate."

"Sure, Byron." He grasped Thomas's skinny arm. "Let's go."

Byron closed the door and turned to Lindsey. She didn't appear to be upset by her ex-husband's visit. The opposite, in fact. There seemed to be a new serenity in her smile. "You're all right, aren't you?"

"Never better."

When he took a step toward her, Lindsey averted her eyes. When she unfolded the documents Thomas had wanted back, squinted at them and ran her hand through her hair, her unconscious gesture charmed Byron. The soft light from a lamp glowed on her flesh, glistened in her hair. The night suited her, he thought, for she was a woman with secret, mysterious passions.

"I really don't remember this investment."

"Would you like me to look over them?"

"Yes, please." Without hesitation, she thrust the document toward him. "I hate legal paperwork."

With one hand, Byron took the sheaf of papers. His other hand enclosed hers. Ever since he'd returned with the children, he hadn't trusted himself to be near Lindsey, had avoided her gaze. He didn't want to push her or embarrass her. Nor did he wish to create confusion for Amanda and Sonny. But his suppressed desire had become almost painful. Standing this close to Lindsey, he had to touch her.

Her wide-eyed gaze melted into his. "You were pretty macho with Thomas."

"He's an ass. He mistreated you when you were young and vulnerable."

"Thank God, I've grown up."

"And no one can hurt you now."

"I didn't say that. Your private army is testimony to the fact that nobody is ever completely safe."

"It's a shame," he said. "But to be completely honest, there are some things I don't want to be protected from."

"Such as?"

"The feelings I have for you. Lindsey, I want—"

"Don't say it. We can't. Not now."

"Why not?"

"The children must be worried about us. And Kirsch's men are probably hovering outside the door at this very moment. We're not alone, Byron."

His thumb stroked the palm of her hand, a small solace for the throbbing desire that churned within him. He would have traded almost anything for an hour of privacy with her—his fortune, his possessions, years off his life. But he could not compromise his children's safety. And so the guards would stay at their posts.

"Someday," he whispered, "this danger will pass. We'll have time alone. Just you and me."

"But now, we ought to get back."

With an effort, he forced himself to release her hand, and they moved apart. There should have been special words he could say to her, but his throat felt numb.

He was silent until after they entered the dining room and confronted the children. Sonny's chin jutted forward, and he fired a hostile glare at Lindsey. "She kicked in my door."

Amanda giggled.

"Shut up," he snarled at his sister. "Did you hear me, Dad? The ninja nanny kicked in the door to my bedroom."

"You're lucky, Sonny, that I don't kick you in the pants," Byron said. "When the alarm sounds, you are to respond. No questions. No hesitation. For all Lindsey knew, you were being attacked in your bedroom."

"Geez, Dad, if it's really that dangerous here, why don't we go somewhere else?"

"Because the danger could follow."

"I hate this!" Sonny pushed away from the table, overturning his chair. "I don't want to live in a prison."

"Sit down, Sonny."

"Why?"

"Because I'm your father and I say so."

As he spoke, Byron cringed inside. At one time, he'd sworn that he would never be the kind of father who made peremptory statements, especially not the infamous "because I say so." He'd vowed to be sensitive, hoped thoughtful dialogue would define his relationship with his son. But there were times, like now, when it was necessary to pull rank.

"Amanda," Byron said, "will you please find the McHenrys and ask them to bring Mr. Kirsch to the table."

"But, Dad, I want to watch you get mad at Sonny."

"I'll come with you," Lindsey offered. She took Amanda by the hand and went to the kitchen.

Byron faced his son. "Let's get a few things straight, young man...."

Ouch, Byron thought, there was another of those "typical" authoritarian remarks. What was it about a crisis that brought out the worst in parents? He started over. "Please try to understand, Sonny. People are trying to kill me. They have weapons. They wear masks. And they are vicious enough to try to get to me through you. All this security isn't a game.''

"Yeah, yeah, yeah. Aunt Estelle always has a security guard and nobody has ever attacked her.''

"This is different. Estelle thinks a security guard is some kind of status symbol. A man with a gun broke into this house, and Lindsey had to kill him.''

When he spoke Lindsey's name, Byron noticed a tensing in his son's shoulder. "You don't like Lindsey.''

"But you do,'' his son accused.

"Yes, I like her a lot. Not to mention the fact that her life is in danger because she protected me.''

"Big deal. That's her job.''

Byron wanted to inform his son that he'd damn well better learn to like Lindsey because she was the first woman who had touched his heart since the death of his wife.

But before Byron could say another word, the McHenrys, Kirsch, Lindsey and Amanda filed back into the dining room. He appointed seats and called their council meeting to order.

In fairly short order, several decisions were made.

Reg McHenry mentioned areas that couldn't be trod upon.

The children agreed to run to the vault whenever the foghorn alarm sounded.

Kirsch discussed areas that might be difficult to watch over, and everyone agreed to avoid those zones.

The most complex discussion centered on feeding the security force. Finally, they settled upon setting up picnic tables in the far garage. Food would be ordered by Helen McHenry and delivered to the gate for lunch and dinner. Helen would prepare breakfasts.

"Is that all?'' Byron asked.

"What about Lindsey?'' Sonny demanded. "I'm too old to have a nanny telling me what to do.''

"Fine," Lindsey said quickly. "After we have established acceptable behaviors, I'll expect you to take responsibility for following them. Since you are old enough to understand, then I shouldn't have to tell you anything."

"What behaviors?"

She smiled sweetly at him. "We needn't take up everyone else's time with this."

"Meeting adjourned," Byron announced. "Tomorrow after dinner, we'll meet again to make sure everything is running smoothly."

They disbanded. Kirsch accompanied the McHenrys to their cottage on the grounds. Sonny stomped up to his bedroom. And Lindsey accompanied Amanda upstairs.

Byron sat alone at the dining room table, allowing the turmoil within him to settle. Though the basic domestic problems were dealt with, Sonny was still driving him crazy. And Lindsey? He groaned. In a totally different way, she was also destroying his grasp on sanity.

Distractedly, he took the documents from his pocket that Thomas had given her. After reading the general information, he studied the fine print thoroughly. Incredible. If his memory proved correct, this was a remarkable coincidence.

He leaned back in the chair and rubbed his eyes. *My God, Lindsey will be shocked.*

Chapter Eleven

Despite a full eight hours of sleep, Lindsey had not recuperated. And it wasn't because of the bruise on her hip or general aches and pains from yesterday's exertions. She awoke feeling itchy and uncertain. Off kilter.

Coming face-to-face with Thomas had left an aftertaste of guilt, but their meeting wasn't as devastating as she'd always expected it would be. Their marriage had failed. But, after seeing Thomas again, she knew why. And she was glad.

Thomas wasn't at the root of her confusion. It was Byron.

She was attracted to him. Who wouldn't be? Beneath his eccentric and physically appealing exterior, he was a caring man, a loving father, a strong person who could cope with whatever life threw his way. And he was rich.

So what's the problem? He'd made it clear that he liked her. With a groan, Lindsey dragged out of bed and into the bathroom where the white tile wall gleamed spotlessly. On the wall opposite the windows and the elegant tub was a humble shower. She crept inside, welcoming the streaming massage of hot water.

While she finished her morning dressing, she argued with herself. Why not have an affair with Byron?

Because she wanted more than a superficial relationship.

Why shouldn't she allow herself to fall in love with Byron?

Because it was impossible. They came from different worlds. She was his employee. Though she believed the old saying that a cat may look on a king, very few monarchs deigned to become seriously involved with alley cats.

A serious relationship with Byron would be like walking a tightrope over the lion's cage. If she fell, she'd be devoured by all the people who suspected her, disliked her and wanted to kill her.

Dressed for the day, she headed downstairs for a restorative cup of coffee and found Helen McHenry whizzing around the kitchen, preparing breakfast for the private army. Lindsey was vaguely envious. At least Helen had a mission in life. "I'm up and ready to help," she announced. "What can I do?"

"Mind the sausages. When the timer goes off, take the bread pudding out of the oven. I need to find Kirsch and arrange for all this food to be taken to the far garage."

While Lindsey took up a position in front of the griddle where neat rows of sausage links sizzled, Helen dashed off, carrying tablecloths like white flags of surrender.

Lindsey poked at the plump little sausages with a fork. Should they be crusty? Or merely tinted brown? Though she loved to eat and thoroughly appreciated a gourmet menu, Lindsey had never learned to cook. Her culinary skills were best suited for making mud pies with the children.

It was almost a relief when the phone rang and she answered, "Cyril residence."

"Of all the nerve. It's you," the piercing voice accused. "This is Estelle Dumont speaking. Would you please put someone else on the line."

"Sorry, there's no one else around."

"Fetch Byron or Helen."

"Gee, I'd love to," Lindsey said, "but I'm watching the sausages."

"You think you're pretty clever, don't you? Well, you don't fool me. I saw that newspaper photograph, my girl, with you looking soulfully at Byron." Her laughter was brittle. "Your little seduction game won't work, dearie. Oh, you might manage an affair with Byron. But he'll never marry you. You're so beneath him that it doesn't merit contemplating."

"Good, then why don't you forget it."

"I shall order him to terminate your employment. Of course, if you had one iota of decency, you'd leave of your own accord. The very idea! Carrying on an affair in front of the children!"

"Ah, yes. The children." Lindsey well remembered Estelle's lack of concern for the children and the tarnished example of proper adult behavior that Estelle set by carrying on with Dan-dan.

"Put Helen on the phone."

"She's not here. She's gone to feed Kirsch's men."

"Who or what is Kirsch?"

"We were attacked again yesterday by a gang of professional hit men. Mr. Cyril hired a private army to protect the villa, and Kirsch is the head of security."

"Hit men?"

"Mercenaries. Men who can be hired to commit murder."

There was a moment of silence, then Estelle said, "Byron hired an army? Whatever do you mean?"

"Nearly forty men. Sharpshooters and security specialists."

"Appalling," Estelle pronounced. "That type of man is certainly not to be trusted. I shall have to instruct Helen about locking up the silver. Oh, this is dreadful, perfectly dreadful."

Apparently, Lindsey thought, one security guard like Dan-dan was tasteful, but an army was tacky.

"But why stay at the villa?" Estelle asked. "Surely, it would be wiser to leave the island."

Lindsey surprised her by saying, "I agree. But Mr. Cyril is determined to stay here and have his month with his children."

"How ridiculous! Byron can be such a stubborn man. He is ruining me with his stunts. I can't sleep. I can't eat. But why should I tell this to you? You're probably on his side."

Silently, Lindsey nodded. That much, she was sure of. She was on Byron's side.

"I must speak to him as soon as possible. I shall call again." Without a goodbye, Estelle hung up.

The scent of burning sausage sent Lindsey from the phone to the griddle. After they were turned, the sausages didn't seem too badly damaged, but an eye-stinging haze had filled the kitchen.

Helen returned at a gallop. "Good grief, Lindsey. What have you done?"

"I'm sorry." She handed over the spatula. "Estelle Dumont called and I was talking to her."

"She's a distraction," Helen agreed. "Why don't you take fruit from the refrigerator and put it in bowls?"

Like a good supervisor, Helen adjusted her instructions to Lindsey's abilities. Between them, they managed to serve the makings of a hearty breakfast for forty. When the last tray of bread pudding had been carried from the kitchen by Kirsch himself, Byron appeared.

He wore his swim trunks and had a towel slung over his shoulder. "Good morning, ladies."

"Perfect timing," Lindsey grumbled. "All the work is done."

"You wouldn't want me in the kitchen anyway," he said. "I'm a disaster."

Helen confirmed his statement with a nod of his head. "That's something you and Lindsey have in common."

"Maybe that's not all we have in common," he said with a mysterious wink. "I'm going to take an extra-long swim this morning. Last night's was interrupted. And who knows about tonight."

He sauntered toward the pool, and Lindsey could hear him shouting, "It's all right, Kirsch. It's only me."

"How can he be so chipper?" Lindsey sank onto a stool and drooped over the counter. "He hasn't even had coffee yet."

"Nor have you." Helen poured a cup for Lindsey and a cup for herself, then sat. "I need to call the caterer and order large chafing dishes. And groceries. Tons of groceries."

"You're doing a wonderful job, Helen."

"It's nothing. Before Reg and I were married, I had a restaurant. Just a tiny place, not fancy, but wholesome."

"Health food?"

"Lord, no. I don't care for tofu and whole-grain things that sit like rocks in your belly. I like food that is, well, traditional." She patted her round tummy. "I guess it shows, but Reg likes me this way."

"He's a wise man."

"And a dreamer. Reg has such plans." She frowned with concern, then changed the subject. "That man who showed up last night. He was your ex-husband, wasn't he?"

"Second ex-husband," Lindsey said. "And my second failure."

"From the looks of him, he was the failure. But, oh my, two divorces." Her round face radiated compassion. "I'm so sorry, Lindsey. Were there children?"

"No."

While Helen told Lindsey how lucky she was not to have gone through a custody battle, Lindsey studied a swirl of coffee in her cup and fought back a familiar pinch of sadness. She'd always wanted children. Now, in her thirties and with no relationship, that dream was fading.

"You must have come from a large family," Helen said.

Surprised by her deduction, Lindsey glanced up. "I was an only child."

"But where did you find the experience to become a nanny?"

"At first, it came from books. I took a couple of child-psychology courses in my senior year in college. Funny," she said. "I spent four years earning a degree in English only to discover that I really wanted to be a grade school teacher."

"Then you became a teacher."

"No." Then she'd run off to Europe to escape Thomas. "I don't know where I learned, Helen, but I love working with kids. There's something miraculous about watching a child grow."

"But you have none of your own." Helen frowned. "You've had a hard time of it, haven't you?"

"Not really. I've made my share of mistakes. But I've always found that it's never too late to pick up and start over."

"What do you mean?"

"Like trying to figure out the situation here. First we thought the intruder was the danger. Then came the complication with the NORAD plans. Then Jerrod. Now it seems that Rankin is the danger. But he's not."

"No?"

"It's like knots in a necklace," she said. "Every time I think I've got it untangled, there's a new twist. So I pick up and start over."

Helen shuddered. "Let's not think of it. We're safe now. With Kirsch protecting us."

"But who hired Mikey Rankin? Who wants Byron dead? You must have some ideas, Helen. Has anything unusual happened recently, in the past few months?"

"Well, of course, Byron's father died. Reg and I went to the funeral in Detroit. There were hundreds of people and a lovely buffet." Her forehead wrinkled in a frown. "I remember. I was standing by the quiches, and Byron got himself into a nasty argument. Something about the family inheritance. Isn't that terrible! Fighting about money at a funeral."

"Who did he argue with?"

"Jerrod Blake."

No surprise, Lindsey thought. Byron and Jerrod were combustible as a flame and a stick of dynamite. "Who else was at the funeral?"

"Lots of family, of course. And corporate people from Continental Auto. And I remember seeing Byron's in-laws— Bart and Julia Dixon. Those poor souls! You know, they still haven't gotten over their daughter's death."

"The death of a child is a terrible tragedy," Lindsey said.

"I wish they were closer to Byron. Might be a comfort."

When Byron whisked into the room, the two women went silent. He looked questioningly at them while he toweled his hair. "Have you two solved the problems of the world?"

"Not even the problems of this little corner of Catalina Island," Lindsey said. "Nice swim?"

"I feel great." He accepted the mug of coffee that Helen offered. "But not as great as you're going to feel, Lindsey. Last night, I studied that document that Thomas brought for you to sign. It seems that nine years ago you made an investment of about five thousand dollars."

"I did? Five thousand?" Five thousand dollars? There was only one time in her life that she'd amassed that kind of cash. "I remember. It was a speculative thing. I checked it out with four different people and they all said it was a good deal."

"A private offering," Byron said. "Initial investment money for a company that was just starting production."

"Whatever. It was right after we first got married. And Thomas said, 'Oh, my dearest, you don't need your own car. And, oh, my sweet, you don't need your own furniture. And, oh, my darling, let's get rid of those clothes.' So, I sold everything."

"And gave him the proceeds to invest?"

"I wasn't that much of a fool." A slow anger simmered within her. "I insisted that the investment be made in my name alone. Not that it made a bit of difference."

"Why do you say that?"

"Because when I wanted the money back so I could go to school, Thomas took great glee in telling me that the company folded and my investment was lost. Every penny." Remembered frustration simmered within her. "The investment went sour."

"That's not exactly true," he informed her. "The company turned out to be profitable. Thomas needs for you to sign that document so he can collect the monies that were due to you."

"How much?"

"I'll have to check with my brokers, but it's somewhere in the neighborhood of fifty thousand dollars."

Lindsey gasped. She gulped. Her outrage erupted as she leapt from the stool and paced. "Fifty thousand dollars? How could he have lied to me when I needed that money! That worm! If I ever see Thomas Peterson again, I'll—" She gave a swift karate kick. "Fifty thousand dollars?"

"Or thereabouts."

"How did you figure this out so quickly?"

"I know the company," he said. "In fact, I made a similar investment. This company has since gone public, their stock has split and they are highly profitable."

Her sputtering rage turned to a deep-throated laugh. "But this is impossible. I've never won anything in my whole life."

"I'm as sure of the facts as I am of my own name. The company is JerBee International, and it promotes certain inventions that have been adapted for use by the military. By the way, JerBee stands for Jerrod Blake."

"I'm fifty thousand dollars richer because of some weird invention of Jerrod's?" She caught both of Byron's hands in hers. "This is too good to be true."

"We shouldn't break out the champagne until my attorneys go over the document," he agreed. "But all indications are positive."

"Congratulations, Lindsey," Helen piped in. "What are you going to do with the money?"

"I don't know."

Her gaze sparkled a reflection in Byron's dark eyes. Excitement tingled through her. It was magic. Like winning the lottery. Or stumbling across a gold mine.

Byron's expression echoed her joy. For once in her life, she felt playful and impulsive. She wanted to kiss his smiling lips. To hug him close to her. To share the almost-physical thrills that were zinging through her.

But, of course, she couldn't do that. Not in front of Helen. Not with the children ready to come downstairs at any moment.

Byron cocked his head to one side. "Do you hear music?"

She pretended to listen. "Why, yes. I believe they're playing a victory march."

"Listen again. It's a waltz." He whirled her into a ballroom dance position. One hand tucked firmly on her waist, the other grasping her own. "Shall we?"

"I'd be delighted."

He hummed as they swooped through the room in wide graceful arcs, and Lindsey felt dainty as a rose petal. In his rhythmic humming, she heard a symphony with whispering violins and rumbling bass. In a blink, the living room transformed to a glittering ballroom. Her khaki shorts were a taffeta gown. His long-tailed shirt and swim trunks became a tuxedo.

Not since she was a child had she indulged her imagination so completely. When Byron arched her in a dramatic move with his lips tantalizingly close to her own, Lindsey saw magic in his eyes—the power to make every mundane moment into a beautiful fantasy.

They danced together in perfect harmony, exact rhythm. Her mind replayed visions of fairy-tale castles on the Rhine, a costume party given by one of her former employers, Paris at dawn. In her life, she'd seen magnificent sights, but she'd never been a part of them.

His hand on her waist directed her with a masterful yet gentle touch. Then he changed the rhythm.

"Tango."

Cheek to cheek. She'd never danced a tango before, but the moves came to her like an inspiration. And she was aware of his torso pressed close against hers. She felt the dampness of his hair. The strength of his arms.

Her body was pressed close to his. Their gazes locked. He took a step backward. She followed, matching her long-legged stride to his. Another step. His breath tickled her cheeks. Another step. A ferocious heat burned behind her eyes. Pure desire. Another step.

They toppled backward onto the sofa. Long arms and legs flailed at the air until they ended in a crumpled heap.

From the kitchen, Helen was applauding.

A high-pitched child's giggle joined hers. And Lindsey heard Amanda cheering and clapping. "My turn. It's my turn."

Byron and Lindsey untangled themselves, and he went to Amanda. He bowed from the waist. "May I have this dance?"

She had her life-size teddy bear beside her. "What about the bear? He wants to dance, too."

Lindsey took the furry paw of the stuffed animal. "Mr. Bear will be my partner. If he doesn't mind."

"He'd love it," Amanda said.

And so Lindsey danced with a large stuffed animal. In her thoughts, she cherished the moments in Byron's arms. Truly a magical memory that would last for a lifetime.

Even when Sonny stomped into the room and demanded breakfast, her happiness was not diminished. She did, however, end her dance with the bear and sit beside Sonny at the counter.

"Good morning, Sonny. We're celebrating."

"Why? I thought somebody was trying to kill you?"

"Well, we can't be terrified all the time, can we?"

"I don't care," he said.

Those three words—I don't care—became the hallmark of her relationship with Sonny.

Over the next two days, she heard those words so often that she thought she'd scream, but "I don't care" was better than "I hate you." And Sonny was doing as she asked.

Other routines also became established. The breakfast serving was easier when Amanda and Byron pitched in to help Lindsey and Helen. During the days, they were often outside in the island sun. In the evening—at Kirsch's recommendation—they confined themselves to the house, playing board games or watching movies on videotape.

On the evening of the third day, after Amanda and Byron had retired to bed and Helen had returned to her cottage, Lindsey and Byron sat alone in the living room.

"This has been wonderful," he said. "It's almost like we're a family again."

"Except for Sonny," she reminded.

"He'll come around. Didn't you notice what happened today when we were playing baseball with the security men? Sonny was pitching to you and he didn't throw one beanball."

"Only because the score was close and he didn't want me to get a free ride to first base. What I noticed was that Sonny laughed hysterically when I tripped in the outfield and almost broke my neck."

"Still," Byron said, "this has been everything I'd hoped. The security guards seem to have solved our problem."

She had to agree. The alarm had gone off twice in the past two days. Both times, it had been reporters. Though Detective Murtaugh checked in daily with reports that Rankin had not been apprehended, Lindsey felt safer. No one could get past Kirsch's army, especially not since they had installed their electronic sensing equipment.

Byron's grin portrayed smooth contentment. "Not even Jerrod—with all his inventions—has been able to sneak through. He promised to try, you know. The minute I told him that we were surrounded with an unbreakable security system, he said that nothing was unbeatable and vowed to prove it to me."

Lindsey remembered the sniper on the hillside, courtesy of Jerrod. And the bugs. And the fake intelligence agents. And the fact that Rankin had located them through Jerrod. She didn't trust Byron's uncle. "The army should have taken him into custody for impersonating an officer."

"Instead," Byron informed her, "they're ready to give him a medal for testing their ID verification. As you mentioned before, he's good at slipping out of tricky situations."

"How did you happen to be talking with Jerrod, anyway?"

"Didn't I tell you? He called yesterday, supposedly to discuss the solar engine, but his real reason for calling was to make an offer on your stock shares in JerBee."

A little surge of pleasure brightened Lindsey's eyes. She'd never had this sort of power before, the power that came from cash value. Jerrod was seeking something from her, and it would please her immensely to turn him down. She lolled luxuriously in her chair. "Should I accept his offer?"

"Unless you're in a rush to get your money, it might be best to wait. There might be someone else who wants to counter Jerrod's offer. The market value is—"

"Forty-eight thousand dollars," she said.

"Right. And Jerrod only offered five thousand more. Oh, yes, and there's something else we should discuss. My attorneys discovered a rider on your investment—an insurance policy. If you died before collecting the money, it would become the sole property of Thomas Peterson."

"That sounds like Thomas. Fussy, fussy, fussy. He insured and double insured everything."

"Think about it, Lindsey. Thomas is not a wealthy man."

Her airy rich-lady attitude collapsed like a house of cards. "Oh my God. Thomas wants me dead so he can collect. Is it possible that Mikey Rankin was hired by Thomas to kill me? Not you?"

"We ought to consider it. Although Rankin himself said the hit was on me."

"And Thomas would have no way of knowing where I was." She frowned. "But that's not exactly true, is it? He sent me letters after the European publicity over the attempted kidnapping of the Vanderhoff kids. Of course, I returned his letters unopened, but he might have contacted someone in the Vanderhoff household. He might have learned that I'd be here for a month."

"On the other hand, my people have checked, and there have been no large cash withdrawals from his accounts to pay for a hit man. And I don't suppose Mikey Rankin would work on credit."

"He might if he was real hard up for cash. Can we find out more about Mikey? Was he a pro?"

"According to Murtaugh, he's a pretty nebulous figure." Byron sighed. "In fact, there's a possibility he was involved in espionage."

"NORAD again?"

Byron nodded as he sprawled out on the sofa. Though suffused with contentment on a personal level, Byron was dissatisfied with the slow solving of their dilemma. Yesterday, he'd laid it out on a computer program, trying to discover connections between all these complex events. But cause and effect were lacking. Each element had evolved its own unique structure.

"Byron?" Lindsey called softly. "If this is my fault, if the hit man was coming after me, I don't know how I can apologize for putting you and the kids in danger."

"Thomas isn't really a likely suspect," he said.

"Maybe I should leave."

"No." His answer was swift and emphatic. Life without Lindsey? He couldn't imagine it. She was a part of them. Amanda loved her. Sonny was getting accustomed to her. "You're family now, Lindsey."

"Thank you, but it's not true. A week ago, you didn't even know me."

"Only a week?" It felt as if they'd been together forever.

He sat up and looked at her. The past few days in the sun had darkened her tan, despite the heavy sunblock she insisted upon slathering over herself and the children. Her neat blond hair seemed brighter. "I won't let you leave."

"But I can't put you all in danger."

In her words, he sensed a different kind of peril. Though he'd been careful not to approach her or touch her since the morning when they had celebrated with a dance, Byron couldn't help feeling a magnetic pull toward her. And he was certain that she felt the same way. "I won't let you run away from me, Lindsey. We're safe here. Nothing is going to hurt us."

She nodded and rose to her feet. "Let's think about it. Good night, Byron."

"Good night, Lindsey."

He sank back on the sofa. Every evening, it was the same. A chat—short and sweet—and then she was off to bed. Escaping from the dangers of intimacy.

But what else could they do? The time wasn't right for a relationship. Not with a threat still hanging over their heads. And, he acknowledged, not with the children watching.

Byron climbed the stairs to his own solitary bed.

In his bedroom, he heard Lindsey running water in the tub and forced himself not to imagine her bathing preparations. Would she brush her hair? Was she wearing a robe, or nothing at all? Commanding himself to stop thinking, Byron flicked on his bedroom light.

His eyes went immediately to the king-size bed. Amanda's life-size bear stretched across the spread. A sleek dagger protruded from the bear's chest.

Chapter Twelve

The bear's silly grin beckoned to Byron. He couldn't look at the fuzzy creature without imagining Amanda clinging to its fur and laughing. Amanda! Oh, God, if anything had happened to his daughter...

He raced down the hall to her bedroom, stumbled and crashed against the wall, flung open the door. Light from the hallway slanted across her bed, revealing a still form. He crept to her bedside, trembling from within. Was she all right? God, she had to be all right.

Gently, he touched her shoulder and felt the sweet living warmth of her body. She shifted beneath his hand. In her sleep, she murmured, "Daddy?"

He kissed the silky strands of hair above her dainty pink ear. "It's okay, honey. Go back to sleep."

Byron backed away from her bed and stood paralyzed in the doorway, staring at his daughter. She was safe, but for how long? Did he dare to leave the room, even for a moment? He must have been crazy to delude himself into thinking he could protect them. Never in his life had Byron felt so vulnerable.

"Byron?" Lindsey came up behind him. "Is something wrong?"

Without speaking, he nodded.

"What is it? What's happened?"

"Check Sonny. Please check in Sonny's room."

Lindsey padded down the hallway and eased Sonny's door open. Immediately, the boy bolted upright in bed. "What do you want?"

"Go back to sleep, Sonny. I was just checking."

He flicked on the bedside lamp and squinted against the light. "I don't want you to come in here unless I say so."

"You're right. You are entitled to your privacy."

"Some privacy. Ever since you kicked the door down, I can't lock it." His slitted eyes gleamed with anger. "I wish you'd never come here."

Byron stepped into his son's room. "Stop it," he hissed. "You'll wake your sister."

"What's going on? How come you two are sneaking around in the middle of the night?"

"I'll explain later."

"You always say that, but you never do explain." Sonny sprang from his bed and confronted his father. "Stop treating me like a kid."

"But you are a kid."

"I want to be a man. Just tell me, Dad. What's going on?"

His skinny shoulders were thrown back and his pajama bottoms made a puddle of material around his ankles. Byron wanted to protect his son, to shield him. But the threat was too near. It was better for Sonny to know. "All right, I'll explain everything. But first I need to talk to Lindsey. You go to Amanda's room. Keep an eye on her. If you see or hear anything unusual, call me."

"You got it." Sonny gave a thumbs-up sign.

As soon as Amanda's bedroom door closed behind Sonny, Byron guided Lindsey into his bedroom. He pointed at the bear.

For a moment, she just stared. Someone had attacked the stuffed bear? This was more than a little sick. But the bear had not been mutilated. It's furry limbs were neatly arranged on the covers. The dagger wound was precisely centered. The very neatness of the act scared her.

"They're coming after my children," Byron said.

"Don't panic. Did you find the room like this? Both windows open?"

"Yes."

She approached the bed. The silver dagger speared a sheet of lined yellow paper from a legal pad to the bear's fuzzy chest. Words clipped from magazines were glued to the paper. Not only an ugly warning, Lindsey thought, but a specific one. She read aloud. "'I will kill you real slow. You will die by inches. You are not safe.'"

"I've got to get my kids out of here." There was a rough edge to his voice. "I was a fool to bring them here."

"Calm down, Byron. We'll get Kirsch up here and he can dust for fingerprints."

"We know who did it," Byron said. "Rankin."

His eyes flicked around the room, as if he expected to see Rankin. Every muscle in Byron's body was tensed. He tasted blood in his mouth. Rankin had been in Amanda's room. He had stabbed Amanda's bear.

"Byron!" Lindsey snapped. "You can't stop and think about this. We have to act."

"I thought we were safe." Byron felt like he was speaking from the bottom of a deep well. "I didn't think . . ."

"It's not your fault. We'll figure it out later, but right now we need Kirsch."

"Don't you understand?" Everything was upside down. Crazy. Disoriented. Things like this couldn't happen—not when he'd taken all the precautions. "Rankin was here in this room. He touched my daughter's things."

"Stop it, Byron."

"This is wrong." His voice was a jumbled whisper. "Can't run away. Never. I know that. Maureen's death taught me." It was inconceivable that he had failed. He felt cold, ice cold, and numb. If anything happened to his children...

He saw Lindsey draw back her hand. In slow motion, he watched her swing in a wide arc. His brain considered ducking or blocking the blow. But his reactions were numb.

There was a loud crack when she slapped his face. He felt a sting. Sensation flooded back through him. "Dammit, Lindsey, why did you do that?"

She stalked to the balcony window and opened it. In a loud whisper, she called, "Hey, Kirsch. Are you out here?"

"I'm here, Lindsey." At night, Kirsch usually stationed himself near Byron's room, since he figured that Byron was the likely target. "What's wrong?"

"Get up here," she said. "Byron's room."

When she came back to Byron, he was still rubbing his jaw. "Sorry," she said. "It seemed like the right thing to do."

"If you think I'm going to say, 'Thanks, I needed that,' you're sadly mistaken."

"You were wide-eyed and spacey, Byron. And there wasn't time to talk you back to earth. Maybe whoever did this is still on the grounds. If we can keep it quiet, Kirsch might be able to organize a search party."

When Kirsch came into the room and saw the bear, the ruddy color drained from his face, leaving only the freckles behind. "This isn't possible," he said. "Nothing could have gotten past our security. Nobody."

"Keep it quiet," Lindsey instructed. "Amanda is still sleeping."

"Impossible," he muttered. "Nobody could..."

Good grief! Was she going to have to slap Kirsch, too? "Somebody did," she said. "We'll get the kids and go down to the workshop. You and your men make a search of the grounds. Right?"

"Right." A muscle in his square jaw twitched. "We'll nail this pig."

"Good," Lindsey said. "I don't want Amanda to see her bear like this. If I take a pillow case and remove the knife and the note, it won't mess up fingerprints, will it?"

"No. And we won't get prints from the bear." Kirsch turned to Byron. "When was the last time you were in this room?"

"I changed clothes after my evening swim. Must have been about eight o'clock."

"And it's eleven now." Kirsch shook his head. "That's a long time frame to hope that somebody's still around."

"Even if you don't catch them," Byron said, "I want this place searched from top to bottom. And I want to know how the hell they got in here." As Lindsey took a pillow case and reached for the dagger, he halted her. "Wait! Sonny should see this."

"Are you sure?"

"Maybe then he'll understand that we're not playing a game."

Byron took Lindsey by the hand. At Amanda's room, Sonny and Lindsey traded places, leaving her to stand watch over Amanda.

While Byron led his son down the hall, he explained, "Things have been tense around here this week. And I know you think that calling in an army of security guards was overanxious on my part. So I want to give you an idea of what we're up against."

"What happened, Dad?"

"Somebody got in here. They left a message."

At the door, he paused. It seemed like only yesterday that Sonny was a chubby toddler. Now he was nearly grown. His voice squawked. He was tall. But was he a man? "I want you to know that there's real danger here."

Sonny entered the room cautiously. His reaction, Byron thought, was odd. Instead of horror or fear, Sonny marched right up to the dagger and read the note. His eyes were bright when he turned back to his father. "This is major, Dad. Really weird."

"I'm so glad you're concerned."

"I mean, this is psycho time. Somebody who attacks a stuffed animal? In-cred-i-ble."

Byron's eyebrows raised. "May I assume that you're not going to have nightmares about this?"

"I can't believe this. A note from cut-out paper?" He shook his head, obviously dazzled. "When the guys ask what I did on my summer vacation, I'm going to have something to say."

Maybe the boy wasn't ready to be a man, Byron thought, but he certainly wasn't a toddler anymore. "Don't tell your sister, all right?"

"Yeah. Sure, Dad."

Using the pillowcase, Byron removed the dagger and the note and placed them in his upper dresser drawer.

"You're doing that in case there are fingerprints," Sonny guessed. "This is great. Hey, Dad, thanks for telling me. You know, I'm not a kid anymore. I can handle a lot more than you think I can."

"Apparently so."

His son's attitude had gone from sullen to cheerfully threatened, and the transformation extended to his acceptance of Lindsey. While they crept downstairs to the workshop with Byron carrying a half-asleep Amanda, Sonny nudged Lindsey's arm and said, "I *bear*ly went to sleep. You know, *bear*ly."

She shot him a confused glance. "That's terrific, Sonny."

Snickering, he continued, "Do you think the Chicago *Bears* have a *stab* at the Super Bowl?"

"Hush, Sonny, you'll wake Amanda."

"Don't worry." He gave Lindsey a wide, friendly wink. "I won't tell her a thing."

Swell, Lindsey thought. Her first friendly communication with Byron's son was because of a psychotic hit man who stabbed stuffed bears. No matter how long she was a nanny, she would never understand the workings of the adolescent mind.

In the workshop, Byron placed Amanda on the cot they'd set up for just such a purpose. Sonny closed the door and locked it. He was talking a mile a minute, quietly so he wouldn't wake his sister, but so fast that his words made a hushed and senseless blur.

But Lindsey wasn't attempting to listen to Sonny. She'd sensed another presence in the workshop—nothing she could point to, but it felt like someone else was there with them—observing them, sharing the air they breathed.

Scanning the room, she saw nothing unusual. And there was virtually nowhere to hide—no doors to other rooms, no windows, no rafters across the high ceiling. The air ducts were too small for a person to hide inside. There was only the Volkswagen and the helicopter.

Cautiously, Lindsey went to the toolbench where Byron kept his gun. As far as she knew, it still wasn't loaded. But their intruder—if there was an intruder—wouldn't necessarily share her knowledge.

Armed with the pistol, she stalked silently around the Volkswagen. Nothing there. She turned toward the helicopter.

"Hey, Lindsey," Sonny cheerfully announced. "What are you doing? Looks like you're going to karate chop the helicopter."

"Lindsey?" Byron echoed his son. "Is something wrong?"

"Probably not." She abandoned stealth and marched to the front of the helicopter with her pistol leveled and ready.

She was right. There was someone sitting inside the open cockpit. Jerrod Blake looked down his nose at her.

"All right, Jerrod," she ordered. "Climb out of there and move real slow."

"Guns aren't necessary," he said as he eased down from the cockpit and straightened the collar on his black jumpsuit. Despite the blackened smears on his face and a black knit cap covering his white hair, he maintained his aura of unapproachable dignity.

Sonny had bounded to Lindsey's side. "Uncle Jerrod? Did you kill the bear?"

"What?"

In Lindsey's opinion, Jerrod's confusion seemed real. But he must have been responsible for placing the bear and the note in Byron's room. There couldn't possibly have been two intruders on the same night. Or could there have been? Two? Or more?

"The bear," Sonny repeated. "Did you kill Amanda's bear?"

"I'm not Davy Crockett, Sonny. Despite this primitive-looking garb."

Byron was in no mood for witticisms. His fists were clenched. His dark eyes flashed as he strode toward his uncle. "Don't play the innocent with me, Jerrod."

"Wait!" Lindsey warned. "He might be armed."

"I'll frisk him."

"Should you?" Jerrod asked. "I might have rigged my body with explosive devices."

Despite his rage and his forward momentum, Byron brought himself to an abrupt halt. Jerrod was crazy enough—and brilliant enough—to rig some kind of detonation device. Byron eyed the old man with flaming hostility. "There's nothing on your jaw," he said. "Give me one good reason why I shouldn't break it for you."

"Don't be childish, Byron. You lost. Take it like a man."

"What the hell are you talking about?"

"I bet you that I could foil your so-called impenetrable security, and I did. You really ought to be grateful. I've illustrated the flaws in your system."

"Why? Why go to all that trouble? Why would you?"

Jerrod declaimed, "As Mallory said when asked why he wanted to climb Mount Everest, 'Because it is there.'"

"Dammit, Jerrod, this isn't a game."

"All of life is a game," Jerrod continued in a vaguely philosophical vein. "Unfortunately, the odds are stacked against us poor mortals. No matter how we play the hand we've been dealt, we will lose in the end. All of us must die. Though we might dream of eternity, we—"

"How did you get in?" Lindsey interrupted.

"Nothing terribly clever. I used one of mankind's oldest and most effective inventions, money. I bribed one of your stalwart guards."

Byron smacked his open palm against the roof of the Volkswagen. A simple bribe. That was all it took to overcome this complex arrangement of patrols and dogs and electronic surveillance. And he'd been blind enough to think they were really safe! What the hell was he going to do next? Byron paced the concrete floor of the workshop. Even if Jerrod were no threat and had merely chosen to appear because Byron told him not to, the implication was clear. Anyone could offer a bribe. Anyone could get inside.

"But why did you kill the bear?" Sonny asked.

"My dear young man, I haven't the vaguest idea what you're referring to. Is 'kill the bear' some new teenage slang?"

When Lindsey explained the reference, a strange expression of concern covered Jerrod's bravado. His eyebrows drew into a frown. "I didn't kill the bear, Sonny. Which means I'm not the first or the only person to breech your father's supposedly foolproof security system."

"Not the first?" Lindsey questioned. "How do you know you're not the first?"

"I arrived only minutes before you came down here. Ergo, someone else was inside earlier, stabbing the bear."

"Come off it, Jerrod." Lindsey's tone was harsh sarcasm. "You don't expect us to believe that you and another

intruder just happened to choose the same night to sneak
inside.''

"Let me think," he said.

"Go right ahead."

"Put away that stupid gun."

Though Jerrod had given her no reason to believe he was
trustworthy, she doubted that he was responsible for the
bear incident. Otherwise, he would have egotistically
claimed credit for being the first and only person to break
the security system.

Lowering her unloaded gun, Lindsey backed off and took
a seat on one of the workbenches. Silently, she watched Byron and Jerrod. The family resemblance was interesting.
Both men were tall, both were handsome in their own ways,
both shared an attitude of utter concentration as they paced
and pondered. Would Byron someday become exactly like
Jerrod? Crochety? Self-indulgent? Dignified but demand-
ing?

Definitely not. Though their genetic root was similar,
Byron had branched in a different direction. His love for his
late wife and for his children had saved him from becoming
selfish and willful like Jerrod.

Byron suffered for his emotions, but pain made the
heartwood richer. Eccentricity might be the Cyril heritage,
but Byron's love for his family caused him to grow straight
and strong.

"I've got an idea," Jerrod said.

They gave him their complete attention.

"Suppose," Jerrod hypothesized, "that the security
guard who assisted me in penetrating the system had received a similar bribe from another potential intruder. If he
escorted both of us inside, he would double his profit. He
might have arranged the situation so we would both enter at
a similar time."

"Too much of a coincidence," Lindsey objected. "There are nearly forty men on the grounds. What are the odds against both of you selecting the same guy?"

"Mine was not a random choice," Jerrod said. "I'll admit that bribery is rather crude, but my methods of selection were—as always—highly technical. Using a sophisticated computer search, I accessed police records for your guards and chose the man whose record indicated he was likely to be corrupt."

"You broke into police records?"

"Rather an untraceable crime, isn't it?" He smiled. "In any case, the guard who helped me was an obvious choice. Especially since I observed your operations and noted that this guard also happens to be the one who assists the caterers in delivering lunch and dinner. Which meant he was stationed near the gate and was therefore approachable." He concluded, "I consider it likely that another intruder came to the same conclusions I did. And that intruder—your bear stabber—approached the same man."

"I doubt that Rankin used a high-tech computer," Lindsey said. "But if this particular guard had a record, he might have been a plant to begin with."

"Does it matter?" Byron sighed. "Bottom line is that it's possible for intruders to get into the grounds. We're not safe. So, what do we do next? Lindsey?"

"I'm blank. Some kind of escape—"

"Running away," Byron said. "Perhaps, you're right."

"I can tell you what not to do," Jerrod put in. "Don't take off on your yacht. It's the most obvious of all escapes, and the most easily traceable."

"That's right," Sonny added. "Anybody with a submarine could attack us." He brightened. "Or frogmen. Or dolphins carrying explosives."

"Indeed," Jerrod said as he sat on the workbench beside Lindsey. "One must always be aware of the possibility of kamikaze dolphins. In any case, I should like to speak with this young lady while you consider your alternatives."

Eyebrows raised, Lindsey turned toward him. What could Jerrod possibly have to discuss with her?

"JerBee," he said. "It has come to my attention that you are considering a substantial stock return, and I would like to make an offer on your shares before they go onto the open market."

"Why?" she asked suspiciously.

"Over the years I have lost control of the company, mostly to family members. And I want it back."

"From which family members?"

"Any and all of them. The Cyril parasites. Individuals who are incapable of independent thinking beyond their next purchases. Merchandise maniacs."

"Who?"

"Estelle Dumont is one," he said. "She sold out at a ridiculously inflated price to a hostile party who wants to buy JerBee merely to close it down. In any case, I am prepared to offer you five thousand dollars above market value."

"I'll consider it," Lindsey said.

"Excellent."

Jerrod pulled a document and pen from a pocket of his jumpsuit. Carefully, he smoothed the paper on the workbench between them. "Sign this and the deal is done."

"I said I'll think about it. Maybe tomorrow."

"I'd prefer that you sign right now."

"Why?" She met his dark-eyed gaze, so similar to Byron's but so utterly different, so lacking in humanity. "What's the rush, Jerrod?"

"All things considered." His smile was cold. "You might not live to see tomorrow."

Chapter Thirteen

Despite Jerrod's dire and obnoxious prediction, Lindsey lived to see another dawn—a beautiful dawn at sea.

The Pacific breeze whisked through her hair as she stood at the gleaming rail of the McHenrys' fishing boat. Sunrise colored the skies with bright magenta that faded to soft yellow and distant eggshell blue at the horizon. Yet, Lindsey alternated scowls with irritated clicks of her tongue against her teeth. Unable to appreciate the beauty, she stared into the waves and worried about possible attacks from submarines and frogmen.

A heavily-armed Kirsch joined her. "I don't like this," he said. "I don't like this one single bit."

"Seasick?"

"You know what I mean. Out here, there's no cover, no protection. I could have gotten the situation back at the house under control. But this?"

"It won't last long," she said.

Their plan was to sail up the coast to San Francisco, where Amanda and Sonny would stay with their grandparents. Though Lindsey had some questions about leaving the children with Bart and Julia Dixon—mostly because it seemed like the most obvious place to leave them—she had no ready alternative. And their escape from the villa seemed to be successful. No one was following them. Their getaway had been easy. Too easy, Lindsey thought fretfully. It was almost as if someone wanted them to make this move.

Last night, after Kirsch had reported no evidence of intruders but confirmed that one of his men had gone missing, Byron had taken action with such speed that Amanda barely had a chance to waken. Under the cover of darkness, they had all hidden in the car that was supposedly being used to escort Jerrod from the premises. Kirsch drove them to Avalon, where they borrowed the McHenrys' boat and headed north.

Incredibly simple, but Lindsey found herself counting the flaws in this plan. Even if Rankin had not been watching the house and had not seen them leave, several people—Jerrod, the two guards who were watching him and the McHenrys—knew the family had fled. Though they hadn't sailed away on Byron's easily traceable yacht, it wouldn't take a genius to guess that they'd used the McHenrys' boat.

"I just don't like it," Kirsch repeated.

"Better than being sitting ducks," Lindsey said, forcing an optimistic grin. Perhaps no one had followed them. Perhaps she had overestimated the cleverness of Rankin. And she was relieved to finally be on the run. Escape was positive movement. Truly, she did prefer this method of evasive action.

When Byron came to the rail and stood beside them, Kirsch glared. "Who's driving the boat?"

"Sonny. Don't worry. He can handle this craft. My boy has been on the water since he was a baby."

"And he's not much more than that now," Kirsch grumbled. "Listen, Byron, I understand the reasons for taking the kids out of the house. But why not put them on a plane? Or a bus?"

"I didn't want to leave a trail."

Kirsch nodded. "Okay. But after we get to San Francisco, then what? If Rankin—or whoever it was that hired

Rankin's brother—wants to come after the kids, they'll check the grandparents. It's the first place they'll look."

Byron shrugged in dismissal. "Why don't you go below and have something to eat, Kirsch? The larder is well-stocked, courtesy of Helen McHenry."

Muttering and mumbling, Kirsch followed Byron's directive.

Lindsey watched him go, then turned toward Byron. "I agree with Kirsch. Not only because sending the kids to stay with their grandparents is too transparent an escape, but also because I'm not sure the Dixons can be trusted." She took a breath. "Helen has told me about your disagreements with Bart Dixon."

"Disagreement is a lighthearted description for what went on between Bart and me."

"Tell me."

"It was after Maureen's condition was diagnosed as hopeless. She didn't want to participate in a whole series of agonizing experiments, and I supported her decision. Her father, a doctor, never understood. He thought I was a coward, that I had given up."

"Sounds like the opposite," Lindsey said. "It takes a brave man to stand and face his destiny."

"Bart didn't see it that way."

She touched his arm. "Byron, if he dislikes you so much, is he the right person to take care of the children?"

"Are you suggesting that Bart Dixon hired the hit man?"

She shrugged. "Isn't it a possibility?"

"Not at all. Hiring a hit man is an act of insanity, and Dr. Dixon isn't crazy. Besides, at my father's funeral, we took the first steps toward reconciliation. I don't think we'll ever be close buddies, but we're not blood enemies."

"Think about this, Byron. After you made arrangements with Bart, we took off. Didn't our escape seem too easy?"

"Maybe we've finally gotten lucky."

His brow furrowed as he gazed toward the golden eastern skies, and she sensed that he was shutting her out, keeping something from her. "All right," she snapped. "What's going on?"

"What?"

"You've got something up your sleeve, and don't deny it. I should have guessed. By now I ought to know that you're the original master of the complex Byzantine scheme. This was too simple and straightforward for you to have planned it."

He shrugged. "Maybe I'm adapting the level of my thinking to Rankin's IQ."

"You're plotting something else. There's some other scheme waffling around in your head, something you haven't told me."

He leaned his forearms against the railing and counted white caps in the sea. Their route was close enough to shore that gulls swooped overhead; their screeching could be heard over the purr of the boat's engine. *Free as a bird*, Byron thought. Would he ever feel that way again? Or had he ever felt so unencumbered?

"Well?" Lindsey queried. "What haven't you told me?"

"Have I mentioned that you look lovely this morning?"

"Oh, sure. Staying up all night does wonders for the complexion."

"On you, it looks good." Not a lie. He was one hundred percent sincere. She was beautiful in the sunlight. And in the night. When this was over, he meant to tell her again and again until she finally believed him. But now, there were other concerns. "We're not really taking the kids to San Francisco."

"Ah-ha! I knew it! And when you made that telephone call at the pier, you weren't really contacting their grandparents, were you?"

"No. Someone else is meeting us. In about a half an hour. At Santa Barbara."

"Who?"

"An old friend. He's an actor, but very safe." Byron chuckled. "He's played a cop on a television series for six years. I told Sonny, and he's ecstatic."

"What else?" she urged.

Byron took a deep breath. This was the part of his plan she wasn't going to like. "After you and the kids are dropped off, I'll return to Catalina. I should be back before noon."

"You're going to leave me with the kids? With your actor friend?"

"That is correct. Lindsey, I feel like hell for getting you involved in this mess. Let me clean it up."

"Aren't you forgetting something? Rankin is after me for killing his brother. Maybe more than you. If I stay with the kids, Rankin is sure to come looking for me."

"No one will find you," he said. "My connection with this actor isn't well-known. Besides, he has an efficient security system to protect himself and his family from rabid fans."

She held up one slim finger. "Number one—a fan in search of an autograph is hardly in the same category as a professional killer." She raised a second finger. "Number two—security systems fail, as we've just learned." Her other fingers splayed before him. "Numbers three, four and five—I won't do it. If you're going back to Catalina to offer yourself as live bait, I will be with you. That's my job—to protect you."

"Your job," he corrected, "is to be a nanny for the children. As your employer, I insist that you follow my instructions."

The words tasted sour in his mouth. He didn't think of her as an employee anymore. To be honest, he'd had trouble remembering that she was the nanny from the first time he saw her on the rear terrace with her gauze skirt blowing seductively around her knees.

"I quit," she said.

"What?"

"You heard me. I hereby tender my resignation. I'm not your nanny anymore and you can't tell me what to do."

"But—"

"I'm coming back to Catalina with you, Byron. And that's that. If you'll excuse me, I want to talk with the children."

She pivoted, but before she could stalk away from him, he caught her arm and twirled her around to face him. "Lindsey, I didn't mean to insult you."

"I gave you good reasons why I should come with you." She shook off his grasp. "And I will be at the villa, Byron. Either you take me back on this boat. Or I'll find my own way."

"No, Lindsey. I'm doing this for your own good. For your safety."

"Thank you very much, great lord of the manor." She dropped a sarcastic curtsy. "But I'll decide what's best for me."

"It was your idea to run from Rankin," he pointed out. "You wanted to hide out until this blew over."

"I've changed my mind."

Her eyes shot blue flames, kindling a spark within him. But it was not the heat of anger that swept through Byron. At that moment, she was the most exciting woman he had ever seen. Like a force of nature, she exuded an innate power. Her inner strength was a match for the waves and the wind and the sky.

How could he—a mere mortal man—expect to protect a goddess? Yet, he had to try. "Stay with the children, Lindsey. They need you more than I do."

"They need their father. Sonny needs a male role model. Amanda needs a daddy to hold her and to be there for her. I'd be doing your children a terrible disservice if I allowed you to put yourself in the path of danger."

"But you're not their nanny anymore," he reminded. "You quit."

"That doesn't mean I've stopped caring for them. I'm concerned about the children. And about you. Even though you're acting like a male chauvinist, mucho-macho ass."

"So you care about me?"

"Of course." She rolled her eyes as if he'd asked the most idiotic question in the world. "I care about you in a humanitarian sense—the way I'd care about a fly caught in a spider's web. Or a helpless puppy—"

"I'm not helpless."

"No, you're not." She lowered her gaze, then looked back at him. The heat of anger colored her cheeks. "Byron, if anything happened to you when I was running away, I couldn't stand it."

He raised his hand to her shoulder and glided it down the slippery sleeve of her windbreaker until he caught her fingers and held them. "Is it possible, Lindsey, that you care about me the way a woman might care about a man?"

Her lips parted, ready to fire a snappy comeback. Yet, she did not speak. Her tongue flicked out to moisten her lips. She breathed heavily, causing her breasts to rise and fall. Behind the fire in her eyes, he saw a sensual glow. And he knew that he was right. She did care.

Yet she broke away from him. Still running? "We can talk about it on our way back to Catalina," she said.

When she left the deck, the spell was broken. Byron was left with his practical concerns.

Though he was anxious to pursue the topic of caring with her, he was determined that she stay with his friend in Santa Barbara. There would be another time for them. When the danger was past, he would take Lindsey for a long cruise. They would swim together in the ocean. They would lie on the deck and watch the stars appear in the night skies.

But now, dammit, there were other matters to attend to.

His plan was to return to the villa, to dismiss all the guards except Kirsch, and to make a stand against Rankin. Very heroic, Byron thought. Or very suicidal.

But what other options did he have? He'd already proved that security systems could be broken. Likewise, no hiding place was impenetrable. And he couldn't stay on the run, looking over his shoulder, seeing Rankin in every crowd and wondering whether death could come from a bullet or a knife.

He had to face Rankin. Surely, he and Kirsch were a match for that small-time crook. The more difficult prospect, Byron thought, was to learn the identity of the person who had hired the hit man. Byron's plan was complicated by the fact that he wasn't setting out to kill Rankin but only to capture him. And to question him. This madness would not truly end until Byron found out who arranged for Mikey Rankin to assassinate him. He needed to know who hated him enough to want him dead.

Kirsch joined him on deck. A mug of coffee was clenched in his meaty fist. "Lindsey told me to come up here and talk sense into you."

"That won't be necessary. Here's the plan. We will drop off the kids and Lindsey with a friend of mine in Santa Barbara. Then you and I will return to the villa. We'll dismiss all the other guards. And we will prepare for an assault by Rankin."

"Have you ever done anything like this before?" Kirsch sipped his coffee and gazed out to sea. "Ever been in combat?"

"No."

"On paper, it looks simple. Or in a movie where you hear a gun go pop and you see a man go down. Nothing to it."

"I don't expect this to be easy."

"You know I was in the infantry. In Nam. And I was a cop. I've killed before. And I'm here to tell you that pulling the trigger is hell. It's not easy for a decent human to commit murder. You never forget." He cleared his throat. "You better think long and hard before you decide to take on professional killers."

Byron's resolve was unwavering. "I'm not planning to kill anybody. I want to capture Rankin or one of his men so I can find out who is behind all this."

"Excuse me . . . ?" Kirsch gaped. "Did I hear right? You think you can catch one of these guys and get him to talk?"

"That's right."

Kirsch shook his head from side to side. "Why?"

"Because Rankin is only part of this. I need to find the person who hired Rankin's brother. Otherwise, I could kill Rankin, then find another assassin on my doorstep."

"You're crazy, man. Rankin's not going to tell you who hired his brother. No way."

"Maybe not. But I've got to try to find out. Listen, Kirsch, if you don't want to join me, I'll understand."

For a long moment, Kirsch studied Byron. "There's something you ought to know about. The gun that Mikey Rankin was carrying had an unusual mark on the handle— a sign used by an international terrorist organization."

Byron's eyelids clicked open and closed as he digested this piece of data. "How did you find this out?"

"From Colonel Wright. He asked me not to tell you until he made certain of the connections with these terrorists."

"And has he?"

"No. But you see what I'm getting at? It's possible that Mikey Rankin wasn't hired as a hit man."

"Because he might have been a terrorist who was after the NORAD plans," Byron mused. "If that's so, would Wright help us set a trap?"

"Negative. He'll offer protective custody. But he won't agree to a plan where you use yourself as bait. The army doesn't do that with civilians."

"Not even if it meant catching Rankin? He must be part of the terrorist group, too."

"Not necessarily. He might be a terrorist who's completing the assignment his brother bungled—" Kirsch sipped at his coffee "—or he might be out to revenge his brother's death."

Strong motives, either way. But not nearly as fierce as Byron's need to protect his children and Lindsey. Automatically, Byron factored the complications. Terrorists meant a larger and more sophisticated force, more effective weapons, a more complex attack plan. Byron's strategy would have to adjust, but the fact that Rankin might be the spearhead of a terrorist organization didn't alter his basic direction.

"I'm still going back to Catalina," he said. "Are you with me, Kirsch?"

"It's going to cost," he warned. "Four times what you're paying me right now."

"Done."

They shook on it. Kirsch almost lost his gruffness when he said, "I might be making a big mistake, but I can't leave you with your rear unguarded."

"Good choice of words," Byron said, "because I need you to back me up on one more thing. It's Lindsey. She wants to come along."

"Okay with me. From what I've seen, that lady can handle herself just fine."

"You misunderstand me. I don't want her to be there. This is my fight. I thought maybe you could talk her out of it."

Big, strong Kirsch—former cop and Vietnam veteran—visibly backed off. He held up one big hand, calling a halt. "Whoa, there. I'm not telling her."

"Come on, Kirsch. She might listen to you."

"No way, Byron. Talking to Lindsey is your problem."

He swung around and left Byron alone on deck.

The morning mist had lifted on a bright new day. Byron saw the shoreline coming closer. They were only minutes away from the destination he had set.

Byron went toward the wheelhouse to help Sonny navigate the last few miles, but he did not enter the cabin. He paused for a moment at the side window and watched.

His son stood at the control console with his attention focused on the tasks before him. His long, skinny legs balanced against the roll of the sea. Amanda was beside her brother. She'd climbed onto one of the chairs that was bolted to the deck and peered intently through the windshield. Her lips were moving, probably chatting and giggling over their adventure, but Byron could not hear her voice over the boat engine's whir.

In silence, he observed. What if his plan didn't work? What if Rankin succeeded in murdering him and he never saw his children again?

His eyes stung, blurring his vision when he realized that he might never see Sonny attain manhood, might never again hear Amanda's musical laughter, might never feel Amanda's arms thrown around his neck. Losing them was more painful than the thought of his own mortality. How could he take that chance? But how could he not?

Unless Rankin was dealt with, Sonny and Amanda were at risk. Their young lives could be cut short by an assassin's bullet. Or worse. They might be kidnapped, terrorized, held until he submitted to Rankin's demands. Fear sucked the air from Byron's lungs, and his knees felt watery as he stumbled against the bulkhead.

Inside the cabin, Amanda turned away from the windshield. Her face lit with a smile. Byron saw her clamber off the bolted-down chair, but it was as if he were watching her through a telescope. Though near, she seemed faraway, distanced from him.

Amanda bounced toward Lindsey, who stood at the rear of the cabin, at the farthest edge of Byron's vision. His daughter was gesturing vivaciously and talking and laughing.

Then Lindsey hugged the little girl. Byron's tension began to melt. Even if he weren't here, it would be all right. Lindsey would make sure that nothing bad happened to his children. She cared about them.

Stepping away from the window, he breathed in a lungful of fresh sea air. Sunlight danced a shimmer across the waves. Everything would be all right. The world would continue without him. His children would grow and flourish.

Lindsey had come from the cabin and stood beside him. "Byron, we need more directions. Sonny says he's completed the course you gave him."

"You can't come with me back to Catalina," he said. "The children need you. If something should happen to me—"

"That's why I should go. So nothing will happen."

"If something happens to me," he repeated, forcing a strength he did not truly feel, "I want you to be there for them. To help them adjust. Will you do that?"

"Nothing is going to happen to you. I won't let it."

"Just promise me."

When he stared at her, Byron had never felt so ferociously, steadfastly determined. He aimed every ounce of his will at her. "Promise."

Slowly, she conceded, "All right, Byron. I'll make sure that the children are taken care of."

"Stay with them."

"For a time. But I can't promise how long."

Half an hour later, as the boat pulled away from the private dock where Amanda, Sonny and Lindsey stood waving, Byron remembered her words. Wouldn't promise how long? Was she planning to settle the kids at this new place and then return to the island?

Contradicting emotions collided in his brain. Though he wanted her to be safe, he also wanted her to be with him. Not to share the danger, but simply to be at his side.

There were questions he had not asked her. Hours he had not spent gazing into her sky-blue eyes. His body went taut as he considered the feelings he had not shared with Lindsey.

Byron turned his attention out to sea. A clear day. A sailor's delight. He wished he could spend it with her. Instinctively, he knew that he could not allow himself to dwell on the possibilities with Lindsey. He would need all his vigilance to defeat Rankin.

And he had to win. If anything happened to him, he would miss the future he might share with Lindsey.

Chapter Fourteen

He was leaving her. Watching Byron sail away from the secluded pier near Santa Barbara, Lindsey had a crazy urge to dive into the Pacific and swim after him. She felt abandoned, lonely. But that was absurd. How could she feel homeless when she'd never really had a home of her own?

For the past eight years in Europe, she never acquired more possessions than could be packed into a suitcase. As a child, she hadn't fit into her mother's world—that dingy little apartment was someplace she wanted to escape. Her husbands' houses had belonged to them and she had been merely passing through. Even when she had had her own apartment, it was only a stopping-off place. Not a home.

Why then—as she watched Byron sail away—did she feel as if her roots were being sheared out from under her? What caused this unfamiliar sense of loss?

If anything happened to him...

The McHenrys' tidy fishing boat became a dot on the horizon, then disappeared. She should be watching the children, should be scanning the palisade for snipers, should be questioning Byron's friend. But if anything happened...

He had been wise, she told herself firmly. The single most important factor in all this craziness was the children's safety. It was right that she stay with them and be certain that their new surroundings were secure.

She blinked, ordered her eyes to focus on the present moment. The future was beyond her control.

The short pier was on a private beach that lay beyond the view of Highway 1. At this hour of the morning, they were alone on the pale sand. Sonny and Amanda waded in the surf. Two security men in casual shirts and sunglasses silently observed. And Scott Winfield, Byron's friend who played a tough, cool cop in a television series, stood a few paces away. His chiseled jaw and striking blue eyes were less impressive than the attitude of masculine strength that radiated from him.

Briskly, she turned to him. "I hope Byron hasn't downplayed the seriousness of our situation. The men who are after him are deadly."

"I understand."

"Does anyone else know that you and Byron are friends?"

"I doubt it. We're not bosom buddies."

She hesitated. If there were no connection between the two men, how could Byron call upon Scott for this rather huge favor? "I don't understand."

"Byron saved my life," Scott said simply. "We're not pals. We don't have much in common. But I would do anything—I mean, anything—for him. I owe him."

Natural skepticism kept her from accepting Scott at his word. Though he sounded bluntly sincere, he was an actor and therefore was adept at convincing people. "Tell me, Scott, have you mentioned the story of how Byron saved your life to many people? Is it common knowledge?"

"No way." He squinted across the waves. "I'm supposed to be a hero. That's my profession. And I'm not exactly proud of the way I behaved when Byron stepped in and saved my butt."

If that were true, Scott was the perfect person to help them. No one knew of his connection with Byron. If Scott's home was well-protected, she'd feel confident in leaving the children and returning to Catalina. "Perhaps," she said, "we ought to invent a cover story for Sonny and Amanda. No point in announcing to the world that the Cyril kids have arrived."

"No problem. We'll say they're cousins, visiting my daughters. Both my kids are fairly responsible, but we better not tell them the entire story, either. Teenage girls have a tendency to run off at the mouth."

On the ride to Scott's house, Lindsey explained to Sonny and Amanda that they were not to identify themselves as Cyrils. Though Amanda was confused, Sonny loved the idea. In moments, he'd created a complicated secret identity.

After spending a day at Scott's ranch-style house, Lindsey was satisfied with his guardianship. His security system was low-key but effective. His guards had been with him for years, and their loyalty stemmed from more than their salaries. As an added bonus, Byron's children were thoroughly enjoying the company of Scott's teenage daughters.

They were safe. But if anything happened to Byron . . .

Lindsey was itching to leave. To return to Catalina. Her imagination had conjured dozens of horrifying scenarios where her presence rescued Byron. After lunch on the second day, she informed Scott of her plans. "I've got to go back to Catalina."

"The island of romance?" he teased.

"Not hardly. I'm returning because I believe Byron needs physical backup from someone he can trust."

Scott set aside the script he had been studying and peeled off his reading glasses. "You care about him, Lindsey."

"Well, of course. And I feel responsible. If I hadn't been so quick on the trigger, if I hadn't killed Mikey Rankin, we wouldn't be in this position."

"You're a brave lady. You don't have to be afraid of your own feelings, Lindsey."

"That sounds like a line from a script."

In a rare flash of actor's egoism, Scott grinned at his own cleverness. "It does, doesn't it? Maybe we can use it. I'm going to have a love interest this season."

"When does your hiatus from the series end?"

"In a week. Of course, Sonny and Amanda are welcome to stay for as long as they want. But I won't be here."

"In a week," Lindsey promised, "this will be over."

She told Sonny and Amanda that she would be visiting with their father for a few days and that they would be in touch. Though Sonny had been comradely toward her, Lindsey knew he wouldn't be terribly upset if she left him alone with the two attractive Winfield daughters.

But Amanda's little face pinched with worry. "Why hasn't Daddy telephoned us?"

"He's being very careful," Lindsey explained. "He doesn't want to do anything that might hint where you are. Maybe when I go to Catalina and join him, we can hurry things up a bit."

"Yes, Lindsey. Please." Amanda forced a grin. "And you better take care of Smokey the cat. Dad probably isn't feeding him right."

Lindsey nodded. "Anything else?"

"My bear. Say hello to my big teddy."

Lindsey hugged the little girl. "I will. And your father and I will be back before you know it."

Without looking back, Lindsey rode away from the house with one of the security men. Travel was second nature to her, and she managed easily to find a rental car, drive south on Highway 1 and—wearing a disguise—she caught the ferry to Catalina Island. It was early dusk when she telephoned the villa from a public telephone in Avalon.

Kirsch answered and immediately reprimanded her. "The phone is probably bugged. I thought we agreed not to be in contact with each other."

"I'm calling from a safe place."

"Don't tell me where. And don't call again."

He hung up.

Angrily, she redialed. Being safe was one thing, being rude was quite another. "Don't hang up, Kirsch. I'm coming in from the cold."

"What?"

"It's spy jargon for returning to the nest, homing in, coming back to the coop."

"You want to come back here?"

"Bingo."

"You can't, Lindsey. We've rigged the grounds with booby traps. We're holed up inside."

"Give me a break, Kirsch. I want back in."

"No," he said gruffly. "You're supposed to stay away. You agreed to it. And that's final. Don't come here."

Again, he hung up.

If anything, his strict orders to stay away made her want to be there even more. What did they really know about Kirsch? Could he be trusted? This time, she telephoned the McHenry residence. The phone rang several times before she gave up.

So the grounds were booby-trapped, were they? A mine field? Trip wires? What? With Kirsch's tactical understanding and Byron's inventive skill, they might have created an impossible maze. But nothing was unbeatable. She'd find a way inside.

Lindsey wandered over to a festive little tavern sandwiched between souvenir shops. Beneath cheery Japanese lanterns, she sat at an outdoor table and concentrated. How could she break into the villa?

Though dusk was falling, she kept her over-size sunglasses—part of her disguise—perched on her nose. Lindsey was confident that no one could recognize her in this cheap floppy hat, screaming red lipstick and garish sundress. But the truly inspired touch in her costume was the altering of her body shape. She'd bought a cheap spandex girdle a couple of sizes too big and stuffed it with her other clothing, creating a huge mound at her belly. She looked nine-and-a-half-months pregnant.

While she had been arranging her disguise, Lindsey wondered if her faked pregnancy might be Freudian, reflecting a secret desire for children. Or to make babies. With Byron. She touched her mountainous belly. Maybe. But she'd have to find Byron first.

She could parachute in via helicopter, but Byron probably had invested in anti-aircraft guns. What if she simply took a taxi to the gates and demanded to be allowed entrance? She shook her head. Bad idea. Both she and Byron would be easy targets if Rankin and his men were watching the villa. An approach by sea was equally impossible.

It was infuriating to think that Jerrod had accomplished a break-in. And so had someone else—the person who had stabbed Amanda's teddy bear. Unless that had been Jerrod, too.

After thinking it over, Lindsey was pretty much convinced that Byron's uncle had pulled that stunt. It was unbelievable that two break-ins had occurred simultaneously. But why? Was Jerrod behind all of this? From the sniper on the cliff to—

The sniper! She knew how to get into the villa. They couldn't have booby-trapped the cliffside opposite the house with any sort of explosive; the rocky shale was too fragile and a collapse of that cliff might undermine the very foundations of the house. More likely, they had rigged a surveillance on the hillside.

And, she reasoned, as soon as they recognized her on the cliff, Byron would find a way to bring her inside.

With a bouncy pregnant waddle, she set out to complete her mission before nightfall.

INSIDE THE VILLA, an alarm buzzed. Byron was immediately alert. He checked the status board they'd set up. A flashing red light told him the attack was coming from the cliff opposite the house.

With practiced ease—for he and Kirsch had run through their strategic maneuvers dozens of times—he went to the upstairs window that offered a view of the cliff. Finally, something was happening. This constant, unrewarded vigilance was getting on his nerves.

He aimed his binoculars at the cliff. Though dusk had settled and it was difficult to identify shapes, Byron finally spotted the intruder, standing on the bluff. A pregnant woman?

Kirsch bolted into the room beside him. "Do you see them?"

"I must be hallucinating," Byron said. A pregnant woman who was waving both arms and grinning?

Kirsch raised his own binoculars. "What in the—"

"A visit from the stork? Maybe she needs help."

"And maybe she's a decoy."

The woman yanked off her hat, revealing sleek blond hair that fell into shape with characteristic neatness.

"It's Lindsey," Byron said. "Didn't you say that she'd called earlier?"

"Yeah, but I thought she was still in Santa Barbara."

Byron stood at the window. It was the very place she'd been standing when she fired her gun on her first day at the villa. He should have been angry with her for putting herself in danger. Instead, he was happy, delighted. He wanted to see her. As he watched her vigorous waving, a new energy coursed through him and the tension of the past days sloughed away.

"Cover me, Kirsch. I'm going to get her."

"Bad move, Byron. But I don't see that Lindsey has given you much alternative."

Some women were like that, Byron thought as he raced down the stairs. There was no alternative but to jump when they wanted you to jump. Such magnificent, unpredictable creatures.

He darted through the French windows. Using the shrubs and scrubby pines for cover, he hurried across the grounds toward the wrought-iron fence that separated his property from the neighboring bluff. Apparently Lindsey had remembered the directions he'd given on the first day because she stood on the upper bluff, not far from the house.

Though moving swiftly, Byron meticulously avoided the booby traps. Thus far, they had no indication that the villa was being watched, but he was careful not to make unnecessary noise or to step out from cover. The attack might come at anytime.

Lindsey stood beside a natural path leading to a gate in the fence. Though she appeared wary of the fence, he called a warning. "Stay there. We've rigged explosives all along here."

In a moment, he stood opposite her, separated by tall iron spikes. She looked wonderful. Her eyes never seemed brighter. The last rays of sun on her hair were a miracle. Sweet anticipation shuddered through him. He wanted to touch her, to hold her. The hairs on his arms prickled. His heart beat at double time.

"We can't cross here," he said. "There's only one safe place."

"I missed you, Byron."

He went to a camouflaged control box and deactivated the switch that controlled the detonator. In an instant, he was back at the fence. "It's safe now. But you'll have to climb over."

She raised her hand, palm toward him, and eased it between the iron spokes. "Touch me."

He fitted his palm against hers. Then the other hand. Their light connection electrified him. Without an embrace or even a kiss, he had never been so instantly aroused.

"Was there an explosion?" she whispered.

"You bet."

Following his instructions, she scaled the fence at the gate. When they embraced, joining their bodies, he couldn't help laughing at the pregnant bulge.

"My disguise," she said.

"Cute." He wanted to kiss her, to consume her, but now was not the moment. "We'd better get back inside where it's safe. I'm going to reactivate the traps. You'll have to follow me exactly so we don't accidentally set off any alarms or explosions."

Attempting to tread in his footsteps, Lindsey followed. She hadn't planned for this sudden outpouring of desire, hadn't expected it. But when she saw Byron, she wanted so much to make love, to express the passion that had been secretly building. There must have been an instinct stronger than logic or duty that impelled her back to Catalina.

The island of romance? Maybe Scott was right. Maybe she was scared of admitting, even to herself, that she cared deeply for Byron. Why be afraid? Unconsciously, her chin thrust pugnaciously forward as they wended through shrubs and birds of paradise.

There was nothing to fear. Byron was a free agent, and so was she now that she'd quit her nanny job. Making love would be perfectly natural. But a tiny voice in her head chirped, *Whatever you do, don't marry the man.*

As long as she remembered the lessons of her past, she was safe.

The moment they entered the house, they heard Kirsch thundering down the stair. He met them in the kitchen.

He glanced at Lindsey's belly and chortled, "Wish I had a photo."

"Of what?" Byron said.

"Ms. Independent Lindsey Olson trailing behind you like a respectful squaw with her belly bulging out to here."

"For your information," she said, "being pregnant is a great disguise. Nobody looks twice, except for other women who, for some reason, feel compelled to relate the horrors of their own labor-room experiences." She headed toward the half bathroom off the kitchen. "Besides, it was fun to have a gallant young man give up his seat for me on the ferry. Now, if you'll excuse me—" she ducked into the bathroom "—I'm about to give birth to a pair of shorts and a couple of T-shirts."

In a moment, she'd wriggled out of the stuffed girdle and yanked the ugly sundress over her head. It felt marvelous to be free from that restrictive, hot padding.

Though she'd always figured it would be uncomfortable to carry a child, Lindsey felt strangely bereft as she gazed down at her slim figure. A baby? *Don't even think of it,* she warned herself. Children were wonderful and she truly adored them. Why else would she become a nanny? But childbearing was one instinct she refused to indulge, no matter how loudly her biological clock was ticking. A woman alone—like her mother—had a tough time bringing up children, and Lindsey had already proved to herself that she was incapable of finding the right mate.

Byron? The thought of him sent a wave of tenderness crashing in her mind. When she stood at the iron fence, she had yearned so much to feel his arms around her. The simple touch of his hand against hers was bliss. Oh yes, he was a man she desired and admired. A terrific father to Sonny and Amanda. And as a husband? No doubt, he'd be loving and warm when he wasn't busy with some crazy invention or running his multinational company. But she didn't mind his varied occupations. In fact, she found his competence to be exciting. His intelligence held a strong appeal.

The more apt problem concerned her ability to be a wife. Lindsey yanked on her shorts. She wasn't very good at staying married; two divorces proved it. And, therefore, she probably ought to dismiss these fantasies of being a pregnant mommy. Without marriage, she refused to bear children.

She splashed cool water on her face, ran a comb through her hair and emerged from the bathroom. Calm, collected and back in control. "All right," she said. "Tell me about the security system."

"Hungry?" Byron asked, holding up a sandwich.

"Famished." She perched on a stool at the counter and dug into the corned beef. "Where's Kirsch?"

"It's his shift at the upstairs vantage points. We have tiers of defense, and I'm supposed to stay down here and keep an eye on the electronic warning system." He gestured at the large status board that stood beside the table in the room with French windows. "So far, nothing has happened."

"And Helen? Where have she and Reg gone?"

"I packed them off on an extended vacation. Reg wanted to stay and help, but I couldn't allow it. This isn't his fight. And he doesn't have the experience that Kirsch does."

Curiously, he watched her. There was a difference in her attitude. She'd gone into the bathroom as a soft, desirable woman and returned as a female Rambo.

"The kids are fine," she informed between bites. "Having them stay with your friend Scott was the perfect choice for a hiding place."

He nodded. "He's a good man."

"Tell me how you saved his life. He wouldn't say a word about it."

"No big deal."

"Apparently he thinks so. Come on, Byron. I promise not to tell the tabloids."

"Scott used to be a stunt man, specializing in car tricks. About seven years ago, I was on a movie set as a representative of Continental Auto. Scott was supposed to flip a limo, land it upside down and detonate a small explosive charge that would cause the car to spin. Talk about stupid tricks. Do people really enjoy watching that nonsense?''

''They seem to,'' she said.

''Well, I knew the stunt wouldn't work. The limo was manufactured by Continental and I could see from the specs that the roof was not structurally able to withstand that sort of abuse. I told them, but nobody believed me, including Scott. It was incredibly frustrating. Dammit, I told them all about the explosion trajectory and explained the fulcrum balance.''

A smile touched Lindsey's heart. Though she had never been on the set of a Hollywood movie, she imagined that someone like Byron would not fit in. His absorbed attitude would be alien among people who made their living from visual appearances.

''Anyway,'' Byron said, ''I couldn't allow the stunt to be performed. The night before, I rigged up a remote control device on the limo so it could do the stunt without risking someone's life behind the wheel. In the morning, when the stunt men and cameramen arrived, I wouldn't let Scott into the car. He was furious, said he was running on a tight budget and needed the bonus money for doing the stunt. We almost came to blows.

''Then, without their permission, I started the car. It flipped. The charge detonated. The roof caved in after the first spin and the limo exploded. If Scott had been inside, he would have been dead ten times.''

''And you became friends?''

''Not exactly. He exploded higher than the limo. Took a swing at me.''

Lindsey gulped down the last bite of her sandwich. ''You were in a fist fight with Scott Winfield?''

''It wasn't really fair. He was too angry to be effective.''

''He's twice your size.''

''Not really. We're the same height. He's just heavier.''

Aghast, she sized Byron up as a potential combatant. He was strong, but his muscles were long and smooth—swimmer's muscles. In contrast, Scott's upper body was heavily developed. "What happened?"

"I guess you might say that I won."

"No wonder he doesn't want to talk about it."

"But we've gotten together once or twice since then," Byron said. "To talk about cars. We've both apologized, and I'm sure he doesn't hold a grudge."

"No, he doesn't. And I think he was glad that he could pay you back by taking care of Sonny and Amanda." A strange friendship, but an effective one. "I'm sure that they're very safe with him."

"Good. That's a great relief." He placed his hand tentatively on her arm. "But what am I going to do about you?"

"I'm here. So you'll have to make the best of it." Disregarding his touch, she finished her sandwich, wiped her lips with a paper napkin and moved away from the counter, pretending great interest in the status board.

A silence settled between them.

Byron stepped up behind her. "You shouldn't be here, but I'm glad you are."

"That doesn't make sense." She tried for a light tone, reminding herself that she was not wifely material. But when she dared to turn and face him, her resolution faded. Sheer physical need rose to take its place. Oh, my, she wanted him with every fiber of her body. "Byron?"

"Yes, Lindsey?"

Her body yearned toward him. If she allowed him to touch her again, if she accepted his embrace, there would be no stopping. "We really can't . . ."

"Can't make love?" he finished her sentence.

"Right," she said uncomfortably. "I like you, Byron. I like you too much to pretend that I could give you a real relationship. I've failed so badly in the past."

"That was then," he said. "This is now."

He moved a pace closer and her inner warmth became an unbearable heat. When he touched her cheek, she nearly moaned with suppressed passion. "It's not right. You deserve something more substantial than I can offer."

"Let's not worry about the future, either."

"But we can't forget it. We have to be responsible, to think about tomorrow—"

"Hey, Lindsey, we might not have a future. If Rankin attacks, we could be dead before morning." He held her face in both his hands. "All we have is the present. In this moment, you are everything to me."

Perhaps she was making a mistake, but Lindsey was beyond thinking and caring. Her desire to be close to him blanked everything else from her mind. Her eyelids closed. Her lips parted, inviting his kiss.

When his mouth slanted across hers, her desire erupted in a warm sensual flow. She glided her arms around him, matched the length of her body against his firm, lean torso.

"I've wanted to do this," he murmured. "From the first time I saw you."

She sighed and leaned against him. Was it possible that her knees felt weak? That she'd forgotten that they needed to be alert? To stay on watch?

"I'd like to carry you up to bed." He placed a tickling kiss on her earlobe. "To seduce you on billowy sheets where I could see the moonlight on your hair."

"That's a beautiful thought," she murmured.

"But an impossible one. We have to stay down here and keep an eye on the status board."

He gazed at her, drinking in her loveliness. The glow from her eyes made him feel like he'd been parched for years, stranded in an emotional desert. Now, a flood of caring surged through him, nearly overwhelming his sensible thoughts.

Lightly, he kissed her again. Did he dare to make love to her tonight? When the threat of danger was so near? Her mouth was so pliant and warm. Her desire for him was apparent.

But Byron had to pull himself away. The instant his body separated from hers, he regretted the inches between them. "I'm sorry, Lindsey. I shouldn't have started anything. We can't risk not being on our guard tonight."

"I know." Her gaze was direct. Her words were straightforward. "But I'm glad you kissed me."

He laced his fingers through the silky texture of her hair. So beautiful. But not a delicate creature. Her femininity was the strength and beauty of a healthy female animal. When she leaned toward him again, Byron feared that his resolve was lost. He wanted so much to make love to her, to treat her with incredible tenderness.

But the moment vanished when he looked over her shoulder. The red lights on the status board were flashing in warning bursts.

Chapter Fifteen

Lindsey stared at the board, not fully comprehending the significance of the red blinking lights. After Byron's kiss, it seemed somehow appropriate that there should be flashing lights. And bells. And sirens.

Her small reverie ended when Byron stepped away from her with quick efficiency. He ran to the stairs and shouted, "Kirsch, the board is lit. Somebody's on the grounds."

He came back toward her, but didn't glance in her direction. His attention was fastened on the status board.

"What do we do, Byron?" She stood beside him, forcing herself to recognize the urgent peril of their situation. "What's the drill?"

"I'm not sure. All the lights are flashing, but that's impossible. It would take an army to surround the house so completely." When he looked at her, his dark eyes gleamed as hard as anthracite. "Dammit, Lindsey, I wish you weren't here."

"It was my decision."

"And you made a bad choice. If anyone hurts you..." He pivoted and stalked to the foyer where he froze, listening. "Do you hear that? It's a helicopter. That's why all the lights are blinking. Must be some kind of electric impulse."

Kirsch thundered down the stairs. "Helicopter."

"Upstairs," Byron said. "We'll need a vantage point."

On the second floor, Byron opened a door Lindsey hadn't noticed before and they ascended a narrow staircase. The third floor was half attic and half garret-sized rooms. The wood floor was covered with dust. Every corner was draped with cobwebs. The air felt thick, musty and hot.

Byron led them to a small room with a surprisingly large window that looked out from one of the gables. "Don't turn on any lights," he said. "We don't want them to know where we are."

They didn't need artificial light. The glow of a three-quarter moon illuminated a computer with a large keyboard and a huge thirty-six-inch screen. The program covering the screen mirrored the status board downstairs. Byron activated a switch and a blue light flickered in the lower right corner of the screen. "This is a direct link, alerting the local police that we're under siege."

"And the rest of this equipment?"

"Like the board downstairs," Byron explained, "the computer indicates position and allows me to detonate light explosive charges designed to stun. This is second line of defense in case anyone makes it through the initial booby traps. Also, by punching in a combination, I can flood the lower floors of the house with tear gas."

"Do we have gas masks up here?"

"Of course."

They also had heavy-duty artillery—several high-powered Winchester rifles with Leopold scopes, a grenade launcher and several wooden crates filled with ammunition.

When Kirsch held his rifle at the ready, Byron tapped his shoulder and cautioned, "Wait before firing. We don't know who's in that helicopter."

Above them, the whirling rotors hovered. Markings on the side indicated U.S. Army issue.

"Wright?" Kirsch questioned. "Why would he come here?"

"Maybe it's not Wright," Byron said. "It might be a trick. Let's wait until they've landed and we can identify them."

They huddled together in the stifling gloom. A bead of sweat trickled down Lindsey's neck, and she arched toward the night wind that played outside the window. The breeze became a cyclone as the helicopter descended. It touched down, swirling the grass and shrubs and palm fronds. Then the rotor blades stopped and the night was again still and quiet.

The spotlights in the front yard showed Colonel Wright disembarking, and Lindsey exhaled with relief. Wright was a nasty inconvenience, not a threat.

Byron tapped Kirsch's arm. "Let's go downstairs and see what he wants."

"I don't like this, Byron. Why didn't Wright contact us before coming?"

Kirsch's voice was low, a trembling whisper, and Lindsey could see that he was still in the grip of tension. The waiting and the constant vigilance had affected him. His eyebrows were fixed in a fierce scowl. The tendons on his arms stood out.

"Tell me that," Kirsch demanded. "Why didn't Wright let me know what he was doing?"

"What difference does it make?" Byron said impatiently. "Wright is not the enemy."

"You don't know that."

"Yes, we do," Lindsey said. She kept her voice low and calming. "It's okay, Kirsch. Colonel Wright is one of the good guys. He hasn't been much help, but he is on our side."

"Shows how much you know," Kirsch replied. "Wright suspects you, lady. That's one of the reasons I'm here. To keep an eye on you."

"What do you mean?" She was under suspicion? Familiar fears welled up inside her. Her time had come. The authorities were coming for her. "What does Wright suspect me of doing?"

"He knows all about your first husband. His name was Grakow. He was a radical, a leftist."

"That was over fifteen years ago," she said.

"Yeah, but you've been living in Europe. And in the Middle East. Wright thinks that being a nanny is a real good cover. He figures that if anybody is involved with terrorists, it's got to be you."

"Terrorists?" She felt like laughing and screaming at the same time. "That's the dumbest thing I've ever heard. I take care of little children. I play with dolls. How could anybody think I was a terrorist?"

"Wright does."

"You're tired, Kirsch," Byron said, coldly. "You haven't gotten more than two hours of uninterrupted sleep in the last two days. You don't know what you're saying."

"Yes, I do. I like Lindsey. But facts are facts. She has been associated with known criminals. None of this stuff started happening until she showed up."

From downstairs, they heard the doorbell ringing.

"Why did you come back here tonight, Lindsey?"

"I wanted to help."

"Maybe." Kirsch held his hand before his eyes, watching his fingers shiver before he squeezed them into a fist. "Maybe not."

"Why do you think I came back?"

"I don't know. But Wright isn't the only one who thinks you're up to something. Detective Murtaugh suspects that you're part of a setup."

"Why?"

"Because you were ready for the first intruder. That killing in the bathroom was too neat. Not many women go around armed."

"You're right." She stiffened. "But I'm not like most women."

"You can say that again."

"And what am I supposed to be setting up? A plan for Rankin to attack me at the Riverside Airfield?"

"Nobody understands the setup. Not yet. That's the problem. That's why you're walking around free."

"And that's enough." Byron stepped up to confront Kirsch directly. Though Byron was nowhere as large as Kirsch, his self-possession made him far more imposing. "You're wrong about Lindsey. The waiting is getting to you, Kirsch. You don't know what you're saying."

"Facts are facts. Maybe you'd better take a real hard look at what's going on here."

"I have. I trust Lindsey. I'd trust her with my life."

From the lawn below came a shout from Wright. "Anybody here? Hello? Byron, are you here?"

"What's it going to be, Kirsch?" Byron demanded. "You can leave with your friend, Wright. Or you can stay here with us. Me and Lindsey. Are you in or out?"

"I don't know."

"You've got to decide. Now."

"I'm tired."

"I know you are." Byron had been through a lot with Kirsch and he wanted to believe that this was only a momentary lapse of loyalty. He needed Kirsch to stay. "I've never been in combat the way you have. But I'm trusting you with my life, buddy. I can't be watching my backside."

"If I leave, will you quit?"

"No."

"Then, I guess I'm still in. I always was a sucker for lost causes." He took a deep breath and exhaled loudly. His large body seemed to deflate like a balloon. "I'm sorry, Lindsey."

"Accepted."

Byron leaned his head out the window. "We'll be down in a minute." He turned back to Kirsch. "You used me, buddy. I hired you because you were recommended by

Wright and Murtaugh. And you've been spying for them, right?''

He nodded. "Nobody expected this to get so hot." With a heavy tread, he lumbered toward the staircase. "Let's see what Wright wants."

Byron followed, but paused at the top step and turned to Lindsey. "Are you all right?"

"Yeah, sure."

But she wasn't. Her stomach ached with the stab of a cold, steel knife that would never go away. The impaling blade wrenched within her, painfully reminding her that the errors of her past would never leave her alone. No matter how far she ran, escape was impossible. Always, forever and always, a part of her would be a tough street kid who had grown up to marry the wrong men.

"Lindsey? I'm sorry for what Kirsch said."

Chin lifted, eyes dry, she replied, "It doesn't matter. I've been accused of worse."

"It matters to me."

The glow from his eyes burned through her. She wanted to believe him, to think that Byron offered the love she had been searching for all her life. But they were so different. How could she expect him to accept her past? "I'm really okay, Byron. Just forget it. Let it go."

He gripped her upper arms. "I won't let you go. When this is over—"

"Then, it will be over. Done with." Sharply, she broke away from him. "Finished."

Downstairs, Kirsch had unbolted the front door and Wright had taken possession of the foyer. Lindsey watched the colonel suspiciously. The stated reason for his visit was an offer to take Byron and Lindsey into protective custody.

"Why?" Byron asked.

Wright cleared his throat. "After more investigation, we have discovered that your Mr. Rankin is peripherally involved in a sale of arms to terrorists. The connection is tenuous, but it's enough to justify protective custody."

Lindsey frowned. Wright's explanation didn't sound exactly correct. "Excuse me, Colonel. But do you think Rankin and his brother were after the blueprints?"

"Apparently so."

"But Byron doesn't have the blueprints anymore. He didn't have possession of them when Martin Rankin attacked us at the Airfield."

"Rankin's motive might have been revenge for his brother's death. Or it might be a case of honor among terrorists. They pledged to kill Byron, and they mean to make good on their promise. Even if the reason no longer exists."

"It's an interesting theory," Byron said. "But irrelevant. I don't want protective custody. I won't be locked up while you go through procedures."

"I can't let you stay here, Byron. It's suicidal."

"And it doesn't look good for NORAD if civilian contractors are being threatened on their behalf. Sorry, Colonel. Your orders don't apply to me."

"I hate to do this, but you leave no alternative." Colonel Wright turned to Kirsch. "This man is here at my request. If I withdraw him, you and Lindsey will be helpless."

Kirsch laughed. "Believe me, they're far from helpless. And, by the way, Colonel, you don't have jurisdiction over me."

"I happen to have thrown some excellent government-related work in your direction, Kirsch. I'd advise you to stay on my good side."

"There are things more important than contacts, sir." Kirsch positioned himself between Byron and Lindsey. "I'm staying."

Wright stepped back a pace to regard them, standing there like the three Musketeers. Slowly, he shook his head from side to side. "Gentlemen and lady, I wish you luck."

He gave a wry salute and turned on his heel.

"Sir?"

"Yes, Kirsch?"

"I wondered if there was a reason that you didn't telephone before your arrival."

"Oh, didn't I mention? Your phones are dead."

Usually, Lindsey thought, a dead telephone was a simple inconvenience. In these circumstances, it was cause for fear and suspicion. Why were the phones dead? Had the wires been cut? "Colonel Wright, would you mind contacting the telephone company for us?"

"Already have. And I told them it was an emergency. They said a repairman would arrive first thing in the morning."

"Tomorrow? Why so long?"

"It may seem to you, young lady, that the military is the most bureaucratic organization on earth. However, I assure you, there are other organizations that make our procedures seem streamlined."

"Meaning?"

"The phone company will get here when they get here."

Wright exited through the front foyer. The whir of the helicopter's rotors announced his departure.

Byron, Lindsey and Kirsch retired to the sitting room. While Byron and Lindsey collapsed on the sofa, Kirsch reset the alarm system.

"About those telephones," she said. "Do you think the wires were cut?"

"I'd count on it." Byron stretched and yawned. "But there's not a lot we can do about it tonight. We can't go chasing around in the dark, looking for downed wires."

"Agreed." Kirsch sprawled in a chair. "And it's probably better to let a repairman mess around with fixing it. Tomorrow morning will be soon enough."

"And tonight?" Lindsey questioned.

"We wait," Byron said.

His weariness was evident, but there was nothing else to be done. Waiting and wondering. Lindsey hated the inaction.

Briskly, she approached the electronic surveillance board. "You should familiarize me with this board so I can take a watch while you both catch up on your sleep. When the lights flash, does it indicate some kind of movement?"

"That's right." Byron hauled himself off the sofa and stood beside her. "Sensors are placed throughout the grounds. The indicators light when something disturbs the equipment. It's rigged to screen out little movements, like leaves blowing, but the cat has managed to set it off a couple of times."

"Why did all the lights flash when the helicopter was approaching?"

"I'm not sure," Byron said. "Kirsch?"

"Beats me."

Lindsey looked from one to the other. "If you two didn't rig this thing, who did?"

"We initially rigged it when the other security guards were here," Kirsch explained. "A couple of those guys were specialists in electronics."

"So it was here when Jerrod broke in?"

"That's right." Byron nodded, then frowned. "Kirsch? Why didn't the sensors pick up Jerrod's movement?"

Kirsch offered a simple explanation. "The guard who Jerrod bribed—a guy by the name of Tito—must have lain low in his position and sent Jerrod on the route he was supposed to walk. The board was timed to allow the guards to move from one place to another on a fixed schedule."

Though Byron nodded in comprehension, Lindsey continued to stare at the lights. Something didn't make sense. Something didn't fit. "I don't quite understand."

Byron went to the kitchen and placed salt and pepper shakers on the counter. "The pepper is Jerrod. The salt is Tito. And this fork is the sensor." He placed the salt and pepper side by side. "Here are Jerrod and Tito together at the gate. Tito is scheduled to cross the sensor—this fork—at a certain time. Instead of going himself, he sends Jerrod." Byron moved the pepper to the fork. "Jerrod crosses the sensor on schedule, and nothing is indicated at the board."

Lindsey placed a sugar bowl beside the pepper. "Okay, but let's say the sugar is the other person—the person who got inside and attacked Amanda's teddy bear. How did he get through?"

"On one of Tito's earlier rounds?" Byron guessed.

"No." Kirsch moved to join them. "Tito was accompanied on all other rounds."

"Lindsey's got a real good point." Byron tapped the lid of the sugar bowl. "How did the second intruder get past the sensor?"

"Could there have been another bribe?" Lindsey suggested. "To one of the other guards?"

"I doubt it," Kirsch said. "When I let the other guys go, I offered a reward to anyone with information about Jerrod or the other break-in. And this was a reward that came with a guarantee of no prosecution. They could take the money and walk. There were no takers."

"Maybe there was no other intruder." Lindsey whisked the sugar bowl off the counter. "No other person."

"In that case, the person who stabbed the bear had to already be inside the house."

"It had to be Jerrod," Lindsey concluded.

"What about the terrorists?" Kirsch asked.

Lindsey exchanged a glance with Byron. "It's possible that this terrorist threat exists," she said. "But Byron and I met Rankin. And he didn't strike me as a zealot."

"Not at all," Byron agreed. "He's a thug, but he also seemed to regard crime as a business."

"Okay," Kirsch replied. "If Rankin is a businessman, how come he's wasting all this time and effort to get you?"

"Maybe he's been hired to kill me. By the same person who hired his brother." Byron reached across the counter and picked up the pepper shaker. "Jerrod."

"Maybe," Lindsey said.

"Consider the data," Byron said. "Jerrod bugged the house. He sent the phony intelligence agents—which could have been a ploy to make me seek him out. We picked up Rankin as a tail after leaving Jerrod's. Jerrod arranged that weird meeting in the deserted airplane hangar. Jerrod stabbed the bear."

"However," Lindsey said, "Jerrod was bonked on the head at the hangar."

"It could have been staged."

"Why? Why fake an injury when nobody in their right mind would expect us to get out of there alive?"

Byron grinned. "I think the operative words are 'in their right mind.' Jerrod hardly qualifies for that. And he has a motive—*Solar One*."

His eyes took on a faraway cast—the look that showed he was thinking, concentrating, following steps toward a solution—and Lindsey ached when she beheld that familiar expression. There were so many sides to Byron and so little time to explore them.

She swallowed hard and shook her head. "Can't be *Solar One*. He told us that he was further with his solar engine than you were. And he saw the computer plans."

"Then, there must be another reason. But what?"

Kirsch dragged himself upright. "I'll leave you two to figure. I'm going upstairs to keep watch. I'll be in the second-floor bedroom above the front entrance. The fancy one."

"Estelle's room," Byron explained.

"I'll be up to relieve you in five minutes," Lindsey said. "You need some sleep, Kirsch."

"You're right." He dragged toward the foyer, then turned. "If you two are going to play detective, you got to keep a couple of things in mind. First, the terrorist's mark on the assassin's gun. Also, Jerrod was checked out by both Wright and Murtaugh. They found no connection whatsoever between your uncle and either of the Rankins."

"Don't you want to help us figure this out?" Lindsey asked. "After all, Kirsch, you're the real detective among us."

"Yeah? Well, we real-life detectives just gather information. We aren't much on mind games." He stumbled toward the stairs. "Five minutes, Lindsey."

She checked her wristwatch. Five minutes alone with Byron. Who would he be? Lord of the manor or an inventor? Architect or the head of a giant corporation? Would he be lover or stranger?

"There is a reason for Jerrod to want me dead," he said. "The most blatant motive in the world—greed. With me out of the way, my family has a better shot at getting their sticky fingers on my father's inheritance money."

"That's a real ugly thought."

"But disgustingly logical. So why don't I believe it?"

"Maybe because it's too circumstantial. We're speculating, and we don't have the facts about Jerrod's bank accounts and investments." She stretched the muscles in her back. "I'm afraid that until we have a confession from Rankin or one of his men, we won't know anything for certain."

"We'll catch him," Byron said.

"Oh? And how are you so sure?"

"Hey, no problem. One of Rankin's men will trip on a booby trap. He'll be stunned. We'll pick him up, ask politely and he'll tell all." Byron snapped his fingers. "Piece of cake."

Lindsey knew he was lying. The danger, if and when Rankin and his men attacked, would be intense. She or Byron might not come away from the confrontation alive. Yet, she wasn't afraid. Rather, she felt poignant, filled with bittersweet awareness that she might not have a future to consider. "Byron? Where will you be while I'm upstairs on guard duty?"

"Down here with the board." He sat close beside her on the sofa and wrapped his arm around her shoulders. "We have three minutes before you go upstairs to relieve Kirsch. Let's not waste them."

She placed a finger crosswise on his lips. "Will you come upstairs after Kirsch has rested?"

"I'm not sure if that's wise. I have to sleep, too. And if you're nearby..."

"I won't keep you awake. Please, Byron. I want you to be with me. Even if you are asleep."

When their lips met, Lindsey didn't want the moment to end. No matter how inappropriate their attraction, she came alive in his arms. If only they had more time.

"Only thirty seconds left," he whispered.

She kissed him lightly and rose to her feet. "Later?"

"Count on it."

After she relieved Kirsch, Lindsey sat quietly at the upstairs window and stared into the star-spangled night. Watching and waiting. The possibility of an attack by Rankin threatened her life. The possibility of caring for Byron undermined her image of herself. She hadn't expected to want a lasting relationship with a man. After two divorces, she'd assumed it wasn't in her cards.

Three hours later, Byron came to her post. His eyes were bleary. Despite his bravado, he was so exhausted that he could hardly stand. "I left Kirsch downstairs watching the board, and now it's my turn to sleep."

Very neatly, she tucked him into Estelle's bed. He was asleep before she pulled the sheets up to his chin. Lindsey watched the regular rise and fall of his chest as he breathed deeply. While he slumbered, she whispered, "I love you, Byron."

She returned to her watch by the window. Unless she stayed alert, they might not even live to see tomorrow. And she desperately wanted a future.

At three in the morning, Byron awoke and traded places with her. Though she expected to be restless, the long night had sapped her energy. Almost immediately, she drifted off to sleep.

When morning came, she was awakened by Kirsch. "My turn," he announced, looking like a different man. "Rise and shine."

"Sadist." Yawning, she grumped out the bedroom door. Halfway down the sweeping staircase, the tantalizing sizzle of frying bacon put a new spring into her step. And when she found Byron in an apron, minding the griddle in the kitchen, a genuine smile touched her lips.

"Cute outfit," she said. And it was. Impossible as it seemed, he looked masculine in an apron. "But aren't you supposed to be keeping a watch?"

"I can see the board from here, and the buzzer alarm would get my attention in any case." He flipped a dish-towel over his arm. "Would madame care for breakfast? The choices are bacon and scrambled eggs. Or scrambled eggs and bacon."

"Why such diversity in your menu?"

"Because that's all I can cook."

"Then bacon and scrambled eggs will be lovely."

Lindsey yielded to luxurious stretching. Amazingly, everything looked better in the morning. She hardly believed they were in danger until a red light flashed on the board.

"Front gate," Byron said. He hurried through the foyer and up the stairs to the window where Kirsch sat watching.

"It's the telephone repairman."

Using high-powered binoculars, Byron studied the familiar white van with blue logo. There were no cars on the island, except for residents and local businesses, so Byron was certain that the van was authentic. He stared through the windshield but couldn't see the driver's face. The man was wearing a cap, also with the phone-company logo.

"Here's a piece of strategy we didn't work out," Kirsch said. "Since we clipped the remote control that opens the gate, one of us is going to have to go out there and manually open the damn thing."

"I'll go," Byron said.

"Forget it." After catching up on his sleep, Kirsch was his old gruff self. "Nobody wants to kill me. Remember?"

Lindsey joined them. "What is it?"

"Repairman," Kirsch said. "I'll go to the gate."

"Okay. I'll stay here with the rifle. And you, Byron, should go back downstairs before your bacon burns."

While Byron ran downstairs with Kirsch following close behind, Lindsey sighted down the barrel of her rifle. There was no movement on the lawn, no sound other than the blaring of the telephone repairman's horn.

A beautiful morning. She envied Kirsch as he drove toward the front gate in his golf cart. The palms wafted gently in the island breezes. She could hear the surf and cries of sea birds.

When Kirsch reached the gate, she took her binoculars and sighted in on the repairman. Though he didn't wear a uniform, his face was shaded by the visor of a cap.

She adjusted the focus on the binoculars. Kirsch was at the gate, checking the man's credentials. He fed in the code. The gate opened.

For just an instant, the repairman looked up and Lindsey had a clear view of his features. It was Rankin.

Chapter Sixteen

Lindsey shouldered the high-powered Winchester rifle, flipped off the safety catch. She hated the kick from rifles and would have been more comfortable with a pistol, but small firearms didn't have the range. She aimed, but Kirsch stood directly in her line of fire.

"Move," she whispered. "Come on, Kirsch, step aside."

She could fire a warning shot, but that would alert Rankin and maybe put Kirsch in greater danger.

"Byron!" she yelled. "Byron, I need you."

Rankin made his move. Pistol drawn, he got the drop on Kirsch. Moving quick as a snake, he pinned Kirsch's arm behind his back and used the larger man's body as a shield. Helplessly, Lindsey watched the macabre pantomime.

Byron burst into Estelle's bedroom. "What's going on? The board downstairs is lighting up."

"The phone repairman is Rankin. He's got Kirsch."

"Dammit!" Byron peered through the window in time to see Rankin maneuver Kirsch toward the van. "He must have stolen a van from the phone company. But how did he know we were expecting a repairman?"

"Byron, what should I do?"

"Shoot out the tires. We're going to catch this guy."

She sighted through the cross hairs of the scope. The sophisticated rifle felt unfamiliar in her grasp. Yesterday, she should have taken some time to practice, but it was too late for that now.

She fired. The gun pulled slightly to the right and up. Her bullet shattered the right front headlight. "Missed."

On the grounds to the south, there was an explosion. And a yell. Apparently one of the booby traps had been set off. Which meant Rankin wasn't alone.

Lindsey took another shot. It went wide. "What's wrong with these guns?"

"They're state of the art."

"Whose state?"

Despite her misfires, the gunfire had spooked Rankin. He shoved Kirsch away from him and dove for the driver's side of the van. Kirsch rolled to the ground, sprang to his feet and began running in a bent-over posture.

Though it seemed like hours had passed, Lindsey knew it was only a few seconds. Less than a minute. Her reflexes felt sluggish, as she tried to find a clear shot at Rankin. He'd thrown open the door to the van, using it for cover. Through the rifle sights, she watched, riveted.

Rankin jumped away from the door. She lost him in her sights. Her vision blurred. Lowering the gun, she blinked. Seconds ticked past. Before she could refocus with the scope, she saw Rankin with her naked eye. He aimed his handgun at the running figure of Kirsch.

"No," she whispered. But she heard the sharp report of Rankin's pistol. Kirsch fell to the ground.

With clear eyes, Lindsey took aim. Rankin was back in the van, crouched over the steering wheel as he drove through the gates. A gutsy move. He was coming right at her, daring her. She fired. The windshield of the van broke apart, but Rankin didn't slow down.

Her mind flashed a picture. Red blood on white tile walls. No! She couldn't think of that. Not now! She blasted at the front tires. Direct hits. The van crunched to a halt.

"Up to the third floor," Byron said tersely. "Let's go."

She followed him into the upper garret where the grenades and other high-powered weaponry were located. Though their plan was to capture Rankin or one of his men, they were well prepared for warfare. It didn't matter that the phone lines were dysfunctional. Byron needed only to flick a switch to alert the local police, via closed circuit radio, and another switch would flood the lower floor with tear gas. With the most expensive equipment that money could buy, he had prepared for this moment.

Byron flung open the door of the garret room.

It was empty.

Lindsey circled the room. "This can't be. None of the alarms went off last night. I was on watch. Nobody could have gotten in here."

"Too late to worry about it. Let's go."

"Where? This window is as good a vantage point as any."

"Our ammunition is gone, Lindsey. We have two rifles and that's it. And all the indicators on the status board were flashing. You heard the explosions. If the sensors are right, Rankin's men are coming at us from every direction except the sea."

"I say we stay here and make a stand."

"We're surrounded, Lindsey. We've got to find cover."

She wasn't ready to give up. Bracing her arms on the window sill, she aimed at the van. Useless. Nothing was moving out there. Rankin must be hidden behind the van. Or walking up to the front door.

She scanned the grounds in front of her, spotting movement near the gates. "It's Kirsch. He's okay."

"Good. Maybe he'll go for help."

Byron grabbed her hand. This time, she didn't resist. They raced down the stairs two at a time. Through the house. No one was inside, but she heard shouts. It was only a matter of time. Minutes. Seconds. Byron led her to the workshop.

When he slammed the door, she shook her head. "We're not safe here. If they're working for Jerrod, he's told them how to defeat the lock, the same way he did when he broke in previously."

"You're right. Let me think, Lindsey."

Fighting for control, she stalked away from him. Her heart beat in staccato. She wrapped her arms around herself as if to physically keep herself from flying into a million pieces.

This wasn't fair. She'd fought all her life, and now she finally had her own money from the JerBee stock, her chance at happiness with Byron. For the first time in her life, she looked forward to the future.

Clinging to self-control, Lindsey knew she wouldn't give up. She'd find a way out of this. Somehow. Then she spied Amanda's life-size teddy bear, seated on a workbench and smiling placidly.

A low chuckle rippled from her, relieving her tension. They were going to make it. They had to. She exhaled. "We'll figure something out, Byron."

"You're sure about that?"

She gestured toward the bear. "He seems to think so. Or else why would he be smiling?" She straightened. Her voice was clear. "Have you got a plan?"

"Let's review our situation." His tone was heavily ironic. "Despite all my precautions and a major outlay of money, we only have a few rounds of bullets. We're heavily outnumbered. And we're trapped in this room."

"Kirsch might make it to a telephone."

"Even if he does, we can't count on seeing reinforcements for another half hour to forty minutes. And I don't believe we'll have that much time."

"Then there's only one chance." She gripped his shoulders. Her marksmanship, her karate, her escape-driving training didn't mean anything in this situation. "It's up to you, Byron. You've got to get creative. Invent something."

"Just like that?" On a subliminal level, he knew she was right. He'd spent most of his life puttering, designing and inventing. But now, when his ingenuity could save his life, Byron's mind was blank.

"Think," she said. "There's a lot of stuff in here. *Solar One*. That old Volkswagen. Unloaded guns. Tools. Amanda's bear—"

"And a partridge in a pear tree. I'm sorry, Lindsey. I can't think of anything."

"You've got to."

His brain was as useful as the stuffing in the head of Amanda's teddy bear. And what about Amanda? And Sonny? Byron's jaw clenched as he considered the possibility of never seeing them again. Slowly, the wheels in his brain began to turn. He could engineer an escape. Like in the movies. He remembered Scott and the limousine stunt that should have killed him.

"I think I've got it."

He grabbed tools from the workbench and hustled Lindsey over to the Volkswagen that sat beside *Solar One*. "Get into the car," he said. "Stay down until I give the word. Then you drive like hell toward the front gate."

"But why? I don't get it."

"Drive fast and reckless. I know you can do it."

When he dashed to the workbench and picked up Amanda's teddy bear, Lindsey was certain that he'd lost his mind. "What are you doing, Byron? We need a workable plan."

"Just be ready to drive, okay?"

"Not until you tell me what you're doing."

Further argument was cut short by a terrible sound—a heavy thud against the steel door.

"Oh, no," she whispered. "They're here. They're already here."

"We can make it, Lindsey. All you have to do is drive."

"Don't be absurd. If somebody is banging at that door, it means they know where we are. Don't you suppose that they have men posted at the outer door? The minute you open it we're going to be mowed down by twenty thousand bullets.''

"But they can't kill us if we're already dead.''

She stared at him. ''You want to run that by me again?''

A steady thumping shook the steel door.

"Okay, Lindsey.'' He opened the passenger door of the Volkswagen and placed their rifles and a couple of the blank-firing pistols inside. ''I'm going to open the outer doors. *Solar One*, the helicopter, is going through. I'll operate it by remote control.''

"Remote control?''

"Yes. Like I used with the stunt limo that almost killed Scott. You don't really think I was risking my life by flying this helicopter, do you? It's on remote.''

The steel door was beginning to give. The crashing thuds echoed through the room.

"Whoever is posted outside will shoot at the helicopter,'' he said. ''Then, I'll explode it. They'll think we're dead. In the confusion, you use your fancy escape-driving techniques to go past them.''

She massaged her temples with her fingertips. His plan was utterly crazy, the last-ditch effort of a real eccentric. But it was better than standing here and waiting to die. ''Let's do it.''

He sat the stuffed bear behind the controls of the helicopter and jumped into the car beside her. With the flick of a switch, he set the outside door in motion. Before it had completely risen, he started the helicopter's rotors.

The roar within the room was deafening. Lindsey clapped her hands over her ears. Loose papers whirled through the air with cyclone force.

The instant the door opened, *Solar One* burst through.

Lindsey heard the firing of several guns. One sounded like an automatic weapon—a machine gun. She peeked over the dashboard and saw three men, including Rankin. As Byron predicted, their attention was focused upward as they aimed and fired repeatedly. The helicopter soared beyond her vision.

"Get down," Byron ordered. He tossed another switch and counted down, "Four...three...two—"

A huge explosion rocked the Volkswagen. Though she'd hidden beneath the dashboard, Lindsey could see reflections of orange flames. Fire! She heard the sound of confusion from outside.

With adrenaline running high, she was unaware of pain as she picked chunks of safety glass from her hair. Several small cuts on her arms were bleeding.

"Now," Byron ordered. "Hit it."

She started the engine. Racing with death. In a Volkswagen? She had to be at least as crazy as he was. Slamming the transmission into first gear, Lindsey jammed down the accelerator and the car burst from the garage.

One of the men stood directly in her path. Fighting her impulse to swerve, Lindsey plowed straight toward him. "Move it," she muttered under her breath. "Come on, buddy, move it."

Byron fired a warning shot through the space where the windshield had been.

In the nick of time, the man jumped aside.

Bullets pinged against the side of the Volkswagen bug and Lindsey hunched her shoulders.

Byron returned their fire, using one of the pistols loaded with blanks. But his plan was working. Slowly, the distance between them and the gunmen lengthened.

Only a few more yards. They'd be at the gate in a few yards. And they'd left Rankin behind.

"It worked!" she shouted. "You're a crazy eccentric, Byron. But it worked!"

"Can you go faster?"

"No, it's floored."

Then she saw something that bristled the hairs on her bleeding arms like a shock of electricity. It was Helen McHenry. Why was she here? Byron had told Helen and Reg to stay away. Helen ran toward the house, parallel to the Volkswagen. Her arms waved like a windmill.

"Helen, no! Go back!" Operating on sheer instinct, Lindsey swung the car in a half circle and swerved toward Helen. But the ground was too rugged. Shrubs and rocks banged against the undercarriage. Just in time, she jumped the little car back onto the asphalt driveway. "We've got to do something, Byron. They're going to kill Helen."

"I'm out of ammunition."

Evasive action, Lindsey thought. She slowed the Volkswagen to a stop and leaped out. "We're over here, Rankin. Come and get us."

Helen had reversed her course and was heading toward her cottage. As Lindsey had hoped, all the gunmen turned their attention toward Lindsey and Byron.

Lindsey jumped back into the car and turned the key in the ignition. It wouldn't start. Rankin and his men were rapidly closing the space between them. She cranked it again. Nothing. She swallowed hard and turned the key. The bug roared to life, and Lindsey drove hard and reckless. But not too fast.

"Can you get more speed?"

"This is it."

"One of the bullets must have hit the engine. Keep going." In spite of the hysteria around them, Byron was coolly sardonic. Using a pistol loaded with blanks, he returned the fire of Rankin and his men. "They don't want Helen. They're after us."

At the gate, Lindsey craned her neck, searching for Kirsch. There was no sign of him. Maybe he'd made it to the McHenrys' cottage. Maybe he'd managed to escape. She had to believe that he was all right.

"Hold it," Byron said as they drove through the gates.

Again, she braked, but this time she kept the engine running.

From the control box inside the grounds, Byron touched the switch that automatically closed the gates. Before they shut, he ran through. They clanged shut and he smashed the outer controls with a rock, effectively disabling the equipment. Then he rejoined Lindsey in the car.

"It ought to take a few minutes for them to break through that damn gate."

"Do they have cars?"

"Probably nothing but that dead van. The vehicle limitations on Catalina are working in our favor. I think we're going to make it."

"Or die trying," Lindsey said grimly.

"Straight down this road," Byron said. "We're four miles from another house."

Glancing in the rearview mirror, which had miraculously survived the gunfire, Lindsey saw Rankin at the gate. He'd been injured. The front of his blue shirt was bloodied, but he was not out of the action. Lindsey saw him aim his rifle. Her foot jammed to the floor, but the Volkswagen simply wouldn't go any faster.

Rankin fired. The steering wheel jerked in her hand. "He got one of the rear tires."

"Keep going," Byron said.

Another shot. The other rear tire was gone. Lindsey squealed round a curve in the road and they were shielded from the house by an outcropping of mossy rocks and twisted shrub cypress trees.

"What are we going to do for brakes?" she asked. "With the back tires gone, disc brakes aren't going to catch."

"We hardly need worry. Whizzing along at ten miles per hour, I don't think we'll have any trouble stopping."

Forward motion was certainly the greater problem. They went only a couple of hundred yards farther when they encountered a rocky incline leading up to a ridge. Riding on the rims with both rear tires gone, the little car slowed from ten to five miles per hour. Before they reached the crest, it coughed and died.

Byron flung open his door. "Come on, Lindsey. Let's get the car out of sight."

Even with the rear tires gone, they managed to shove the little car off the road and into a thicket. It wasn't completely hidden but wasn't readily obvious from the road.

Byron took her hand and hustled her to the other side of the road. From behind the hill, she heard an explosion.

"The gate," Byron said. "They'll be here in a minute."

She followed him down a hill into thick shrubs and weeds. After a moment's stumbling, he found a path that roughly followed the same direction as the road. Lindsey was completely disoriented. If given a city street with back alleys and fire escapes, she could have found a million ways to escape. But lost in nature? Weren't you supposed to swing on vines or something? She stopped to catch her breath and stooped down in the high grass. "Are there snakes out here?"

Byron took two deep breaths. His regular swimming gave him excellent lung capacity and he was far less winded than she was. "Trust me, Lindsey. Being bitten by a poisonous snake is the least of your worries."

"But I really hate snakes. Tell me the truth, Byron. Any snakes?"

"Afraid so. Rattlers. And wild boar. And a buffalo herd."

"Great," she muttered. "I'm a city kid, Byron. Not Sheena of the Jungle."

"This is hardly a jungle. In fact, I wish there were thicker cover."

He huddled down beside her as a majestic black Cadillac roared past on the two-lane road. Peeking through the branches, Lindsey saw through the open window of the car. The man in the back seat was armed. "How many do you think there are?"

"There were three on the front lawn, including Rankin. There had to be at least two more battering at the workshop door."

"Five of them? That's not too bad."

"There might be twenty-five. We have no way of knowing. Let's keep moving."

She didn't move. "Wait a minute, Byron. We can't follow the road. Those guys are ahead of us and could set up an ambush outside your neighbor's place."

"You're right. We'll double back toward the house." He remembered, "The status board showed that they weren't attacking from the sea. We'll head for the cove on the south side of the house. The McHenrys' boat is there."

"Why can't we just hide out here? All we have to do is stay alive until help arrives. Either Kirsch or Helen will get through to the authorities."

"I sure hope so. But we can't count on it."

"Why not?"

"If the phones in the main house are out, the McHenrys' phones are dead, too. And Rankin's men saw Helen. They certainly wouldn't allow her to summon help." Lindsey didn't want to consider any other possibility. What was Helen doing at the house anyway? Lindsey's mind turned to a more hopeful track. "What about Kirsch? He'll find a way to help us."

"Facts are facts," Byron said, echoing Kirsch's statement of the night before. "He might not be on our side."

"What? Rankin shot him."

"Lindsey, you and I both know that Kirsch is the only person who could have taken our equipment out of the attic room. Maybe he's not working for Rankin, but he's not working for us, either."

Kirsch? Last night, he'd admitted that he was spying for Wright and Murtaugh. Was there someone else? Yet another danger? Lindsey couldn't believe that Kirsch would harm them. But nothing made sense anymore. It seemed that no one could be trusted. Except for Byron. She fell into place behind him.

Byron slipped through the pines, aiming toward the rocky palisades and pocket-sized beaches that defined the western side of the island. If they could make it back to the house and down to the sheltered dock area... If the McHenrys' fishing boat was still moored there... If...

No point in speculating. They would make it. The boat would be their means of escape. Or their final resting place.

Chapter Seventeen

Though he knew Lindsey was tired, Byron pushed her to keep moving through the rugged outback of Catalina. They couldn't slow down. As soon as Rankin's men discovered the abandoned Volkswagen, they would search the surrounding area. And, on an island, there were precious few places to hide.

Byron concentrated on finding the most direct route through scrubby underbrush and patches of cactus. His thinking scaled down to finding the next path forward, toward the sea. On the run. Dammit, on the run.

Rankin had bested him. A small-time thug had beaten Byron's high-tech weaponry, sophisticated sensing devices, guards and strategies. His determination had not kept them safe. His wealth had not protected them.

It was ironic that despite all his expensive firepower, they'd escaped by his wits in a stripped-down Volkswagen. At Lindsey's urging. He thanked the fates that brought her back to him. Without her, he would have lacked the will and the inspiration to plan their flight. Alone, Byron was sure he would have died in the workshop, surrounded by expensive toys.

Though they were running for their lives, he had not given up hope, and he felt a strange satisfaction. For the first time in his life, he was unencumbered, free from the burden of possessions and the weight of responsibility. Free.

Survival was a primitive goal. With nothing else to help him, Byron had to depend upon himself. And upon Lindsey, the woman he hoped to make his wife. His aims crystalized with great purity. Nothing mattered but the next step forward.

In the future—if there were a future for him—Byron would not set aside a single month for time with his children. Only thirty days per year? It wasn't enough. The pleasure he felt in their company could not be measured merely in quality time. He would arrange for them to always be near him. With Lindsey as his wife, they would be a family again.

But he had to take the next immediate step. To survive.

They were close to the sea. He could hear the surf and the skree of circling terns. Stepping from a copse of pungent eucalyptus trees, he almost fell from a rocky cliff that plunged steeply to the Pacific. "We're here."

"Good." She panted. "No more jungles, okay? I say we climb down and swim for it. The island isn't that big. We could make it to a phone."

"Can't do it," he said. "The currents are treacherous along here. And the undertow is deadly."

Lindsey gave a small groan and her knees gave out. She sat cross-legged on the bluff. "Are you sure? The water looks tranquil."

"Drowning is a quiet death."

He knelt beside her. She was winded. A criss-cross of scratches marked her long legs. Her arms were a patchwork of dried blood from when the windshield broke inward upon them. When he touched her shin, she winced. And he swore softly.

"I'm okay," she said. "Doesn't even hurt."

"It hurts me."

"Look on the bright side. We haven't met any snakes."

"Except for Rankin."

Keeping to the upper edge of the palisade, he led her to the bluff opposite the house, not too far from where Lindsey had stood the previous day.

For a moment, Byron squatted down in the grasses and considered the terrain. Should they follow the safer course along the upper bluff and risk being that near to the house? Or should they climb down the rocks to the sea? The bluff was an easy hike, but Rankin and his men might still be in the house. The jagged cliff meant a dangerous climb.

Lindsey whispered, "Which way do we go?"

He pointed the way along the rim of the palisade and up to the wrought-iron fence surrounding the grounds.

She shook her head. "We'd have to go too close to the house."

"Then we climb down."

Below them, the Pacific crashed against rocks. Lindsey's eyes blurred when she saw the swirls and eddies so far below. "Down?" she peeped. "Have I mentioned that I'm not terribly fond of heights?"

"The climb down is easy, practically a path. The problem comes when we get to the bottom."

"Why?"

"We have to cross the little beach below, then climb around the point that juts out." The waves thrashed the rocky promontory, sending up sprays of water eight feet high. "On the other side, is the cove. And the boat."

"Down," she said with more conviction than she felt. "Nobody is going to be stupid enough to follow us there. Not even Rankin."

Byron set out, and she gritted her teeth and followed. Apparently he had explored these rocks before because he moved swiftly from one ledge to another. Almost a path, sheltered from the view of the house by another outcropping ridge, it wasn't too bad, she thought, as long as she didn't look down.

"Stop," he whispered.

Ahead of them, the path ended abruptly in a sheer, vertical rock face. Another ledge beckoned, two feet away, but between the jagged rocks was nothing but thin air. Lindsey flattened her body against the cliff. A white-winged gull soared near her, then plummeted to the waves far below to skim the water's surface. "I can't fly, Byron."

"You'll jump. You have long legs, Lindsey. It'll be easy."

Before she could tell him exactly what she thought of his crumbling path and the insanity of leaping through space, there was a sound from the house.

They knelt quietly behind jagged porous stone. Their view of the rear terrace was excellent. And they saw that it was not deserted. Two men with bandages staggered through the doors and sprawled on lawn chairs. Then, Rankin himself appeared.

Lindsey tensed when she saw him. But her desire for vengeance was overcome with dismay. "He's so close," she whispered. "But too far away. I guess we'll never know for sure who hired his brother."

"Or if he's merely one tentacle of a world-wide terrorist organization."

"I don't believe that. A tentacle," she scoffed. "Rankin is a hired gun. A small-time crime boss. Believe me, Byron, I know the type. I was married to one."

"Your first husband?"

"Yes. The only difference between Chas Grakow and Rankin is that Rankin is more honest. Chas had to make up elaborate justifications about how he was fighting against the capitalist machine and helping the average guy on the street. What a joke! His real motivation was power."

"That fits a terrorist mentality," Byron said.

"Maybe it does." She watched Rankin as he stood on the edge of Byron's property, puffing out his chest. "That guy is not a terrorist. Trust me on this one, Byron. Rankin is in this for the money."

"Is that like your first husband, too?"

"Not really. Chas was more excited about having followers. Teenagers, mostly, who would do anything Chas said because they needed to believe in ideals. Or to escape from disasters."

"What, Lindsey? What did you want to escape?"

"Poverty, deprivation, abuse." In a monotone, she tossed off those devastating words. There was a whole lot more, but this wasn't the time for a deep philosophical discussion.

"And you ran from it?"

"You bet I did. I had to. Running was the only way I could survive."

"Whatever happened to Grakow?"

"I heard he was dead. I didn't cry."

That sounded cold. But it was true. She wouldn't lie to Byron. If she seemed like a cruel wife or a coward who always ran from her problems, so be it. She couldn't deceive him into believing that she was something she wasn't. "It wasn't easy being me, but I didn't have it any rougher than thousands of other teenagers. I coped with my life by running. I ran away from my mother, from two husbands and now from Rankin."

"But you came back to Catalina," he said.

"I did." She gazed into the blue sky. Ahead lay a precipice and certain danger. Behind were pursuers. Across the cliffs stood Rankin, a man who wanted to kill her. Strangely, she wasn't sorry she'd returned to Catalina.

"I admire you, Lindsey."

"Me?" She shook her head. "But you're the guy who wants to stand and fight. Who never runs."

"I don't think you were running away, but going toward something, looking for something special and wonderful. There hasn't been much love in your live, Lindsey. But that's going to change." He took her hand and raised it to his lips. "I know because I'm the man who's going to change it."

Was he saying that he loved her? "Well, Byron, you've picked one heck of a fine time to tell me that you're going to change my life. We're probably going to be killed within the hour."

"That's why I have to tell you now. We don't exactly have time for a fancy courtship."

Did she love him, too? The answer sprang like music from her heart. Yes, yes, she loved Byron. But now? Now they needed to think of survival. "When this is over, Byron. When you know you're going to live for more than twenty minutes, tell me then."

They both turned toward the terrace of the house when Rankin barked an order at the other two men. Lindsey noticed that he'd changed from his blood-spattered shirt. Though there was a stiffness in his movements, he didn't seem badly injured. Certainly, he was capable of talking—if only they were close enough to hear a confession.

The other two men went inside and Rankin stared at the surrounding area, seeming to look right at them, then pivoted and followed his men into the house.

"He's not a terrorist tentacle," Lindsey said firmly. "Besides, we already figured out that Jerrod was behind the attack and therefore he must have hired Rankin."

"It wasn't Jerrod," Byron said. "You pointed it out. If Jerrod had been running the show, Rankin would have known how to open the lock on the workshop door. And that didn't happen. Those guys were battering at the door, not unlocking it."

"But if not Jerrod, who?"

"We'll find out. But first, let's get out of here."

He stood. With his long legs, he easily spanned the distance between the two ledges and paused on the opposite side. Nonchalantly, he turned and held out a hand to help her. "Come on, Lindsey. It's not far. You can make it."

She shuffled from one foot to the other. Talk about a leap of faith! The break in the path that hugged the rocky cliff looked a million miles wide to her. But Byron's hand was so near. Her toe probed forward into space. The opposite ledge was one long step away. That was all it was. A single stride.

Then she looked down and the world turned into a dizzy spin, a funnel that would suck her down and down. "I can't do it."

"You can. Trust me."

Eyes closed, she stuck out her foot. Her fingernails dug into the ridges on the cliffwall. She reached out, felt Byron dragging her from the void. She stepped across.

He embraced her, warming her with his body. "I knew you could do it, Lindsey."

"Never again. I am never doing this again."

"I certainly hope not."

The rest of the climb down was easy, a winding path that led down to a small gray beach. "Be careful," he warned. "The rocks near the bottom are real slick."

When they reached the level where sea spray misted, the footing was wetly precarious. Lindsey worked hard at maintaining her balance. One misstep could mean a sprained ankle. And if she couldn't run, she would not be able to escape.

At the beach, they ran across the small stretch of pewter sand and dodged into the shelter of rocks at the foot of the palisade that ran directly below the Cyril Villa. This time, height was no problem. They stayed near the bottom where the ocean churned and spit its froth. A towering wave slapped Lindsey's thighs, taking her breath away in a cold gasp. The salt water in her scratches should have hurt, but Lindsey was too numb to notice pain as her fingers clung to the mollusk-bedecked rocks.

Slowly, cautiously, picking each step, they progressed toward the farthest jut into the ocean. Her fingers slipped. Her feet in sneakers skidded. But she kept from crying out and regained her balance.

Byron rounded the far point first.

"I can see the boat," he said. He gripped her wrist and helped her around the outcropping to a small ledge.

In the small cove, she saw the trim fishing craft that belonged to Helen and Reg McHenry. "Let's swim, Byron. I can't hold on."

"Only a little farther," he urged. "You can do it."

Slowly, with painstaking caution, they crept along the slick gray rocks. Incessant waves splashed higher. Lindsey was drenched, shivering uncontrollably despite the sunshine. Her jaw clenched to keep her teeth from chattering. Her fingers seemed to have lost sensation yet she managed to hang on. Only a little farther. A matter of yards.

From the house above them, another booby trap exploded. And Lindsey glanced upward. For an instant, her concentration was interrupted. And so was Byron's.

Watching helplessly, she saw his feet slide from beneath her. He plunged into the surf.

She counted to three. He did not resurface.

"Dammit." She jumped in after him.

Freezing water closed over her head. Her feet touched bottom and she pushed upward. When she broke the surface, she was shocked to find that she'd already been swept ten feet from the shore toward the open sea. The rhythm of the rushing waves enveloped her in a rolling liquid embrace. Up went the tide, down went the tide. She couldn't swim against it. Fighting with all her strength, she could barely stay in one place.

Byron was in the water beside her. "Relax," he ordered. "We're going to be all right."

Yet when his strong arm encircled her waist, an unreasoning panic tensed her body. She was freezing cold. Her arms flailed. She submerged, took in a mouthful of salty water, gagged.

He kept hold of her hand. "Lindsey. Calm down."

"Can't," she sputtered. "Get away from me."

"You've got to relax or you'll drown us both."

The undertow overwhelmed her. Helpless against the flow and eddy of the whirling sea, she tried to listen to him. She knew he was right. Her fear could kill her. Another high wave lifted her, then pulled her beneath its white crest. She couldn't breathe. Couldn't see. Her eyes stung with salt. The lashing surf roared in her ears.

When she got her bearings, she saw that they were being whisked toward the farthest point of land. Byron held her. He tried to swim. But the sea was too strong, even for him.

"I can't do it," he said.

"You have to." She fastened herself to his waist, freeing his hands, and kicked with all her strength. Her face went under. Cold fear consumed her mind, but her survival instinct was stronger. She forced herself to kick hard with her long, powerful legs.

When she surfaced, she saw a long finger of rock. It was on the opposite side of the cove from where she'd fallen into the water, and Lindsey knew it was their last hope of safety. Beyond the rock was an endless expanse of ocean, miles and miles.

Together, she and Byron fought the water. The last waves were kind, propelling them toward land. When Byron anchored himself to a rock and pulled her from the water, Lindsey gulped in oxygen. She rolled onto her back. She stared at the most beautiful sun that had ever shone. "Am I still alive?"

"Very much so." Catching his breath, he spared a swift glance at her heaving breasts, sharply outlined by the wet fabric of her shirt. "We've got to keep going. We're almost there."

Using her dwindling reserve of energy, she forced herself to her feet. After the ocean's buffeting, her legs wobbled. Her body felt like limp seaweed. "Let's go."

At the pier beside the fishing boat, Byron crept stealthily, suspecting a trap. Yet, there seemed to be no one around. Was it possible that they had outwitted Rankin? He climbed on board, pulled Lindsey after him. They crossed the polished desk, went to the forward wheel inside its cabin. The keys were in the ignition. Byron reached, then stopped himself.

Despite her exhaustion, Lindsey understood his hesitation. "Too easy?"

"Right. Plus the fact that Reg would never leave keys in the ignition."

When the lower hatch door was flung open, Byron realized that he and Lindsey had no guns, no weapons. He braced himself for a fist fight. But it was Reg McHenry who appeared. "For goodness sake," Reg hissed. "Don't start the engine."

"What's wrong?" Byron asked.

"I've just been down below and the engine is hooked up to some kind of explosive. No good trying to unhook it, either. Come with me."

Lindsey overcame her surprise at seeing him. "Helen's all right, isn't she?"

"Oh, yes. Fine." Moving like a quick but wizened elf, he beckoned to them. "Hurry, you two. Come along."

Byron joined the little man on the dock and caught his arm. "Why are you here, Reg? I told you and Helen to leave."

"Sorry to say, Byron," Reg said, his British accent brittle, "but the missus and I thought you were overreacting. We drove to Avalon, stayed a night and decided it was too bloody uncomfortable. We're set in our ways, Byron. Last night, we came back to our own cozy little house."

"How did Helen get back to the house?" Lindsey demanded. "When there was all that gunfire."

"Heaven knows how she managed. But she returned to the house unscathed."

"And no one followed her?"

"Not yet. I came down here to see if we could use the boat for our escape, but I'm afraid it's not possible. On account of the explosives." He led the way up the narrow stair toward the rear of the villa. "Let's hurry, shall we?"

"Be careful of the booby traps," Byron said.

"I will be. It's a good thing you showed me where you'd put those traps and sensors."

At the top of the rough-carved stairs, they were less than twenty yards from the house. Lindsey shivered uncontrollably. The cuts and scratches on her arms and legs had been washed clean by the sea, but felt raw and stinging. The bruise on her hip throbbed.

When she spied Smokey the cat, sunning his fat gray belly in the sun, the peaceful incongruity brought a sardonic smile to her lips. Someday, she intended to waste an afternoon lying in the sun.

They made it past the house.

With Reg leading the way, they followed the well-worn path to the McHenry cottage. Lindsey had been there only once before, visiting Helen, and was charmed by the small idyllic house built of white stucco with a neat red tile roof. Morning glories climbed the walls. The windows sparkled in the sunlight.

At the cottage door, she felt a new warmth. A safety. Here they would find shelter. They could regroup and plan a better escape. She dared to hope that they would succeed.

At the cottage door, Reg turned and faced them. "I'm afraid that's far enough," he said.

He held a gun in his hand.

Chapter Eighteen

"You were the inside man," Byron said.

"Indeed, I was." Reg frowned. "It wasn't awfully clever of you to overlook me."

"No, it wasn't."

Their civilized manner shocked Lindsey. Reg and Byron were chatting like a couple of gents discussing the winning and losing of a chess game. Didn't anybody around here understand that murder and deceit were not acceptable behaviors?

Reg turned to her. "Dreadfully sorry, Lindsey. I do wish you hadn't been forced to go through all this."

"Let me get this straight," she said. "You don't mind, do you? If I ask a few questions before you kill me?"

"I won't kill you, dear. Ask your questions."

"Okay." She pressed a finger to her forehead, trying to calm her brain. "You were able to come and go easily. You had access to the house. Was it you who stuck the dagger in Amanda's bear and left that note?"

"Yes." His head bobbed once.

Why hadn't she thought of it before? Lindsey remembered the bear—stabbed so neatly and arranged on Byron's bed. Neat as a flower bed. Careful as the tending of a rose garden.

"And that ploy worked rather well," Reg congratulated himself. "You see, I knew what sort of person Mr. Rankin was, and I wanted Byron to remove the children from the house so they wouldn't be hurt. I'm not a monster, after all."

Not a monster? That was debatable. "And then, last night," she continued, "you took all the weapons from the third-floor room."

"Slick as a whistle. Didn't even take them out of the house. I simply removed the heavy artillery to another part of the attic. No one goes up there. It was easy to find another room and use my keys to unlock the door."

"But why?" she asked. "Here's the big question, Reg. Why did you do this to Byron? Do you hate him?"

"Not at all. Byron has been quite a good employer, and I truly am sorry about all this. It was a business decision, pure and simple. I've got two kids in college. I was offered quite a lot of money." He fidgeted. "At first, it didn't seem like I was doing anything wrong. I got paid very well for being gone from the house on the night when you shot the intruder, Lindsey. Then, I got a bonus for keeping my mouth shut. That didn't really hurt anybody, did it? Paid again for hiding the weapons last night. And I expect, when I turn you two over to Mr. Rankin, I will receive another bonus."

Lindsey couldn't hold back for one more second. In her opinion, Reg's civilized behavior was worse than open abuse. She planted her fists on her hips. "And I bet you think you're a gentleman, huh?" She jabbed the air. Reg stood carefully beyond the distance where she could reach him. "Well, I'll tell you what you are, mister. Somebody who sells out his friends. You're a liar and a murderer and traitor and..."

"Lindsey!" Byron snapped. "He may be all those things, but he does have a gun."

"I don't care. And don't you tell me to stop, Byron."

"I understand," Reg said. "She had a rough time as a kid. Didn't you, Lindsey my girl?"

"I'm not your girl, you filthy, disgusting little man." Lindsey felt herself becoming harder, sharper, cut back to an inner core of rage. Her lips drew back from her teeth and she spat on the earth beside Reg's feet. "You're no better than the others. Liars. Cheats. I despise you, Reg Mc-Henry."

Byron watched her, and she turned on him. "Don't be shocked, Byron. This is who I am. Not a princess brought up in a castle. This is me. Lindsey Olson Grakow Peterson. The street-smart little girl who grew up to be a woman with a past, a woman with secrets. This is me. The woman you thought you cared about."

"I do love you," he said. "More than ever."

Her hard shell of rage split in two. She was speechless. He could still love her. She flew into his arms, clinging tightly. If they only had a few more minutes to live, she wanted to pack a whole wonderful, loving lifetime into each second.

"This is quite touching," Reg said, "but we really must get on with it."

Smoothly, Byron turned toward Reg. "Whatever you've been paid, I'll triple it."

"Can't take that chance," he said. "You might decide it's better to turn me over to the police. And who's going to support my children in college if I'm in jail?"

Helen McHenry opened the door behind him. Her round face was streaked with tears. "I didn't know," she said quietly. "Didn't know what was happening until today when all the guns started firing."

"It's all right," Lindsey said. She broke away from Byron. Instinctively, her arms raised to embrace Helen.

"Don't you move," Reg warned. "I'll shoot you in the leg, Lindsey. I mean it."

Helen groaned. "Reg, how could you do this? How could you?"

"You'll thank me, dear. When you see those bills paid and our children dressed in college graduation gowns." He shot her a hard glance. "Fetch the car, Helen."

When Helen looked at Lindsey, tears oozed from her eyes.

"Hurry up," Reg said firmly. "We must be on our way, dear."

Helen's steps toward the family car were leaden, and Lindsey sympathized with her. She knew what it was to be caught between committing a crime and trying to please her husband. And Lindsey didn't kid herself that her own decision not to follow her first husband had somehow been more noble than Helen's behavior. Lindsey had been with her first husband for a matter of months. Helen and Reg were married for over twenty years. They shared children. They shared a happy life. How could Helen betray him? Yet, she had to. Lindsey had to convince her.

Reg loaded Byron and Lindsey into the rear of the four-door car. He climbed into the front seat, keeping the gun trained on them while he ordered, "I want you to drive to the gate, Helen. You know the way."

"A hundred thousand dollars," Byron said.

"Damn it all, Byron. I wish I could accept. I like you. I've always liked you. And I admire the way you handled your wife's death."

"Then let us go, Reg."

"You know I can't. I'm in too far, now. I made a bad mistake that first night when I agreed to leave you alone in the house with Lindsey. There's no turning back now."

Lindsey tried to reason with him. "You haven't done anything wrong yet. You won't go to jail. Byron won't press charges."

"Wish I could believe you, but I can't. I'm an accessory, aiding and abetting. True, it's unfair. Life's unfair. It's life that made me into a gardener and Byron into the lord of the manor."

At the wrought-iron gate, which had been blown from its hinges, Helen parked the family sedan. Reg placed another gun in her hand. "You keep an eye on them, Helen. I'm going back to the house to negotiate our fee with Mr. Rankin. If the money's not right, I'll holler to you. Then, you drive about two hundred yards and stop. Understand?"

"Before you go, tell me one thing," Byron said. "Who hired you? Who hired the hit man?"

"Can't say as I know. Before Mr. Rankin contacted me directly, my payoffs have been in cash. And my instructions were on typed notes that came through the regular mail."

"Postmarks?"

"Avalon."

He climbed out of the car, offering parting advice for Helen. "Don't get any ideas about letting them go, my dear. You'd be putting me in prison. And leaving our children without means of support."

Slamming the car door, Reg strutted toward the house.

Tears blotched Helen's rosy cheeks as she turned in the driver's seat and aimed the gun at Lindsey and Byron.

"You know he's wrong," Byron said. "Please, Helen, drive us away from here before this gets worse, before you and Reg are murder accomplices."

"I can't."

"I'll help take care of your children." Byron's voice was soothing. "If I'd known you and Reg needed money, I would have been happy to help you."

"It's too late, Byron. I can't hurt Reg."

"I understand," Lindsey said. "I've told you about myself, Helen. You know about my first husband. And you saw the second. Neither of those men can hold a candle to your Reg, so I know how hard this must be for you. But listen to me."

Their eyes met and locked, sharing the deep pain of betrayed women—an agony that went bone-deep and hurt for a lifetime. Lindsey's heart truly ached for her friend and confidante, Helen McHenry. "Here's what will happen. Reg will be arrested. He may even do some jail time. But he'll be freed. You can start over clean."

"Reg in jail?"

"If we're killed, you'll go with him, Helen. Count on it. Murtaugh and the LAPD aren't fools. They'll find out what happened." Lindsey's voice lowered. "Just because your husband has made a mistake doesn't mean you have to."

"Reg is a good man." Helen's lips quivered. Her eyes filled with tears. But the gun, braced in both her strong capable hands, remained steady.

"Even a good man can make a mistake," Lindsey said. "Reg was trying to do the right thing for you and the children. But he doesn't really want Byron to die. Nor do you."

"I never would have allowed them to hurt Amanda or Sonny."

"Give me the gun, Helen."

When Lindsey slowly raised her hand, Helen stiffened. "Stop right there, Lindsey. I can't let my husband go to jail."

"You can't let him commit murder."

"He wouldn't."

"Don't be blind. When Reg tells that he's captured us, Rankin will kill us. Reg might as well pull the trigger himself."

Helen's wrist went slack and she allowed Lindsey to take the pistol from her. Turning in the driver's seat, Helen leaned her head against the steering wheel and sobbed.

But there wasn't time for grief. Behind them came the putt-putt of a golf cart starting up.

Lindsey grabbed Helen's shoulders. "You've got to drive, Helen. They're coming."

"Wait," Byron said. "I'll drive."

"No time," Lindsey said. "Come on, Helen. Start it up."

Helen responded. She turned the ignition, pushed down on the gas pedal, and they cruised slowly away from the house.

"Faster," Lindsey said.

"But then I'd be breaking the speed limit."

Uncomprehending, Lindsey sank back in the back seat and looked at Byron who confided, "Helen has never in her life had a ticket. And she hates to drive."

Gunfire shattered the rear window of Helen's car. Inconceivable as it seemed, the golf cart was gaining on them. Lindsey swung around in the seat. The small handgun felt natural in her hand.

Before she could aim, Helen shouted, "Be careful. Reg might be with him."

"I won't hit Reg," Lindsey said with the confidence of a woman who was expert with small firearms. She lowered the barrel of the gun.

The golf cart came up behind them. Close enough that she could see Rankin driving with one hand and shooting with the other. No one else was with him. She aimed for his shoulder, confident that she could make the shot.

Then, Helen drove around the curve in the road and the golf cart was hidden by brush and a rock outcropping.

"Oh, no!" Helen shouted.

When she slammed on the brakes, Byron and Lindsey were thrown forward against the seat. Rebounding quickly, Lindsey saw the obstacle in the road that had caused Helen's reaction. The Volkswagen. Their disabled Volkswagen was back on the road, blocking the way of another car. The big, black Cadillac. Beyond the Caddy was another vehicle—a pink taxi with fringe.

"Helluva time for a traffic jam," Byron muttered.

Lindsey shoved open the passenger door and dove into the underbrush. Byron was right behind her.

But Rankin was ready for both of them. A bullet splatted against a rock beside Lindsey's head. She froze.

Rankin jumped out of the golf cart, his pistol ready. "Hold it right there."

Lindsey might have been able to get off a shot, but when another man—the big man Rankin called Terry—came from the Caddy to join him, she knew the odds of hitting both were not good. Hiding the gun on the ground beneath her, she rolled over to face Rankin.

"You are so damn much trouble," Rankin said. "Both of you."

This time, he wouldn't take any chances with them. This time, he would kill expediently. With a sneer, he thrust his arm forward and eased back on the trigger.

Chapter Nineteen

A shrill voice pierced the silent, fatal moment. "Stop this. Immediately."

"Estelle?" Byron propped himself up on an elbow and stared at the beautifully coiffed vision in a crisp Dior suit.

Estelle Dumont dismounted from the pink-fringed taxi and picked her way through the tangle of vehicles to confront Rankin. Imperiously, she announced, "Mr. Rankin, you are fired."

"What?"

"I've changed my mind and your services are no longer required. Of course, I will pay you, but you are dismissed. Effective immediately. Now, shoo. Go back to the rock you crawled out from under."

A mottled red spread dangerously across Rankin's face. "I'm not done here."

"Pul-eeze, dear." Estelle fluttered her hanky. "Don't be tiresome."

The sputter of a car engine cut through the scene as the pink taxi with a fringed awning chugged up the incline and disappeared over the hill. "Dreadful little vehicle," Estelle said. "Can you imagine my embarrassment at having to ride in Minnie's Taxi?"

Lindsey hoped that the taxi driver would have the sense to report this mess, that he'd go for help.

When she started to her feet, Rankin swiveled around. "Stay on the ground, nanny girl." He gestured at Byron with his gun. "And you, too, hotshot."

"You are being so annoying," Estelle said.

Rankin's gun turned on Estelle. "Don't push me, lady."

But Dan-dan had appeared behind Estelle's shoulder. His glittering smile was matched by the gleam of sunlight on the sawed-off shotgun in his hand.

If the situation hadn't been so dire, Lindsey would have burst out laughing. Estelle was prissily treating a professional killer as if he were a naughty chambermaid. Also, she had blithely admitted that she was the person who had hired Rankin. Wasn't she aware that she'd broken laws, wreaked havoc, involved military and civil law officers?

Her behavior was carrying eccentricity a bit too far. Into madness? It wasn't funny, Lindsey told herself. But she wouldn't have been surprised to see Uncle Jerrod pouring tea for the Mad Hatter and the March Hare. Instead, she spotted Kirsch, slumped over the steering wheel of the Volkswagen. Immediately, she sobered. Was Kirsch all right? Obviously, he needed medical aid.

They needed to end this charade. But how? Her fingers closed on the gun behind her back and she thanked her lucky stars that she hadn't fired at Rankin before. He didn't know she was armed, and that might be her only advantage.

"Enough of this crap." Rankin addressed Dan-dan. "Don't even think about shooting, pal. If you hurt me, you're dead. There are two of us. And I've got two more men back at the house. And another three posted along the road ahead who are probably going to stop that idiot in the pink taxi."

"Why should they?" Estelle demanded. "He brought me here and no one bothered us."

Rankin ignored her and spoke to Dan-dan. "Why don't you put down the gun, buddy. Maybe you won't get hurt."

Dan-dan smiled, but Lindsey could see the confusion behind his toothy grin. Quickly, she spoke for him. "Hey, Rankin, have you ever seen somebody who was shot with a sawed-off shotgun. At this range, it would cut you in half. He could probably hit both you and Terry with one blast."

"You shut up." He pointed his pistol at Lindsey.

"I wouldn't do that," Dan-dan warned.

"This was supposed to be so simple," Estelle pouted. "Really, Mr. Rankin, your brother was a more pleasant person to deal with."

Byron sat up, brushed the dirt from the knees of his jeans. "I don't quite understand, Estelle. Did you hire Mikey Rankin to kill me?"

"That's such a nasty way of putting it. But, yes, I did. And you brought it on yourself, Byron, by being so stubborn about dividing the inheritance among your relatives. In any case, I've spoken to Jerrod, and he convinced me that—after all this nonsense—you would be amenable to a settlement. That is correct, isn't it?"

"Anything you say, Estelle."

"Really amenable," Lindsey added in a placating tone. "You've proved your point, Mrs. Dumont."

Byron coiled one leg beneath him, preparing to spring forward. "So tell me your entire plot, Estelle. I guess you arranged for my murder to happen while you were on your way to Cape Cod."

"I believe it's called an alibi," she said. "And I was awfully clever, don't you think? Since I knew you were working on those silly plans for the government, I arranged to have the murderer carry a gun with a special marking on it. He was supposed to leave the gun behind and to do something colorful—like writing a slogan in blood—so the authorities would assume that terrorists were responsible."

"Clever," Byron said.

"I thought so, too." Her smile did not reach her eyes. "Then, of course, I hired the famous Lindsey Olson so that no one could accuse me of leaving you here unprotected."

Dan-dan added his two cents. "She wasn't supposed to be so good. We didn't figure that a girl could be so tough."

Estelle gazed haughtily at Lindsey's damp tangled hair and scratched limbs. "My dear, this experience hasn't agreed with you. You look positively horrid."

"Enough," Rankin shouted. "Listen, lady, you can't call this off now. I'm going to explain once. Only once. You and me, we broke the law in some real big ways."

"Oh, yes, attempted murder," Estelle said dismissively. "But there's really no harm done, is there? Byron certainly won't press charges. Will you, dear?"

"Absolutely not," he said, talking fast. "Listen, Rankin, this may seem unusual, but you might have noticed that our family is a little bit eccentric—"

"A little?"

"They're a lot eccentric," Lindsey mumbled. "But we thought it was an excuse for weird behavior. Not a motive for murder."

"What?" Rankin snapped.

"Might as well leave the nanny out of it," Byron said. "What's important is, as my dear Auntie Estelle pointed out, there's no harm done. And I'm more than willing to let bygones be bygones."

Byron's attitude so effectively reflected the Cyril family's off-center morality that Lindsey almost believed him. If she hadn't known the depth of his sincerity and the warmth of his caring, she might have accepted his pose as an eccentric playboy.

Rankin gestured toward her with the business end of his revolver. "That takes care of you, but what about the nanny? She's not crazy."

"But I'm realistic," she assured him. "The cops think I'm involved with this anyway, and I don't owe them any favors."

Indecision flickered in Rankin's expression. "What about my brother? My revenge?"

"I'm really awfully sorry," Byron said. He pulled up his other leg into a crouch and spread his hands wide. "Perhaps a cash settlement would assuage your grief?"

Rankin frowned, seriously considering the proposition. Then, he shook his head. "No way. I don't believe this stuff." He nodded to Terry. "You take the bodyguard. Byron and the nanny are mine."

Byron shot forward like a coiled spring. The force of his leap knocked Rankin off his feet. They struggled for the gun.

Estelle gave a dainty shriek and buried her face in Dandan's chest, causing his shotgun to wobble off-target.

Lindsey rolled to her stomach, fumbled with her pistol.

Terry, confused by all the action, apparently decided that Lindsey was the clearest danger. He sighted down the barrel of his pistol at her.

A single shot rang out.

Terry looked around in shock. His gun dropped to the ground. His arm dangled limply at his side. Immediately, a blood stain spread from his shoulder. He stumbled back against the golf cart. With an almost peaceful groan, he slid to the ground, unconscious.

Kirsch staggered from the Volkswagen. His rifle—one of the rifles without ammunition—was leveled at Byron and Rankin, brawling on the ground. He yelled, "Stop! It's over, Rankin."

Lindsey went to Kirsch. "Are you all right?"

"No." His face was pale and the freckles stood out in sharp relief. "But it's only a flesh wound." He nodded toward the fight. "Shouldn't we do something about this?"

"Let's not interrupt," Lindsey said. "Unless Byron starts losing."

The two men rolled across the dirt road to the shoulder. When they stopped, Byron was on top. He tore the pistol from Rankin's hand and heaved it into the bushes.

Though Rankin had been injured at the house, he was strong. He flung out an arm and jammed the heel of his hand into Byron's chin. Almost casually, Byron slapped his hand away. He drew back and jabbed into Rankin's face.

Rankin bucked. He clawed, but Byron was quicker. He made a quick neat chop at Rankin's throat causing him to gag.

Byron climbed off Rankin and stood a few feet away, waiting for him to catch his breath. "Get up," he said. "Come on, Rankin. I'm not done with you."

Rankin's nose bled. He curled into a tight ball on the ground, coughing.

"Come on," Byron urged. "Come and get me."

Byron dragged the other man to his feet. Rankin took a loose swing, but his arms had lost all strength. With one more blow to the belly, Byron knocked him to the ground. Rankin lay still.

Breathing hard, Byron stepped away from the man who had threatened his children and hurt Lindsey. It was over. The terror was ended. The fight was won. He couldn't quite believe it.

Lindsey touched his shoulder. "We made it, Byron."

He held her. Her body against his was a miracle.

His gaze searched her face. Even bedraggled, she was the most beautiful woman on the face of the earth. He wanted to hold her in his arms forever, to caress her, to love her. His lips formed words he had spoken only once before in his life: Marry me. Before he could speak, Lindsey offered two words of her own.

"Frisk him," she said.

"What?"

"Rankin's probably got another gun. Or a knife."

Byron nodded as he separated from her and knelt beside Rankin. Surely, his love affair with Lindsey had been the most unusual courtship ever recorded. He wanted to propose, and she wanted him to frisk his fallen enemy.

In Rankin's pockets, he found a derringer and a switchblade. Another knife was hidden in an ankle sheath. When he finished, Byron looked down into Rankin's semiconscious eyes. "If it's any consolation, Rankin, you were right about what I'd do if you surrendered. I would have pressed charges because I want to see you locked up for a long, long time."

He went to Kirsch. "Thanks, buddy."

"It's the least I could do."

Byron glanced at the rust-colored stain of dried blood on Kirsch's upper leg and helped him to Helen's car. "You could use a doctor. Helen will drive you to the nearest telephone and contact the police and an ambulance." He sat Kirsch inside the car. "Okay, Helen?"

"Yes." Her voice was muffled. "I'm sorry, Byron."

"So am I."

Lindsey came to the car window and leaned inside. Lightly, she kissed Kirsch's cheek, then reassured Helen, "You've done the right thing. Everything is going to be okay."

Helen fastidiously fastened her seat belt, turned on her blinker and maneuvered around the black Caddy before chugging carefully down the road.

"Byron, dear," Estelle shrilled. "Whatever did you mean when you said that you intended to press charges against Mr. Rankin?"

"Exactly that, Estelle."

"Well, I must say that's awfully petty of you. You're not dead, after all."

"Not from Rankin's lack of trying."

"But what about me?" Her perfectly outlined eyes widened. "Of course, you can't intend to press charges against me. Or Dan-dan."

Byron was saddened by her complete lack of understanding, her utter self-absorption. Could she really believe she'd done nothing wrong? His Auntie Estelle needed psychiatric help. And Byron figured that he and the legal system would make sure she got treatment. "We'll talk about this later," he said.

"One thing puzzles me," Lindsey said. "Estelle, if you were so broke, how could you afford the services of Rankin and his brother?"

"Well, I sold some of that useless JerBee stock back to Jerrod, of course."

"Did he know?" Byron asked. "Did Jerrod know that you hired a hit man?"

"Obviously," she retorted. "How else could he inform me that you were willing to make a settlement?"

When Byron sighed heavily, Lindsey went to him. It was one thing to know that his crazy aunt wanted him dead, but if Jerrod and numerous other eccentric Cyrils cousins, uncles and in-laws were also involved...

"I told Jerrod yesterday," Estelle said. "And he was rather rude about the whole incident, insisted that I return immediately from Cape Cod and put an end to Mr. Rankin's contract."

Lindsey slipped her arm around Byron's waist. "Nobody else wants you dead," she said. "This is Estelle's plan. She was working alone."

"Seems that you've been doing your share of work, too." Estelle glared pointedly. "An arm around the waist? Perhaps a little kiss on the cheek? Rather seductive behavior for a nanny, isn't it?"

"Rather," Lindsey replied.

"Well, I certainly don't intend to write up good reference letters for you. And it give me great pleasure to inform you that you are fired."

Lindsey threw back her head and laughed. "You can't fire me, lady. I've already quit."

Estelle shrunk down, like a turtle going into its shell.

"However," Byron announced, "I would like very much to offer Lindsey another position."

"No, thanks. I'm taking some time off."

He held both her hands in his. "Would you be my wife?"

"This is appalling." Estelle turned to Dan-dan, her last and best ally. "Don't you think this is appalling?"

His glittering smile was just for her. "I think whatever you think."

"If Byron is going to propose to his bodyguard, I have half a mind to propose marriage to you."

"I accept."

When Dan-dan embraced her lightly, not mussing the line of her Dior suit, Lindsey whispered to Byron. "I'm sure they'll be very happy at the sanatorium of their choice."

"My opinion exactly." He turned her toward him. "And you haven't answered my question."

"I don't know," she said honestly. "I haven't had a lot of luck with husbands."

"And you've done a lot of successful running away. But you didn't run from me. You came back."

"A good thing I did."

"A very good thing."

She snuggled into his embrace, adoring the warm security of his arms around her. After all they'd been through together, how could she refuse him anything? For the first time in her life, Lindsey felt like she had a home.

"Lindsey, my darling," he murmured. "I want to spend the rest of my life with you. Say yes."

She buried her face against his chest. Her whispered answer was drowned in the wail of approaching police sirens.

From *New York Times* Bestselling author
Penny Jordan, a compelling novel of ruthless passion
that will mesmerize readers everywhere!

Penny Jordan

Silver

Real power, true power came from
Rothwell. And Charles vowed to have it,
the earldom and all that went with it.

Silver vowed to destroy Charles, just as surely and
uncaringly as he had destroyed her father; just as he had
intended to destroy her. She needed him to want her . . .
to desire her . . . until he'd do anything to have her.

But first she needed a tutor: a man who wanted no one.
He would help her bait the trap.

Played out on a glittering international stage,
Silver's story leads her from the luxurious comfort of
British aristocracy into the depths of adventure,
passion and danger.

AVAILABLE NOW!

 HARLEQUIN

Take 4 bestselling love stories FREE

Plus get a FREE surprise gift!